THE
BLACK
KEY

∾THE∾
BLACK
KEY

AMY EWING

An Imprint of HarperCollinsPublishers

For Faetra,
I miss you every day.

HarperTeen is an imprint of HarperCollins Publishers.

The Black Key
Copyright © 2016 by Amy Ewing
All rights reserved. Printed in the United States of America.
No part of this book may be used or reproduced in any manner
whatsoever without written permission except in
the case of brief quotations embodied in critical articles
and reviews. For information address HarperCollins
Children's Books, a division of HarperCollins Publishers,
195 Broadway, New York, NY 10007.
www.epicreads.com

ISBN 978-0-06-223584-8 (trade bdg.)
ISBN 978-0-06-256581-5 (int. ed.)

Typography by Anna Christian
16 17 18 19 20 PC/RRDH 10 9 8 7 6 5 4 3 2 1

First Edition

~ One ~

THE MARSH REALLY STINKS WHEN IT RAINS.

Raven and I huddle under a dying tree just outside the walls of Southgate. Fat raindrops pelt down on the hoods of our cloaks, softening the rough-spun fabric, turning the hard-packed dirt beneath our feet to soft mud that sucks at our boots.

The rain doesn't bother me. I want to lift my hood and let the water splash on my cheeks. I want to join with it and feel myself fall from the sky in a million little pieces. But now is not the time to connect with the elements. We have a job to do.

This is the third time we've been to Southgate over the

last few months, since Hazel was taken. With the Auction date moved up from October to April, the members of the Society of the Black Key—the Lone City's homegrown rebel force, led by Lucien—have been working overtime to gather more people to our cause, to stockpile weapons and explosives, to infiltrate royal strongholds in the outer circles.

But none of that will matter if the royalty can just stay hidden, snug behind the massive wall that surrounds the Jewel. That's where we come in. The surrogates are stronger when we work together, and it will take every girl we can get to crumble that huge wall to pieces. To strip the royals of their main protection. To let the people into the Jewel.

Raven and I have traveled to all four of the holding facilities, along with the other surrogates Lucien saved from the Jewel—Sienna, Olive, and Indi. Northgate was the worst—all cold iron and stone floors, drab uniforms, and no personal items allowed. It's no wonder Sienna hated it so much. She didn't like going back there either, but we need a surrogate who knows the facilities, and who knows the girls.

We've been showing them the truth a few at a time, helping them access the elements, changing them from surrogate to something more. Raven has a unique and intangible ability—she can access a special place, a cliff overlooking the ocean, and she can bring others with her as well. It's a dreamlike, magical spot where girls like us form an instant connection with the elements. I've been there more times than I can count over these past months.

We have to be careful with who we choose—only girls going to the Auction, who will be on the trains heading directly inside the Jewel. Lucien got us the lists.

There is no hidden door to Southgate, like the one at Ash's companion house, and no Regimentals prowling outside either. Southgate is a fortress in the middle of a sea of mud-brick hovels. The Marsh is even sadder than I remember it. The sulfuric smell of the mud beneath my feet, the sparse, scrubby trees, the dilapidated homes . . . it all screams *poor* in a way that I never quite understood until I lived in the Jewel.

Even the Smoke and the Farm aren't as bad as this. The unfairness is like a slap in the face. A huge part of the Lone City's population is living in squalor and no one cares. Worse, no one really *knows*. What do the citizens in the Bank or the Smoke know of the Marsh? It's a faraway place where the people who shovel their coal or scrub their kitchens or work their looms live. It's not real to them. It may as well not exist.

"Only three girls left to show the elements to here," Raven says. "Then it's back to Westgate in a few days."

She's cut her hair short again and her eyes gleam with black fire beneath her hood. She is not quite the Raven who left this holding facility with me last October for the Auction, nor is she the hollow shell the Countess of the Stone had tortured her into when I rescued her from the Jewel. She is somewhere in between. She has nightmares about her time spent locked in a cage in the dungeon of the palace of the Stone. She still hears snippets of people's thoughts and feelings—whispers, she calls them—a side effect of the Countess's doctor cutting into her brain over and over again.

But her laughter has returned, and her wit—especially

when she talks to Garnet. And she trains each day with Ash, strengthening her once frail body until her wiry frame has become lean and hard.

She glances up at the immense wall towering over us. Climbing it was never an option. Its stone surface is perfectly smooth, no cracks or crevices for handholds. We spent hours sitting around the dining room table with Sil discussing the best ways to break into the holding facilities. In the end, it was Sienna who came up with the idea. We can't go over the walls, or go through them (at least, not without attracting seriously unwanted attention).

But we can go under them.

The power of the elements has grown stronger in me over the last few months. Sienna is stronger too, as well as Indi, the surrogate from Westgate. Sienna can connect with Earth and Fire, Indi only with Water. So far, no other surrogate besides Sil and I has the power to access all four elements. Olive, the little curly-haired girl from Eastgate, is the only one who still balks at using the elements she connects with, Air and Water. She's the only one of us who still uses the Auguries. And she is the only person in the White Rose who has a good word to say about the royalty.

But Olive, Indi, Sienna, and Sil are far away in the red-brick farmhouse I've come to call home. They're probably all asleep now, snuggled up in warm beds, safe in the wild forest that protects the White Rose.

"Violet?" Raven says.

I nod. "I'm ready," I say, closing my eyes.

It is as easy to join with Earth as it would be to slip into a hot bath. I become the earth; I allow the element to fill me up until we are one unit. I can sense the layers of dirt beneath my feet, a heaviness in my chest. All I need to do is ask and the earth will respond.

Dig, I think.

The earth in the Marsh is different than in the Farm—scratchy, thin, and unhealthy. The pounding of the rain muffles the crack as the dirt before our feet opens. I reach out further with my mind, asking the earth to carve itself out, down, down, down, until I hit soft brown soil. I create a passage easily; Earth is more than happy to accommodate my needs. When I sense the scraping of stone, I know I've hit the bottom of the wall's foundation. I push my tunnel farther—the wall is thick and I must make sure I clear it.

It is such a strange sensation, to be so aware of the tunnel and yet be physically standing high above on the ground. Like I have two sets of eyes, hands, ears, nostrils. I wonder if it's a bit like how Raven feels when she hears the whispers—having someone else's thoughts in her head alongside her own. I sense when the stone falls away and there is only light and dirt above me. My tunnel climbs, the earth and I carving out a space together until, with a little pop, we burst through the mud and out into the courtyard that lies on the other side of this wall.

Once the job is done, I release my connection with the element and open my eyes.

Raven is watching me with a wary expression. "Your face looks so weird when you do that, you know."

"Ash thinks it's beautiful. Haunting, he says, but beautiful."

She rolls her eyes. "Ash thinks everything about you is beautiful."

Of all the people we left back at the White Rose, Ash is probably the only one not sleeping right now. Even though we've done this so many times, at all four holding facilities, he still worries. I imagine him in our loft, staring up at the slats in the barn overhead, wondering where we are, if we made it, if we'll get caught, when we'll be home.

But I can't let myself think about Ash worrying about me. I peer down into the dark tunnel.

"Let's go," I say.

The tunnel is narrow, just wide enough to fit us single file. It's impossible to get a hold on the crumbling dirt, so Raven and I just slide down the sloping wall until we hit the bottom.

It's maybe ten feet under the wall, where we are encased in absolute darkness for a minute, and then we're on the Southgate side, staring up at the tunnel leading to the courtyard. It looks like miles from this perspective.

We scramble up the slope and emerge into Southgate's courtyard, muddy and out of breath.

This is where the real danger is. Outside, in the streets of the Marsh, no one would ever recognize us, except for our immediate family members. No one has seen us since we were twelve. Raven's family is far away to the east, mine to the west, but it's only my mother left to recognize me. My brother, Ochre, is a part of the Society now, working in the Farm. And my sister, Hazel, has been kidnapped by the Duchess of the Lake, to serve as my replacement.

No. I can't let myself think about Hazel right now. I

can't afford to be distracted. I'm doing this for her. To save her. To save all the surrogates.

But still, it's impossible not to worry. Lucien said the Duchess has made an arrangement with the Exetor. An engagement. Between the Exetor's son and the Duchess's future daughter. He said that her surrogate—my Hazel—is pregnant.

And if that's true, then Hazel is dead. Childbirth kills surrogates.

No. I shake my head and glance at Raven. She was pregnant when I rescued her from the Jewel in December. She survived. Hazel will, too. I'll make sure of it.

But now I have to focus on the task at hand.

The building looms up before us, a stark outline against the rain. It looks smaller than it felt when I lived here, though that probably comes from spending so much time among the immense palaces of the Jewel. Besides, South-gate is the smallest of the holding facilities. Northgate was enormous. Even Westgate and Eastgate are bigger than this. Westgate has a huge garden all around it and a solarium in its center. It's actually quite pretty.

"Come on," Raven whispers. We skirt around the mound of dirt I pushed out to make the tunnel—I'll replace it after we leave, hiding our tracks—and make our way to the greenhouse.

The glass structure glistens in the rain and we slip inside and pull back our hoods. Raven shakes out her hair and glances around.

"Are we early?"

I take out Ash's pocket watch. Thirty seconds to

midnight. "They'll be here," I say. It's warm inside the greenhouse, the air thick with the scent of growing things, earth and roots and flowers. The rain patters gently as Raven and I wait.

At precisely five seconds past midnight, I can just make out hooded shapes hurrying across the courtyard. Then the door to the greenhouse opens and the group of girls we've been waiting for floods in.

"Violet!" some of them whisper, rushing over to greet me and Raven.

Amber Lockring strides forward, throwing back the hood of her cloak, her eyes gleaming. "Right on time," she says with a grin.

"Five seconds late, actually," Raven points out.

Amber wasn't one of our friends here, though she lived on our floor. Raven confessed that Amber called me a freak on my first day at Southgate and Raven bent her arm behind her back until Amber said she was sorry. They had never liked each other after that. When we got the list of girls going to the Auction, Raven immediately chose Amber as the first one to reveal this secret to. When I asked why, she narrowed her eyes and said, "She hates the royalty just the way I did. And she was the only other girl in our dorm who wore pants."

I had to smile at that. If they hadn't hated each other so much, they might've been friends.

"You brought them?" I say.

Amber gestures proudly to the figures still huddled by the door, three girls with varying expressions of fear and suspicion on their faces. "Tawny, Ginger, and Henna.

They're the last ones. This is all of us going to the Auction."

I do a quick head count. Only nine out of the seventy-seven girls at this year's Auction are from Southgate. And they stand before me now.

"Did anyone see you?" Raven says.

Amber snorts. "No. Obviously. I have done this before, you know."

"Great job," I say.

"Ready?" Raven mutters.

I step forward.

It's time to show these girls who they really are.

~ Two ~

But before I even get a chance to open my mouth, I'm interrupted.

"Violet . . . what . . ." Ginger gapes at me. She's the oldest of the three new girls, with carrot-colored hair and broad shoulders. "What are you doing here?" Her gaze snaps to Amber. "What is she *doing* here? I told you I didn't want to get in trouble!"

"Stop whining," Amber says. "We picked you for a reason. Don't you want to know why?"

Amber is a bit of a bully, but she was an excellent first choice. None of the girls ever want to argue with her and she knows exactly how to push them.

"Aren't you supposed to be in the Jewel?" Tawny asks.

She's fifteen, with eyes like a doe, and they are so wide right now they seem to take up half her face.

"I was," I say. "But now I'm here to help you."

"Help us?" Henna asks. She's a tiny thing with russet skin and curly black hair. Something about her reminds me of Hazel, and it makes my heart pinch. She doesn't look frightened or confused, but curious. "How?"

"You'll see," a pretty redhead named Scarlet says, putting an arm around her. "It's incredible."

"We've been practicing," Amber says. "Scarlet made a whirlpool in one of the bathtubs the other night. I made a mini tornado in the palm of my hand, like the one you showed me the first time you came."

"That's wonderful," I say at the same time Ginger says, "Scarlet made a what?"

"You better not let anyone catch you," Raven says.

Amber shoots her a smug look. "We're careful."

I would have thought that having so many young girls be opened to the elements in one place would be dangerous, volatile. But it has turned out to be the opposite. I noticed it first with Indi and Olive. They didn't experience the same fitful, destructive sleep that I did when I first changed from surrogate to something more, because Sienna and Sil and I were there. It's like the more of us there are together, the easier the elements are to keep under control. As if we keep one another anchored.

We're lucky. Otherwise some poor girl might have accidentally destroyed her room in her sleep. It would be hard to explain that to the caretakers.

"All right, what is going on?" Ginger demands, folding

her arms across her chest. "How did you get here? Why aren't you in the Jewel? Why did you drag us out of bed in the middle of the night?"

"I knew she'd be the worst," Amber mutters to me. Raven chuckles softly.

I take a deep breath and begin to explain. It's a story I've told many times, and I've got it down quite succinctly. I tell them about what it means to be a surrogate—about the leashes, about the stimulant gun, about the humiliations of being forced to perform in front of the royals. How we are treated as property, as pets. I tell them about Dahlia, killed by the Duchess of the Lake for no reason other than spite. I tell them about Raven, how the Countess of the Stone cut into her brain. Raven leans forward at that point.

"You can still feel them," she says, motioning for Ginger to touch her scalp.

"Feel what?" Ginger asks.

"The scars."

Raven's skull is so covered with them that it only takes one touch before Ginger recoils.

"Violet saved my life," Raven says in a flat tone. She reaches into the pocket of her shirt and pulls out the photographs. This is my least favorite part. "Otherwise, I would have ended up like this. And so will all of you if you are sold on Auction Day."

I keep my eyes trained on a lone curl by Henna's temple. I hate these photographs. I was grateful when Raven offered to be in charge of showing them. I think she knew how much it hurt me to see.

There are four girls, all dead, their lips blue, their skin

waxy. Their eyes are closed but there are deep V scars on their chests. Lucien told me that sometimes, if a doctor was particularly interested, an autopsy would be performed. Not to determine cause of death—they know that already. Just to see what we're like inside. Just because we're different.

Henna gasps. Tawny looks away. Ginger leans forward.

"Are those . . . are these real?" she says.

"Is that Verdant?" Henna gasps again. Every photograph is of a girl from each of the holding facilities. Verdant was sold at the Auction before mine.

My and Raven's faces are the only answer she needs. Ginger takes a step back, her face full of horror.

"They told us the royalty would take care of us," she says. "They . . . Patience said—"

"Patience lied," I say.

"This is the fate of every surrogate who has ever been Auctioned," Raven says. "Childbirth kills us, if another royal House doesn't get to us first. But for the first time in our history, the surrogates have a chance to do something about it."

I reach out and touch Raven's shoulder. "Put those away," I say. "They understand."

Tawny is blinking back tears. "But why? We help them. We give them babies. Why do they want to k-kill us?"

"Our deaths are merely a by-product," I say. "A result of an unnatural pregnancy. We aren't sure why bearing a royal child causes death. Maybe it's the Auguries. Maybe it's because we were never meant to carry children besides our own. Whatever it is, we are only a means to an end for them. They don't see us as people at all. We have no names in the Jewel. Our opinions don't matter.

"But," I continue, "there are people in this city who want change. People who are risking their lives to fight the royalty's hold over us. Why do they keep us separated by walls? Why do they dictate what we do with our lives, where we work, how much we earn? Why don't we have a say in how we live?"

"And it's not just the surrogates who get treated like they're expendable," Raven adds. "There's a whole city out there that's being oppressed."

"Imagine what we might accomplish if we all worked together," I say.

"Excuse me," Henna says, raising her hand as if this is a class. "You said we finally have a chance to do something about this. But . . . we're locked up in here, watched over by caretakers. The only power we have is the Auguries. I don't see how changing the color of something is all that useful."

"Let's take them to the cliff," a brunette named Sorrel says, tugging on Raven's sleeve—she's the youngest of all the girls in this group.

"Yes, the cliff," Scarlet says eagerly.

"I can't believe you knew about this and didn't tell me," Ginger says.

Scarlet looks sheepish. "I couldn't; they made me promise! Once you go to the cliff, you'll see—it's really too dangerous to talk about. If anyone found out . . ."

"All right, enough talk," I say. "It's time to show you."

Amber, Scarlet, and the other girls we've already shown the elements to quickly form a circle. Scarlet takes Ginger's hand with an apologetic look.

"Don't be too mad," she says. "You'll love it when you see it."

Raven squeezes my fingers. I smile and close my eyes. I love going to the cliff.

It is a strange place, somewhere nebulous between the real world and a former Paladin stronghold. The Paladin were a race of warrior women, gifted with the use of the elements and charged with protecting this island. The royalty came in ships, claimed the island for their own, and killed all the Paladin.

Or so they thought. But the Paladin survived. We surrogates are their descendants. Lucien thinks it's genetics that make some women (like me) have the ability to connect with the elements while others (like my mother) can't. He believes it's a recessive trait, like having blue eyes. Sil told him that's crap, and not everything can be explained so easily.

Either way, it doesn't matter. These girls before me are Paladin, and it's time to show them what that means.

The cliff first appeared when I saved Raven's life, after she miscarried. I don't know what took me to that place, if it was fate or chance or pure love, but once I went there, I felt an instant connection with the elements, with my heritage. I understood myself and the world in a way I never had before.

That's what we did with Sienna, and Indi, and Olive. That's what we've done with all the girls in the facilities. Get Raven to them. Take them to the cliff.

A second after I close my eyes, I'm falling. I hear a faint shriek that I think is Tawny, but it's okay, we're already in a place where the sleeping occupants of Southgate can't hear us.

It's nighttime on the cliff, and raining. The weather here often reflects the weather in the real world. Or sometimes it reflects the surrogate's own desire, like when we took Sienna, and it was snowing because Sienna loves the snow.

The drops of rain are warm and run down my cheeks in rivulets as I raise my face to the sky. The ocean stretches out below, and while I can barely see it in the darkness, I hear the waves crashing against the rocks. The trees that stretch out behind me rustle in the wind. And in the center of the cliff is the statue, a monument of blue-gray stone that leaps up in a spiral, a frozen wave reaching to the sky.

I've missed it here, I murmur in my mind.

Me too, Raven replies wordlessly.

Me three, Amber adds. Some of the girls who have been here before run off to do their favorite things. Azure dances under the trees. Sorrel gazes out over the cliff, listening raptly to the roar of the ocean. Ginger stands in a state of shock, Scarlet beside her still holding her hand. Tawny seems torn between fear and excitement.

Henna's eyes are wide as she circles the statue, reaching out a cautious hand to touch it. I know what she's feeling—stone that is impossibly smooth, like water made solid.

Then Henna begins to laugh. She holds her hands up to catch the raindrops, and I smile because she is ours now. She sees who she was meant to be.

Something in her laugh makes Tawny laugh, and then the two of them are running to the edge of the cliff with Sorrel, so close I think they might fall.

But they won't. The Paladin made this place and they protect it. They protect us, here.

Scarlet is making the rain dance and swirl around Ginger's head, to the older girl's delight. It still hits me every time, how free we are here, how wild and unabashedly ourselves. Every time I see a new girl feel it, this connection with one another and the world around us, it gives me hope.

Time to go, Raven says, and we are pulled away, sucked upward until we are back inside the greenhouse at Southgate. Tawny is crying openly and Ginger's eyes are glassy. Henna looks windswept and exhilarated.

"What . . . I . . ." Ginger can't form what she wants to say. I remember the feeling well.

"What *was* that place?" Henna asks eagerly.

"Look down," I say. The three of them do and gasp.

Dark purple flowers bloom at Ginger's feet, pale pink ones at Tawny's. Henna's are a brilliant orange. For several long moments, they stare, enraptured, as the rain patters on the glass above our heads.

"Tell them about the Paladin, Violet," Scarlet says.

"Tell them about the Society of the Black Key," Amber says.

"And you must tell us more stories, Violet!" Azure insists. "We want to know what's happening out there."

"One thing at a time," I say. I take a breath and begin to talk.

Three

"So it's Westgate next," I say, barely stifling a yawn. We were at Southgate all night, until just before dawn. "We'll leave in two days."

"I can't wait to sleep in my own bed tonight." Raven shifts uncomfortably in her damp cloak.

The train car is packed with workers, even though the sun has only been above the horizon for less than an hour. Lucien made all of us forged documents, assigning us as farm labor. The best way to get between the circles of the city, he said, is to hide in plain sight. No one thinks much about workers from the Marsh anyway.

On our first train ride here, I was terrified a Regimental would spot us, see through our flimsy piece of paper and cry, "Arrest them!" But everyone in the Jewel thinks Raven is dead, and no one is looking for me, since everyone thinks my sister *is* me. The Regimental who checked our papers barely gave us a glance.

It was the same with the other holding facilities. No one gave any notice to a few teenage farmworkers.

I watch the sun rise over the mud-brick houses that flash past the train window. This ride is so different from the train I took to the Auction. Back then I was starting a new life in a strange place, full of fear and anticipation.

This time I know exactly where I'm going—back to the White Rose. And I can't wait to get there.

I wonder how this day will be for Ginger and Tawny and Henna. They must feel so strange, so alive, everything vibrant and new, colors more clear, scents more potent. I'm glad they have Amber and the other girls to help, to guide them. Henna connected with Air right away—there was a look of wonder in her eyes as the wind began to swirl around her, reacting to her thoughts. Scarlet showed Ginger how to make little cracks in the earth, and Tawny sent raindrops splashing upward instead of down. It never gets old, seeing these girls wonder at their own abilities. And the more of them Raven and I can get to, the stronger my hope grows.

My stomach rumbles. I hope Sil has made biscuits for breakfast. A warm, flaky biscuit with strawberry jam would be perfect right now. And a kiss from Ash and maybe a hug from Indi. Indi loves hugging.

I don't realize I've fallen asleep until Raven is shaking me awake.

"We're here," she says.

We trudge off the train at Bartlett Station and my heart leaps when I see Sil among the crowd of carts and carriages, her horse, Turnip, shaking her sandy mane. Sil is dressed in her usual overalls and flannel shirt. Her black, kinky hair, streaked with gray at her temples, encircles her head like a wild halo.

"So," she says, after we've climbed into the bed of the cart and she's given Turnip a flick of the reins, "how did it go?"

"The usual. They were scared and stubborn at first, but when they see the pictures and then the cliff, everything changes," Raven says.

"His Royal Keyness will be pleased to hear it, I'm sure," Sil says. She and Lucien have a sort of grudging friendship. But I suspect they each care for the other more than they'd ever admit.

"How are things at the White Rose?" I ask.

She snorts. "You've been gone one night, what, you think Sienna burned the house down?"

"I wouldn't put it past her," Raven mutters.

"Don't think your boyfriend slept much, but otherwise everything's the same. Sienna throwing around attitude and Indi always trying to give me a damned hug. Olive's started sewing another dress. A ball gown, she says. Asked me if there was any way I could get her some chiffon."

Raven and Sil have a good chuckle over that, but Olive's attachment to everything royal makes me nervous, not amused.

Sil loves complaining about the new girls but I think she secretly enjoys the company. She was alone for so long before Azalea, Lucien's sister, found her.

I start to drift off again as we enter the forest. It's going to be a warm day—last night's rain drips from the leaves overhead and Raven pulls up the hood of her cloak. I leave mine down. I love the feel of water in my hair.

The forest grows denser the farther we travel into it. The White Rose is hidden here, protected by some ancient Paladin magic, Sil suspects. She believes they led her to it, to a clearing where nothing but a broken-down farmhouse remained. The trees grow in strange shapes in this forest, their trunks bent at odd angles, their branches sometimes growing straight into the ground.

I feel the tug, the gentle pull in my stomach that signifies that we are close.

Sure enough, a few minutes later we emerge into the clearing, the redbrick farmhouse in its center a welcoming sight. And even more welcoming is the familiar figure standing on the front porch.

Ash is already down the stairs and jogging toward us before we're halfway across the clearing. I jump down from the bed of the wagon and run to meet him. He lifts me up in his arms and I bury my face into his neck.

"You're back," he whispers. I kiss his ear.

"I hope you didn't worry too much."

He sets me down on my feet. "I might have slept for an hour or two. That's an improvement."

I run my fingers through his hair—it's gotten longer in the last couple months—then gently touch the shadows under his eyes. He slips his hand into mine and we walk back toward the house. Sil and Raven have already gone inside. I tell him about the last three girls.

"So now all the Southgate surrogates going to the Auction know they are Paladin," I say. "Any news from the other circles?"

While the Marsh seems to have remained fairly untouched by the strife building in the city, it's getting bad in the Bank and the Smoke. And even though I understand that this is what a revolution entails, I hate seeing the reports in the papers, the bombings, the damage, the death. Every day we hear about more arrests, more violence. The Society is targeting royal strongholds: Regimental barracks and magistrate offices and banks. Trying to gauge reaction time and keep the royalty confused. Never the same quarter or circle twice in a row. Black keys are scrawled on walls and doors. We're hearing more and more reports of unplanned violence, of people making attacks on the royalty on their own.

Ash has been training a swath of Society members in this quarter, but his reach is limited, since there's still a warrant out for his arrest and execution. He can't go to the other quarters, or into the other circles, like I can.

"Mostly the same." Ash's frown is deep. "I can't stop thinking about the companions. If I could just get to them, they could help us so much."

"I know," I say patiently. We've had this discussion before. "Lucien says he's doing all he can for them. But you're still a fugitive."

"Lucien isn't doing anything because he *can't* do anything for them. They won't trust him," Ash says. "That's a fact."

I don't want to have this argument again. Over the past few months, Ash has grown more and more restless, his concern for the companions rising with each new attack in the Bank.

"But you're helping so much here," I say. "Look what you've done for Raven, for the Whistler and his crew, for all the Society members in the South Quarter."

The Whistler, one of Lucien's top agents, runs a tattoo parlor where the Society meets in secret. My brother, Ochre, works with him now. Ash has been training other young men and women to fight, so they can teach those in the surrounding quarters and circles, since he can't leave the South Quarter himself.

"Yeah, only in this quarter, and only at night when no one can see me, and *only* when Sil is going there." Ash stops and sits down on the front steps, rubbing his temple with the heel of his hand. "Rye is in the Jewel, right in the Duchess's own home! If I could just . . . contact him somehow. And don't bring up Lucien again—he's a genius, but companions are notoriously wary of ladies-in-waiting. They can get you in a lot of trouble if they want."

It always surprises me when Ash talks about the behind-the-scenes parts of the Jewel. The sniping among the servants or the illicit romances. The hierarchies that exist among the royalty's underclass.

"You're doing everything you can," I say. "Your very name is enough to get people joining our cause."

Ash has become something of a legend in the Lone City. His wanted status works in our favor. The rogue companion, falsely accused, who escaped the Jewel and the clutches of the royalty—the fugitive who evaded capture. He's a hero in Society circles.

"So I just sit back and let my name do all the work while companions continue to be abused and are dying?" Ash says.

The life of a companion is a hard one. I was shocked when Ash finally told me about it. They often become suicidal, cut themselves, or get high on a liquid form of opiate called blue. Rye, Ash's roommate who helped us escape the Bank, was using it when I met him a few months back.

I put my hand on Ash's neck and try to rub some of the tension away.

"I know it's hard," I say. "But it's the only way. The Bank is too dangerous for you. The White Rose is the only place where you'll be safe."

"But it's okay for you to be at risk?" he asks. "You and Raven and the girls, you travel to the holding facilities. That isn't safe at all."

Before I can reply, the front door is thrown open. "Oh, Violet, you're back!"

Indi wrenches me away and engulfs me in a hug. She is so tall, my head only comes up to her shoulders.

"How was it? Did you find the girls you were looking for?"

"We did," I say, patting her back. "It went fine. I'll tell you all about it, but first I need food or I'm going to fall over."

"Of course, you must be starving. Let me fix you a plate." Her face turns a little pink as she looks at Ash. "Do you want a plate, too?"

Even though Indi's known Ash for months now, she still blushes around him. To Ash's credit, he always acts as though he hasn't noticed.

"I'll be in in a little bit," he says. "Got to take Turnip back to the barn first."

He gives my hand a squeeze, so I know the argument is over for now. Turnip is munching on some grass, still hooked up to the wagon. He leads her off to the barn that sits at the edge of the ring of trees, and I watch and wish there was something I could do for him.

But I won't let him go back to the Bank. That's a death sentence for certain.

"Well, come on, Violet," Indi says, her eyes, like mine, focused on Ash's retreating figure. "I want to hear about last night, and you know the way Raven will tell it, she'll leave out all the good details and just be gruff when I ask questions."

"Indi!" Sil's voices booms from behind the screen door. "Your damned muffins are burning."

Indi gasps and whirls around, vanishing into the house.

I stand for a second on the porch, letting the sun warm my face. I want to hold on to this morning tightly, to imprint it in my brain, a talisman against whatever darkness the future holds.

In this moment, I am safe and alive, and surrounded by friends.

Four

I END UP SLEEPING THROUGH MOST OF THE DAY.

Dinner that night is the noisy affair it usually is.

"Olive, can you pass the salad, please?" I ask.

Where Indi is tall and fair and almost unnervingly optimistic, Olive is dark and small with perpetually red-rimmed eyes from crying so much. Even now I see them start to fill with tears.

"My mistress loved salad," Olive says, passing me the bowl. "One time at the palace of the Stream, we had a salad with candied pecans and fresh goat cheese and there was a lotus blossom on top and when you opened it there was a miniature golden bird inside." She sighs dramatically, glancing to the little pile of lettuce, tomato, and cucumber on her plate.

Sienna tosses a few sleek braids over her shoulder.

"Your mistress loved putting you on a leash, too," she says, flicking open the lighter that Sil bought her as a present. A tiny flame sparks. "Should we start tying you up outside at night like a dog?"

"Put that away," Sil warns her.

Olive slams her fork down on the table and stands. "Don't talk to me like that."

"You know you'd be dead now if Violet hadn't saved you, right?" Sienna says, pocketing her lighter.

"Knock it off," Raven says.

The few candles in the center of the table flare up. Olive's eyebrows knit together, and with a puff, the flames are extinguished.

"Hey," Sil says.

Sienna holds her hands up. "It was an accident, I swear."

"Please," Sil says. "Your control is perfect now. You haven't had an accident in months."

"Let's go over the plan again," I say, and everyone groans except Ash, who is always quiet during dinner. He usually shovels food into his mouth as quickly as possible and then escapes to the barn to be among the chickens and goats Sil keeps. And Turnip.

Turnip was the nickname he gave his younger sister, Cinder. She died a month ago of black lung. Lucien heard about it through one of his contacts in the Smoke, a young boy who calls himself the Thief. He helped Ash get a chance to say good-bye to his sister before we escaped that circle. I guess he kept tabs on her after.

Ash swallows the last of his chicken, shoves a piece of potato in his mouth, and stands.

"Ladies," he says with a nod to the table. He kisses the top of my head and walks over to the sink. Ash has heard all this before. I feel a bite of guilt, after our argument today, that he is not part of this plan, that this is something I intend to do without him. But I can't help that—it's the Paladin who need to take down the wall, and Ash isn't a Paladin.

I go to the side cupboard and take out several rolls of paper. One is a map of the city. The others are copies of the blueprints of the Auction House.

"So," I say, unfurling the map in the center of the table, "in a few days, we'll leave for Westgate. Sil, you'll stay here and coordinate with the Whistler in the Farm.

"We've got four girls left at Westgate, seven at North-gate, and five at Eastgate." I point to the numbers that have been scribbled over each facility, then scrub out the *3* over Southgate with an eraser. "Indi, Sienna, and Olive, once we get to your respective facilities and show the girls the elements, you will—"

"Stay in a safe house until the night before the Auction," Sienna says in a dull monotone.

"Where we will sneak back into the facilities with the help of any girl who can connect with Earth," Indi says brightly.

"And then we hide on the trains until they leave for the Auction," Olive finishes. A gleam shines in her eye. "That's when we take out the caretakers and the doctor."

"You're not killing them, Olive," I say. "Just knocking them unconscious."

"I'm sure we'll be able to manage," Raven says. "It was just Charity and Dr. Steele on our train there."

"Northgate always sends three caretakers," Sienna says.
"They'll still be outnumbered," I say.

"The Regimentals will be waiting for you at the Auction House," Sil reminds us.

"And it's Garnet's job to delay them as long as he can," I say, rolling up the map and taking out the blueprints. "And remember, if anything happens on the train, if you get found out or . . . or anything. Get to the walls. Bringing down the walls is crucial. And even if it's not the wall that surrounds the Jewel, breaking down any royal barrier is a success for our cause."

Olive pouts a little but keeps quiet. There are multiple sheets of blueprints of the Auction House, because not only are there many different rooms, there are several floors beneath it. I pin them down with plates and glasses.

The Auction House is built in a large dome with other smaller domes and turrets piled up around it, various rooms where the royalty are entertained while they wait to purchase surrogates. And of course, the amphitheater where the Auction itself takes place. But there are also—as Lucien pointed out—the Waiting Rooms and prep rooms and a train station on the floors below, chambers for the servants to wait in, and powder rooms for young royal ladies to fix their hair and makeup. And there are secure rooms, safe rooms, in case any danger should befall the Jewel during the Auction. These rooms have thick walls and iron doors. They are where the royalty will run to if threatened. We'll have them trapped, while the city falls around them.

The Auction is the biggest social event of the year. Lucien told us that every married royal is allowed to attend, so they don't need invitations like they would for the Exetor's Ball or a simple House party. Anyone who can attend does. It will be the highest concentration of royals in one place.

"So we'll get in here," I say, pointing to the underground train station, on the blueprint that shows the lowest levels of the Auction House. "And we'll have to be ready right away. Sil is right, there will be Regimentals expecting four train-loads of unconscious girls. And Garnet might not be able to delay them long, if at all. We should expect a fight."

"Yes, and most of the Regimentals he's been able to bring over to our side don't work in the Jewel," Raven says. "He says the Jewel Regimentals are the worst."

Garnet has gone from wild party boy to upstanding citizen in a head-spinning amount of time. While all royal men are technically officers in the Regimental army, it's always been more of an honorary title. No one actually serves. But once Garnet chose to serve in the search for Ash, he discovered a lot of discontent among the Regimental forces, especially in the lower circles. Now he's using that to our advantage.

"I do wish there were an easier way," Indi says wistfully. "One that didn't involve violence."

"You want us to fight them with hugs?" Sienna asks.

"Love is stronger than hate," Indi says.

"Violence is the only option, so there isn't any point in arguing about it," I say, cutting Sienna off before she can retort. "Once we're inside, everything needs to happen at once. We need to contain the Regimentals. We need to cause so much panic that the royalty run and hide in their precious safe rooms. Then we need to get to the wall."

"And you and I set off the signal," Sienna says to me, flicking her lighter open once more.

I nod. "You and I set off the signal."

"And everything goes up in flames," she says. The lighter's flame glows in her dark eyes.

The timing must be precise. In the days leading up to the Auction, bombs will be planted in the final, key locations that haven't been attacked yet. As many Society members as possible will gather in the Bank. The day of the Auction, they will station themselves by the wall that separates the Bank and the Jewel, waiting for the Paladin to bring it crashing down. My job is to get as high up as I can, into one of the Auction House's five spires. Sienna will use Fire while I use Air, to set off a flare of sorts, high enough that everyone in the city will be able to see it, indicating that the bombs should go off. I would do it myself if I could, but we can only use one element at a time.

And after that, as Sienna so aptly put it, everything will go up in flames.

I go over each sheet of blueprints meticulously. I trace my fingers over the various hallways, test the girls' knowledge of what goes where, which staircase leads to what room, how many levels there are in the Auction House, what each one holds, where the safe rooms are, locating every exit and entrance until finally Sienna lets out a loud sigh.

"Violet, we get it, all right? We've gone over this a million times. I could draw these blueprints in my sleep."

"We need to be prepared," I say. "The other girls won't know anything. They won't have seen these. We have to be the leaders. We have to know exactly where we're going. We can't bring them into this only to let them down."

Sienna looks slightly abashed. Indi's brow creases and Olive stares down at her plate.

Raven reaches out and grips my hand. "We won't," she says.

I roll up the blueprints and map and put them away, a deep unease settling in the pit of my stomach. All this to help the surrogates, and yet my sister is still trapped in that palace. Memorizing all the blueprints in the world won't help her where she is.

It's been months since the Duchess announced Hazel's pregnancy. Is Hazel's stomach a tiny bump, like Raven's once was? Is the doctor using that horrible stimulant gun on her? I don't even know if Hazel *is* a surrogate. She was taken before she could be tested at the Marsh clinics. But she must be, otherwise she would be of no use to the Duchess.

If only there were some way I could see her, know she was all right, tell her to hold on . . .

After dinner, Olive begs Sil to bring out The Book.

The Book isn't really a book. More like various fragments from lots of different books. Lucien compiled it for Sil over the years, stealing pieces of old texts from the Duchess's library. All together, it tells the history of the Paladin, of this island before it became the Lone City. And all the girls in this house love reading it. Myself included.

The island was called Excelsior, the Jewel of the Earth.

Olive snuggles into my side as we read the yellowed, crumbling pages. It's strange to me that Olive loves The Book so much—especially since it details how the royalty conquered this island by force and massacred most of the native population. But it talks about a place called Bellstar and another called Ellaria and I think the idea of other places out there beyond the Great Wall appeals to her in the same way *The Wishing Well* story appealed to me as a child. She wants to believe in the magic and the mystery of it.

She doesn't seem to understand that we are part of that magic.

The only sounds are the clink of dishes as Sienna washes and Indi's soft hum as she dries. Sil sits in her rocking chair by the fire, nursing a glass of whiskey. Raven is on the floor at my feet, her head resting on my knees.

"What do you think Bellstar is like?" Olive asks. "I wish there were pictures."

"It must have been very wealthy," I say. "They built hundreds of ships to find this island."

"What happened to them?"

"The people?"

"The ships."

I trace my fingers over the faded letters on the page. "I don't know," I murmur.

Suddenly, the arcana buzzes in my hair. I've long revealed the secret of the arcana to the other girls—it was too difficult to hide it after a while. I pull it out now and the silver tuning fork floats a foot away from my face.

"Hello?" I say. Raven perks up. We never know if it will be Lucien or Garnet on the other end.

"Well?" Lucien's voice is tense. "How did it go?"

I smile. "It was fine. The usual. That's all of Southgate down. Just three more holding facilities left."

"With only about a month to go until the big day."

My stomach squeezes in nervous anticipation. My thoughts fly to my sister again. A month is such a long time. *Hold on just a little longer, Hazel. I'm coming.*

"How is the Jewel?" I ask, which is pretty much always code for, How is Hazel? So when Lucien begins to ramble, I'm immediately on edge.

"Insane, as it always is when the Auction approaches," he says. "Of course, it's worse this year, since the lower circles are in such turmoil. But you'd think the royalty don't read the papers. The Lady of the Hail can't stop boasting about her post-Auction night dinner—it sounds like she's preparing twenty courses, if you believe her, which I don't. She's sent the Electress a hundred invites. And now I have to oversee a shipment from the House of the Flame. Spiced meats, some saffron, and fresh cream from their dairies in the Farm. It's due to arrive tomorrow. As if saffron is something I need to be worried about right now. Meanwhile, there have been three more arrests in the Bank—one was quite a close call, I thought they'd captured one of my associates—and another bomb went off in the Smoke, which I certainly didn't sanction—it was poorly made and full of shrapnel so now that quarter is being levied with food restrictions. Even the Regimentals are feeling the pinch. And meanwhile—"

"How's my sister?" I interrupt.

He pauses. My heart stops as he doesn't say anything.

"Lucien," I say, "what is happening?"

"Nothing," he says. "Nothing I feel you need to worry about."

Raven is sitting up, her dark eyes fixed on the arcana.

Sil has put down her whiskey.

"Why don't you let me decide what I need to worry about," I say.

"I have a . . . suspicion. It's not confirmed but I feel that the Electress is planning an . . . accident. For your sister."

"What?" I jump up as if I can run to Hazel right now, as if I could protect her. I *have* to protect her. "You work for her, find out what she's planning and stop it!"

"I do not know if she is even planning anything," Lucien says. "All I know is that the more enthusiasm the Exetor expresses for this engagement, the more furious she becomes at it. She has made some comments that lead me to believe—"

"She'd do it just out of spite," I say. "She'd do it to get back at the Duchess."

"Yes, but you see—"

"Ugh, these people!" I throw my hands up in frustration. "Don't they get that she is someone's sister, someone's daughter, someone's friend?"

"No," Lucien says dryly. "And I think you'd understand that better than anyone."

His words cut but not as deeply as the thought of Hazel being assassinated. I thought I would have time. Time to get to her, to free her. Time to explain, time to apologize.

Lucien can't save her. He can't watch her twenty-four hours a day. He has other priorities, and as much as he cares for me, he would sacrifice Hazel if it meant saving the city.

"I'm going to the Jewel," I say. "Now. Tonight."

"Violet, don't be—"

"I'm going," I snap, cutting him off. "What would you

do if it was Azalea? It's my fault Hazel is there at all. The Duchess took her to get to me. I know it, I feel it. If I can't protect her now, I . . ." My voice trails off because I can't finish that sentence.

"And how exactly do you plan on getting here?"

"I'll take a train to the Bank. I can burrow under the wall surrounding the Jewel as easily as Southgate." Okay, maybe not quite as easily, but it's the same general idea.

"Not only is that a foolhardy plan that could give the game away, but what do you intend to do once you are in the Jewel itself? Walk up to the Duchess's palace and ring the doorbell? Think, Violet. There are bigger things at stake here than personal struggles."

"And if I don't try and save Hazel now, then I don't know what I'm fighting for at all," I say.

"You would be recognized," Lucien says. "It's too—"

I gasp, an idea occurring to me—a crazy, rash idea that I'm not even sure is possible. But I'm willing to try anything at this point. Without another word I turn and run upstairs, ignoring the shouted questions from Sil and Raven, Lucien's tinny voice demanding to know what's going on.

Ash and I sleep in the barn together, but we keep our clothes in Raven's room. There are other clothes as well, which Sil has collected over the years. One dress I remember distinctly, because it reminded me so much of the servant's dresses Raven and I used to disguise ourselves in the Bank. I comb through the closet, find it, and yank it off the hanger—it is plain and brown, a little small across the chest but it will do. I pull it on and look at myself in the mirror. Slowly, I raise a hand and knot it in my hair.

Once to see it as it is. Twice to see it in your mind. Thrice to bend it to your will.

My scalp tingles as my hair turns from black to gold. The headache that comes with performing an Augury throbs at the base of my skull. This is how I disguised Ash when we sneaked into his companion house. It's strange to use it on myself. I turn my head back and forth, examining the unfamiliar strands of blond.

But it's my eyes that are the real problem. If I can't change them, the Duchess will spot me instantly.

I close them now. I think I can do this without physically putting my fingers on my eyeballs—the thought gives me the creeps. I just need to focus hard enough on what I want. The picture forms crystalline in my mind.

Once to see it as it is. Twice to see it in your mind. Thrice to bend it to your will.

Unlike with my hair, this Augury is agony. I scream and clap my hands over my eyes. They boil in their sockets, burning like little balls of fire. Just when I don't think I can bear it any longer, the pain stops. I stay hunched over for a moment, breathing heavily.

When I open my eyes, a stranger stares back at me in the mirror. A blond-haired, green-eyed stranger with my nose and chin. I quickly use the second Augury, Shape, to adjust the lines of my face. It hurts almost as much as my eyes, but at the end, my chin is a bit rounder, my forehead higher, my nose a little larger.

"Violet, are you—" Raven stops short in the doorway, gaping at me. "What did you *do?*"

"I'm going to the Jewel," I say, walking past her and

back downstairs to where Lucien is probably still losing it on the arcana.

Olive shrieks as I enter the living room. Indi drops the plate she's drying. Sienna gapes. Sil looks shocked for a split second, but then I see the faintest hint of pride in her eyes.

"I told him," she says, over Lucien's voice, which is still coming through the arcana. "You're too damned stubborn."

"What's happening?" he demands. "Why did she scream? Sil, *answer me*!"

"I'm going to the Jewel, Lucien," I say. "I'll get myself to the Duchess's palace. I'll watch over my sister until the Auction."

Lucien starts laughing. In fact, he laughs for so long that Sil and I exchange a worried glance. "I'm sorry," he says. "But this is too much, even for you. How long do you expect to stay free once the Duchess discovers you *in her own palace*? How do you plan to protect your sister when you are a captive yourself? Or maybe the Duchess will simply kill you for fun, now that she no longer requires your body to produce a child."

"Lucien," Sil says, clasping her hands together and resting her chin on them, "in any other circumstance I'd agree with you but . . . I don't think there's any way the Duchess will recognize her."

"And why is that?"

"Because she looks freakishly like a different person."

I didn't realize Sienna had come in from the kitchen. She reaches out and gently takes a lock of my hair. "Color and Shape?" she asks me. I nod. "Did it hurt?"

I grimace.

Sienna grins. "Ash is going to flip his—"

"What do you mean, like a different person?" Lucien interrupts.

"I used the Auguries," I say. "On myself." Tears spring to my eyes and they sizzle with residual heat from the Augury. "Please, Lucien," I say. "Help me. Help me help my sister."

I remember my Reckoning Day, the last time I saw my family as a whole. How angry Hazel was with me, how she thought I'd forgotten her. She didn't understand that I wasn't allowed to write to her, that Southgate had rules.

I understand the rules of the Jewel. And I won't let my sister think she's been forgotten again.

Five

THE SILENCE THAT FOLLOWS IS BROKEN ONLY BY THE
loud thumping of my heart.

"Let me talk to Garnet about this," Lucien says in a
clipped tone. "Wait and don't do anything rash."

The arcana falls silent onto the floor. I pick it up and
hold it with trembling fingers. "I can't leave her there," I
say, sinking onto the couch. Raven sits beside me. "She's all
alone. I can't . . ."

"I know," Sil says, a softness in her voice.

We sit there for what feels like hours. The arcana never
buzzes. Finally, I rouse myself.

"I'd better go see Ash," I say. "He must be wondering
where I am."

I don't think he's going to take the news particularly well. Just as I stand, the arcana rises in the air.

"So," Garnet says. "I hear you're planning a covert operation."

"Hazel's in danger," I say. "I have to be there. I have to do what I can."

"Well, you're in luck," Garnet says. "Because I happen to know of a royal House that is hiring help."

"You do?" I say.

"Yes," he replies. "Mine."

Raven and I exchange a quizzical glance.

Garnet continues. "My wife needs a lady-in-waiting of her own." Raven stiffens almost imperceptibly at the word *wife*. "Coral has been trying to hire one for months and Mother rejects every one she finds. Up until this point I've stayed out of it because there is no point in fighting with my mother over something so trivial, and honestly, I could not care less about Coral having a lady-in-waiting. But now it seems we need one. So I will merely inform everyone tomorrow that I've hired you. It's a very typical me move, a nice touch of arrogance, a dash of indifference for my mother's wishes." I can imagine the gleam of mischief in his blue eyes. "I'll let you know which train to get on tomorrow. I'm sure there will be a new group of servants coming in— everyone is going crazy preparing for the Auction. I'll send out word that we're expecting you."

"Thank you, Garnet," I say fervently.

"Don't mention it. Hey, is Raven there?"

"Thought you'd never ask," she says, stepping forward with a grin.

"Business before pleasure, always. Do you have time to talk?"

Raven laughs. "I'm not the one with the crazy wife and the overbearing mother. I've got all the time in the world."

"Yes, but you've got Sil, and she isn't exactly a bucket of rainbows, is she? Kidding, Sil!" he says quickly before Sil can retort.

Raven takes the arcana to the front porch. I say good night to Sil and the girls and head to the barn to break the news to Ash.

HE'S BY THE GOAT PEN, ONE OF THEM NUZZLING HIS HAND searching for an extra treat, when I enter.

For a moment, I just stand and watch him, the strength of his shoulders, the curve of his arms, the gentleness in his touch as he rubs a black-and-white-spotted goat behind the ears. I breathe in the calm before I break it.

"Ash?" I say timidly.

He turns around and lets out a strangled yelp when he sees my new face. "What—*Violet?*"

"It's me," I say, stepping forward. He comes closer, inspecting my eyes and nose and hair with a little bit of wonder and a lot of confusion.

"The Auguries?" he asks. I nod. "Why?"

I explain what Lucien told me about the danger Hazel is in, and how Garnet is going to hire me to work in the palace. I see his face turn from incredulous to downright stormy.

"You're serious," he says. "You're leaving the White Rose. You're abandoning your own plan and going into the Jewel, into the heart of danger."

I swallow. "Yes."

"Fine." He turns and climbs up the hayloft ladder, tossing a few things he keeps up there down, an extra shirt, his pocket watch, the photograph of his family that he took from Madame Curio's companion house. Then he climbs back down the ladder. "I'm coming with you."

"What? No, Ash, you can't."

"And you can?"

"I don't look like me! I don't have a million Regimentals trying to find and execute me. Garnet will look after me. I'll be safe."

"Garnet has his own role in this revolution," Ash says. "He can't put everything on hold just to watch over you." He starts shoving the items into a small satchel. "Everyone in the whole damned city has a role in this revolution, except me."

He throws the bag over his shoulder and glares.

"So when do we leave?" he asks.

I wait for a few moments, until his breathing has calmed slightly. Then I step forward and place a hand on his cheek.

"Ash, you *can't*," I say. "You'd never make it past the Bank."

"Stop trying to keep me safe all the time, when you clearly don't show the same consideration for yourself." The chickens cluck nervously as he begins to pace around the barn. "You're always telling me to stay here, be patient, be protected, but what if that's not what I want? What if I want to do more, no matter the risk? And you feel like you can just waltz off to the Jewel because Hazel is in danger and expect everyone to understand. Well, I *don't*, Violet. I don't understand."

"She *is* in danger," I say.

"We're *all* in danger!" Ash shouts, and Turnip whinnies, shaking her mane. He runs his hand down her long neck to calm her. "Don't you even see the hypocrisy here? Don't you get how unfair it is, that you are allowed to risk everything and I am not? The companions are my surrogates, Violet. They are *my* people and they are hurting, too, but they aren't special in any way, so who cares? Who cares if they are bright, talented young men being abused and manipulated? They're pretty little things who are only good for screwing, right? Why should their voices matter?"

"That's not what . . . this is *Hazel*, Ash. My sister. You'd do the same for Cinder."

It was the wrong thing to say and I know it immediately. Ash's head whips up, his gaze so fierce it makes me shrink away.

"Don't," he says coldly.

My cheeks burn. "I'm sorry. I'm just saying we all have people we're willing to sacrifice for."

"And who do I have left, Violet? You. Just you." He takes the bag off his shoulder and drops it on the ground. "But you seem to think you are the only one allowed to make hard choices. And you don't seem to get that your choices affect other people, including me."

He stares at me for a few seconds before shaking his head, turning on his heel, and storming out into the night.

WHEN RAVEN STOPS BY THE BARN TO GIVE ME BACK THE arcana, she knows that something is wrong.

I barely even need to explain the fight with Ash. My

whispers must have been broadcasting at full volume. She moves aside the straw dummy Ash has her practice things like chokeholds and punches on and pulls me over to sit on a hay bale, wrapping her arm around me.

"He's scared and angry," she says. "And he wants to help."

"I understand, but it's like he doesn't even realize the danger he'd be in if he left! I'm not saying I don't believe in him—"

"Aren't you?" Raven asks. There is no judgment in her tone but the question ruffles me anyway.

"What do you want me to do, say, 'Yeah, Ash, great idea, go on off to the Bank and fingers crossed no one recognizes you'?"

"There are people he cares about in this city, too. And here in this house, it's all about the surrogates. We never talk about the companions. No one does. Not Lucien, not Garnet . . ." She cocks her head. "We all have our own battles. I don't want you going back to the Jewel any more than he does. I just know you well enough to know when fighting is pointless." She nudges me with her shoulder. "You better take care of yourself. And Hazel. And keep an eye on Garnet for me."

I smile, though the argument still weighs on me. "Yes, ma'am."

"I wonder what his wife is like."

"Pretty dull, from what he's told us." Garnet generally avoids mentioning Coral if he can help it. Especially around Raven.

She hops off the bale. "So you'll be a servant again. Hey,

maybe it'll be an advantage. Maybe you can see if there's any discontent in the royal Houses, you know, and use it for our cause."

I know she's just trying to help, to be positive. And I appreciate it. "Yeah," I say. Then I pause. "Is . . . is he back at the house?"

"No," Raven says. "I don't know where he is."

I give her a parting hug and get ready for bed. I climb up into the hayloft, carrying the satchel with Ash's things in it with me. I lie down, close my eyes, and wish for sleep. But all I see is the Electress pouring poison into Hazel's water glass. Or hiring someone to push her down stairs or suffocate her in her bed or . . .

The Duchess never lets Hazel out though, I remind myself. Shouldn't her confinement be enough to keep her safe?

I open my eyes and stare at the slats in the ceiling, trying to will away my frustration and second-guessing. I always thought doing the right thing would be easy. If not easy to act on, at least easy to identify. But now I'm abandoning my own plan for something rash and half thought-out. I don't even look like myself anymore.

There's a creak on the ladder and I sit up.

"Ash?" I whisper. I feel his weight as he crawls over to me. "I'm so sorry," I say. "I didn't—"

"Shhh." He presses his lips to mine gently and I shiver. I pull him toward me, grateful for his comforting presence, the warmth of his body, the scent of his skin.

"I don't want to fight," he murmurs.

"Me neither."

His fingers trace down my neck, over my collarbone.

I'm only wearing a thin slip, and goose bumps blossom over my skin as his fingers move down toward my stomach.

"Have you ever thought about . . . after?" he asks quietly.

"After?" I ask, only half paying attention because his fingers have circled my belly button and are moving toward my right hip.

"After all this." His lips are on my neck. "After you save Hazel. After the fighting and the tearing down of walls. After this city has been thrown into an upheaval unlike it's ever known. Say we win. The royalty don't run this city anymore. What do you want?"

"I don't know," I say as his hand squeezes my thigh. "I haven't really thought about it."

"All this planning and you don't even have an idea of what you want after?"

"Maybe I don't believe we'll win."

"Maybe you're just frightened of the future."

I find the depression at the base of his neck and kiss it gently. "And what is *your* plan for the future?"

His hand freezes on my knee. "Nothing," he says, pulling away from me.

I'm immediately alert. "Hey," I say, reaching up to twine my fingers in his hair, keeping him close. His eyes reflect the barest hint of moonlight that makes its way into our bed. "You can tell me."

He sighs, then says, "I want to be a farmer."

I wait for more explanation but he doesn't continue.

"Is that . . . all?" I say, not wanting to offend but feeling a bit confused.

"You don't think that's stupid?" he says. "You don't think after all the fine things people like you and I have had access to, the clothes, the food, the wealth, that I'd want something more?"

"I think all those fine things we had came with too high a price," I say. "I'd be happy never to see cloth-of-gold again in my life. Where would you want to farm? I mean, besides the Farm, obviously."

He adjusts himself so that he's stretched out beside me, head propped up on one hand. "There's an old ruin of a place about five miles outside the Whistler's village. Ochre showed it to me once. It's a good spot for hiding the younger boys who've joined us, you know, a day or two before the Auction, when they won't be returning home after their work day. But I thought . . . I thought I could fix it up. Maybe Sil would sell me a couple of chickens and a goat. Get some seeds. It would be nice to work with the earth. And I like animals. I'd like a life of growing my own food, making my own things. Having a real home."

Tears spring to my eyes, as I realize I'm not anywhere in this picture he has painted. "Oh," I say in a raspy voice. "That sounds nice."

"Are you crying?" Ash says, aghast.

"No," I say too quickly, scrubbing the tears away.

I can almost hear his brain click. "Do you think I don't want you there with me?" he asks.

"No," I say again, but it's a clear lie.

"Violet. I did not write you out of my life," he says, "but I would never want to assume my plans would line up with yours. You have the right to choose what you want for yourself."

"But what if that sounds nice to me?" I say. "What if

I want to help you fix up that old place? I bet I could convince Sil to give us Turnip, since she likes you better than Sil anyway. And I could have a chrysanthemum garden, like the one my mother used to have in our kitchen windowsill. I could use Earth to help you with planting crops, and Water, too, to tend them. I could use Fire to keep the house warm in the winter, and Air to keep us cool in the summer."

I can see it, I can see it so clearly it's an actual ache in my chest. A little front porch with a wild garden blooming all around it. A white house with blue shutters. Ash and I working in the soil, ending each day tired and sweaty and covered in dirt, but happy. Having a place of our own.

When Ash speaks again, his voice is thick. "That sounds . . . perfect."

"Of course, Raven will have to live nearby," I say.

"And Garnet, too."

"And Indi."

"Sienna?"

"Yes, but not Olive."

"No," Ash says with a laugh. "Not Olive."

I sigh and lean back against the heavy blanket we sleep on. "I want that life, Ash. I want it so badly I can taste it."

"So do I," he murmurs.

I allow my mind to spin out, to imagine a world where my sister doesn't have to live in fear of her own body and the power it holds, where my brother isn't forced to work in an assigned profession. I try to imagine the walls falling down, the city integrated, its people no longer divided but unified.

I fall asleep with the taste of Ash's lips on mine, and fantasies of a better future dancing in my dreams.

The next morning, however, Ash's good mood has vanished, all the tenderness of last night gone, replaced with tension and anger at my leaving.

I can tell he's trying to hide it, but there's a tightness around his eyes and mouth, a sharpness in his tone.

Ash isn't the only one who is tense. Even Indi is on edge. Once Garnet contacts me about the train I need to take, there are no smiles to see me off except for a forced one from Raven.

I stand by Sil's cart and give each girl a hug, promising to see them soon, reminding them to keep studying the blueprints. Ash crushes me against him and whispers fiercely in my ear.

"Please be careful. Promise me."

"I promise," I whisper.

"I wish there were some way I could tell Rye to keep an eye on you," he says.

"Do you think he'll recognize me?" I ask.

Ash tucks a lock of my newly blond hair behind my ear. "No," he murmurs. "Plus he'll be too busy with Carnelian to pay much attention to a new servant."

"Should I tell him who I am?"

"I don't know. It could be dangerous." Ash's jaw hardens. "And watch out for Carnelian."

"Right." I'm not looking forward to living under the same roof as her again.

"I'm serious, Violet. She's sharper, more intelligent, than you give her credit for."

"Well, I'm happy to avoid her completely," I say. I don't want to talk about Carnelian anymore.

We kiss one last time before Sil gets in the cart and I climb up beside her.

Raven raises one hand in farewell. Ash stays on the porch, watching the cart until we pass under the trees and the White Rose is swallowed up behind us.

"You certainly know how to wreak havoc," Sil says.

"I don't want to fight with you, Sil," I say wearily.

She nods and gives the reins another flick. We ride the rest of the way in silence. I can't help wondering—what if I'm too late? What if Hazel dies today? What if something is happening to her right now? Turnip's pace is infuriatingly slow. The fields stretch out in rolling waves of yellowish brown, never changing.

When we finally reach Bartlett Station, my back is aching from the tension. Sil waits with me until the train pulls up.

"You've got your papers?" she says, and I hold up the forged documents that will allow me to get as far as the Bank. I have to take three different trains today to get to the Jewel. I'm wearing the brown dress, the one that looks like a servant's garb.

"And here are some extra diamantes, just in case," Sil says, pressing the coins into my hands. My throat has swelled up so I nod in thanks.

"Well," she says as the train screeches to a halt and the doors are thrown open. Then she engulfs me in a short but emphatic hug.

"Thanks, Sil," I whisper. "For everything."

"Go on, then," she says, rubbing her eyes and turning away. I join the line of people waiting to board. When I get on, I find a seat by a window. Turnip and Sil are already on their way back to the White Rose.

The train rolls forward and the first step of this journey begins. To get to the Bank, I'm going to have to transfer at one of the Farm's main terminals.

Should I even be doing this? Is the danger to Hazel great enough for me to take such a risk?

But as the farmland flashes past me out the window, I think about waiting here over the next month, so far away from her, not knowing from one day to the next if she's dead or alive, certain of only one thing: it's my fault. I couldn't live like that.

The main terminal is large and loud, packed with people. I find my train, a great gray monster, and take a seat opposite a worker reading the *Lone City Herald*. The headline reads: "Exetor and Electress Promise Spectacular Auction Festivities This Year." At the bottom of the page, I see another article, only a paragraph and in much smaller print: "Five Dead in Bombing; Black Key Society Suspected."

Nerves gnaw at my stomach for the rest of the ride. Especially for one moment in the Smoke, when we pass the ruined shell of a factory near the elevated tracks. One of the bombed buildings. Black keys are scrawled everywhere. A man is being beaten in the street by three Regimentals. Then the train chugs on, leaving the unsettling scene behind us.

But it stays in my mind for the rest of the ride. I haven't seen much of the actual revolution. I've heard stories, from Lucien and Garnet, and read them in the papers, but I've never seen the results of Lucien's efforts laid bare in front of me. It's very different, reading a headline versus seeing the blackened ruin left behind.

When we arrive at the station in the Bank, we're instructed to leave the train and transfer to a different one. My stomach is in so many knots I don't think they'll ever untangle. I'm sweating under my arms and on my lower back. Garnet said there would be a group of newly hired servants coming in, but all I see are men in bowler hats and women with parasols.

Just then a covered wagon pulls up. Girls file out of it, all of them wearing brown dresses. They range in age from a few years younger than me to nearly as old as Sil. A woman in charge is ushering them off the wagon.

Quickly, I slip through the crowd and fall in step behind a girl with curly brown hair. We wait patiently in a group as another train, the one going to the Jewel, pulls up.

Someone grabs my arm.

"Where is your hat?" A girl in her late twenties is glaring at me, furious.

"What? Oh, I . . . I lost it," I say. The lie falls out of my mouth on its own.

She tsks. "Here, I have an extra one." She hands me a white cap with lace fringe on it, identical to the one on her own head. "Take care not to lose this one."

"Right, thanks," I say.

"You're lucky you didn't arrive in the Jewel like that," she says as we begin to board the train. I notice that all the servant girls are entering a smaller, front compartment, separate from the Bank patrons. "The ladies-in-waiting are sticklers about new girls. They might just send you back to the Bank, and you don't want that, do you?"

I shake my head.

"Which House are you assigned to?"

"The Lake," I say.

"Really?" The girl looks surprised. "I didn't know they were looking for more help."

"Garnet of the House of the Lake hired me," I say, taking care to call him by his full title. "For his wife."

"Oh, so he's finally getting her a proper lady-in-waiting, is he? I'd have thought the Duchess would never let her get one." She claps a hand over her mouth, eyes wide. "Don't repeat that. I—I didn't mean it."

"Don't worry," I say, lowering my voice to a conspiratorial whisper. "I won't say a thing."

She grins. "Thanks."

We climb into the compartment, which is standing room only. There are no chairs or benches to sit on. The train whistles and the doors bang shut. A second later, we lurch forward.

"You haven't seen the Jewel before, have you?" the girl says.

"No," I lie.

I must look genuinely frightened because her whole manner softens. "What's your name?"

"Lily," I say. Again, the word comes out on its own, but I'm glad I chose it. A tribute to my blond-haired friend from Southgate. Lily is pregnant and living in the Bank now.

"Well, Lily," the girl says, looking out the window at the posh town houses passing by, "you're in for a real treat."

Six

THE IRON DOORS SCREECH WHEN THEY OPEN.

I hold my breath as the train slowly chugs through the wall that separates the Bank and the Jewel. When I came here for the Auction, nearly seven months ago, I was drugged and unconscious for this part of the journey. Now I can see just how thick this wall is, maybe even as thick as the Great Wall that surrounds the entire island. We are plunged into darkness and all I can think is, *Will eighty-one surrogates be enough to bring it down?*

Not surrogates, I remind myself. *Surrogates are slaves. We are eighty-one Paladin.*

After a full minute of pitch black, I stare out the window in awe as the Jewel comes into view. I'd forgotten just how deceptively beautiful it is.

The buildings that line the inside of the wall are not palaces, but they are glamorous all the same. We pass a restaurant made entirely out of glass, three tiers of people eating and drinking and laughing. There's a croquet pitch— two teenage girls are knocking around brightly colored balls while their ladies-in-waiting (one male, one female) look on. In the distance I can see a rose-colored, domed building with golden spires.

The Auction House.

The train creeps toward the station, which is by far the nicest one I've ever seen. There is a comfortable little house beside it where people can wait for their trains. Motorcars line the road.

We are instructed to stay put and be silent until the other travelers have left and the train is empty. Then we file out in a neat line. There are three wagons waiting for us. The woman in charge begins to sort us into them, depending on which House we are going to. I'm waiting nervously for my turn when I hear a familiar voice.

"Not that one, it's got to have the crest of the House of the Flame on it."

The last time I saw Lucien was at the White Rose, when I asked him to save Sienna for me. That was over two months ago. He looks angry, impatient, his mouth turned down, his forehead wrinkling. His hair is in its usual perfect topknot, and he tugs at the lace collar of his white dress as two men haul the crate onto the back of a glossy coach with the Exetor's crest on it—a crowned flame crossed with two spears.

"Be careful, I said," he snaps at the men. I knew Lucien

ran the Exetor and Electress's household, but I've never seen him like this. He seems . . . mean.

But then his gaze sweeps over the line of girls being sorted into the wagons, scanning them, looking for a familiar face . . . and when his eyes land on me, they register not even the slightest hint of recognition. His face falls ever so slightly.

I suppose I should be relieved. It's a good thing if I'm not recognized. But it stings a little all the same.

"That's the last one, sir," one of the men says.

"Very good," Lucien says, handing him a few diamantes. "House?"

I start. The woman in charge is staring down at me.

"House?" she says again.

"The Lake," I say.

"Wagon three." She points to the wagon on the far right and I duck my head meekly, hurrying over to it and climbing into the back. It's covered with a brown canvas and there are two benches. I sit beside a heavy girl with frizzy black hair.

"Which House are you serving?" she asks me.

"Oh, um, the House of the Lake."

"I'm going to a Founding House as well!" she exclaims. "House of the Rose. Is this your first time in the Jewel?"

I nod.

"Mine too. I'm Rabbet, what's your name?"

The wagon fills up around us. Some girls keep to themselves; others whisper to each other.

I almost blurt out my real name but stop myself at the last second. "I'm Lily."

"That's a pretty name," Rabbet says. "Which circle are you from?"

"The Farm," I say as the wagon lurches forward. Part of me wishes Rabbet would stop talking because I'm so nervous, but in some sense it does provide a nice distraction. "What about you?"

"The Smoke. I started working as a scullery maid in the Bank when I was eight. And then they moved me up to kitchen maid and then chambermaid. My mistress was going to make me her lady's maid, she said. But then she died."

"I'm sorry."

Rabbet shrugs. "Now I get to work in the Jewel! I wonder what the palace of the Rose looks like."

I saw the palace of the Rose very briefly—the Duchess and I drove past it on our way to Dahlia's funeral. It was crafted out of jade and shaped like an evergreen tree.

I can only see out of the back of the wagon and I'm expecting palaces lined up behind golden gates, the way it was on all my drives through the Jewel. But the road we're on is rough and uneven, not at all like the smooth roads I remember. And I can't see any palaces at all, only large stone walls on either side of us. And every wall is topped with vicious spikes.

Are we *behind* the palaces?

That would make sense. The royalty would never want to see this sort of wagon on their streets. They wouldn't want to see the servants at all.

My suspicion is confirmed when we make our first stop.

"House of the Gale," the driver shouts. A blonde and

a brunette jump down off the back of the wagon. There is an iron door in the stone wall, with a bell hanging beside it. The blonde rings the bell as the wagon begins to roll forward. The brunette glances back at us as the door opens, fear in her eyes, before she disappears from view.

I never thought to look for a door in the wall that surrounded the Duchess's palace. And I loved walking through her wild garden.

Then I force my thoughts away from it because all of my memories of the garden are tinged with Annabelle. She was my own lady-in-waiting, but really she was my friend. My first friend in the Jewel. She was sweet and good and the Duchess killed her right in front of me.

The memory of her lying there, dying on the floor of my bedroom, rears up, a monster of guilt and pain inside me. I squeeze my eyes shut for a moment to steady myself.

We make two more stops before it's Rabbet's turn.

"House of the Rose!" the driver calls.

"Wish me luck," Rabbet says breathily.

"Good luck," I say with a tight smile. The wagon lurches forward and two more stops later, the driver shouts, "House of the Lake!"

My knees shake as I climb down and stand in front of the iron door that leads to the Duchess's palace. My throat is dry and I'm having a hard time swallowing. My limbs are numb and clumsy and seem to have forgotten how to work. The wagon rolls away and I stare after it for a moment, panicked, thinking this was a very stupid idea. But then I remind myself that Hazel is behind this door, and somehow, my hand manages to reach out and pull down on the rope swinging from the big brass bell.

Several seconds pass. Then a minute. Then two. Nothing.

I ring the bell again. Then again.

What if Garnet forgot to tell anyone I'm coming? What if the Duchess said, no, he can't hire a lady-in-waiting? What if someone else comes along this road and starts asking questions? What if—?

The door groans open.

"What do you want?" I don't recognize the woman standing in front of me. She is plump and older, with olive skin and wrinkles around her eyes.

"I . . . I'm here to work," I say.

The woman's eyes narrow. "I'm not aware of Cora hiring anyone new."

"Garnet hired me."

The woman claps a hand to her chest. "Oh my goodness! I'm so terribly sorry, when he told me I thought it was just another one of his jokes. Come in, come in, let's get you into some proper clothes. What's your name?"

I almost want to laugh because the last time I was here, not only did no one ask my name, but I was forbidden to even try and say it out loud.

"Lily," I say.

"Well, we'll get you assigned a proper lady-in-waiting name. I'm Maude."

I step inside the walls of the palace of the Lake, and the memories are so strong they threaten to crush me. All those walks I took with Annabelle; the day she showed me the greenhouse; the times when we would just sit together on a bench, listening to the birds chirp and the wind rustle through the trees. Finding out Raven lived next door and gazing up at the wall that separated us. Sending her trinkets, a button or a hair ribbon, anything to let her know I was all right. Seeing Ash kiss Carnelian in the ballroom, the all-consuming agony of realizing he would never be mine. How he followed me into the hedge maze and confessed to me that he hated his life. That was the day I started to realize we were the same.

"The passage to the kitchen is behind here," Maude says, pointing to a crumbling statue of a young archer with a wolf by his side. "But I'll show you the grounds for now. This way."

I pretend like I know what she's talking about. We walk through the garden, buds just beginning to blossom on the trees, the sun filtering through their branches. We pass by the old oak tree, where Dr. Blythe made me practice the third Augury, Growth. The tree was so big, I never thought I'd be able to affect it. But I did. I remember the blood that poured out of my nose while he clapped in appreciation.

I notice new things, too, things I hadn't been able to sense before. The smell of the earth is different here than in the Farm—there's a chemical note to it that makes my nose wrinkle. And what I once thought of as wildness in the way the trees grow now feels contained—this garden may look untamed but every tree was carefully planted. They are as trapped here as I was, all shoved together with no room to breathe. Earth is the element I connect with the easiest and most deeply—the trees around me sense my presence, the way a dog's ears might prick at a familiar noise. I want to reach out to them, to join with them.

We pass the little pond, where I once told Ash I couldn't see him anymore. Bright orange-and-white fish dart around in the shallow water. We emerge out into the tidier area, skirting the giant hedge maze. But instead of going in through the door next to the ballroom—the door I always used when I visited this garden—Maude swerves sharply to the right. There are stairs cut into the ground, hidden by bushes, leading down to a plain wooden door. She opens it and I find myself at the edge of a bustling kitchen.

A large wooden table dominates the center of the room. Several cooks in white aprons are busy shouting out orders or stirring things in pots or chopping vegetables. There are five enormous stoves and something seems to be boiling, simmering, or baking in every one. Scullery maids with soot-smudged faces poke at fires and refill the piles of wood stacked at various points around the kitchen. One girl is kneading an enormous pile of dough. We're clearly in a lower level of the palace—the windows are high up in the walls, long rectangular shafts of light slanting through them. Gleaming copper pots and pans hang from racks on the ceiling. The smells here are delicious; roasting meat and garlic and freshly baked bread. A footman is flirting with a maid in one corner and with a start I recognize her—she's Carnelian's maid. I think her name is Mary.

I resist the urge to touch my face, to make sure it still looks as different as I made it.

"Who's this?" a red-faced cook bellows. She's nearly as fat as the Countess of the Stone, Raven's evil former mistress. But the Countess of the Stone has cold, cruel eyes—this woman bears a much friendlier expression.

"Garnet hired her to serve Coral," Maude explains.

"Good for him," the cook says. "It had to happen sooner or later. Here you go, dearie, have a tart." She motions to a tray of pastries topped with glazed apple slices. I scoop one up and eat it gratefully.

"No time for food," Maude says, leading me away.

"Thank you," I say to the cook, brushing a few crumbs from my lips. She smiles at me.

We walk down a long stone hall, other corridors branching off it, and then up a set of stairs, emerging into the servant's wing of the palace. Maude leads me down the main corridor and then makes a sharp left.

"Here we are," she says, opening the door to what appears to be a combination drawing room and fitting room. There is a three-sided mirror in one corner near a row of closets. In the opposite corner is a couch upholstered in peach silk and a low mahogany coffee table. A pitcher of water and two glasses sit on the table. "Find yourself a dress that fits—I think the lady-in-waiting garments are . . ." She opens a closet door, closes it, then opens another one. "Ah. Here we are."

There are rows of white dresses with high lace collars. A knot tightens in my stomach. This is all becoming too surreal—me being here, under totally different circumstances. I look at the dresses again. Are these the same ones Annabelle wore?

"Come on now, Lily, we haven't got all day." Maude reaches into the closet and pulls out a dress. "This looks to be about your size."

She hands it to me and I realize I'm expected to change right now. I slip off the brown dress, sad to lose the only part of the White Rose I brought with me. The lady-in-waiting dress fits fairly well and I decide it can't have been Annabelle's—she was far thinner than me, and flatter in the chest. The lace itches around my throat.

"That looks lovely. Now just to fix your hair." Maude reaches for my low bun, but I step back.

"That's all right, I can do it," I say. I don't need Maude asking questions about the arcana, which I carry in my hair everywhere I go. I wait until her back is turned and then hastily sweep my hair up to form a tight bun on the crown of my head, just like Annabelle wore, keeping the tuning fork tucked away inside.

"Very nice," Maude says. She spritzes me with some flowery perfume and pronounces me fit to be seen in the palace.

"Her ladyship and Cora are out at the moment," she says. "I'm surprised Cora didn't stay home and wait for your arrival. She usually greets the new ladies-in-waiting."

"She probably didn't believe Garnet either," I say.

Maude chuckles. "You're right, my dear, she likely did not. Well, I suppose it falls to me to show you around a bit, then."

I smile. No Cora and no Duchess and a tour of the palace? This is the perfect time to look for Hazel. Maude might even lead me straight to her.

"That would be lovely," I say. "Lead the way."

~ Seven ~

I FEEL CONFIDENT THAT I'LL MASTER THE TOUR QUICKLY—
after all, I lived in this palace for three months.

But once we reach the end of the servant's wing and pass
through the glass promenade that connects it to the main
part of the palace, Maude pulls back a tapestry depicting
some former Duchess of the Lake, which hangs on the wall
by the dining room. A set of stone steps are behind it, leading to, I presume, the series of corridors I saw earlier.

"I'm sure you know the rules about being seen," she
says as we descend. The air is noticeably cooler, and I'm
reminded of the secret passageway from Ash's parlor to the
library. I wonder if these halls connect with that one.

"Why don't you just go over everything," I say. "I'm sure

both Garnet and the Duchess would want me fully briefed."

This seems to impress Maude. "Smart girl. Very well. We may use the main corridors only at meal times and when the Duchess is out. You may be seen in various rooms—I'll give you a list later—as long as you are cleaning. The Duke's quarters will be off-limits to you, as are the Duchess's and surrogate's."

"Is she all right?" I ask. I can't let any opportunity to find out about Hazel pass. "The surrogate, I mean. After that companion raped her and all." The lie bites at my throat—it's the Duchess's lie, the one she told the world when Ash escaped. It's strange to think that, as far as Maude knows, the surrogate is still *me*.

Maude stiffens. "The surrogate is fine. That's all you need to know."

"Of course," I say quickly.

We reach the bottom of the stairs and Maude begins to rattle off hallways.

"The dining room, the library, the ballroom, the main gallery, the drawing room . . ." Everything looks the same down here. When I was living in the plush surrogate quarters, I nicknamed the hallways based on what they contained—the hall of flowers, the hall of portraits . . . for the servants, every hall seems to be the hall of stone.

However, unlike the ones I nicknamed, these halls are bustling with people. Chambermaids and laundry maids and scullery maids and footmen and that old butler (James, that was his name) and I even see a Regimental. He is big and burly and he nods to Maude.

"Six," she says. "How are things with the newlyweds?"

He smirks. "The same. I think Garnet would rather have married a turtle to be honest."

"This is Coral's new lady-in-waiting," she says with a wink. The Regimental's eyes pop.

"They finally got one for her, did they?"

"Garnet arranged it himself," Maude says.

"Good luck," the Regimental says to me.

Then he turns and walks off down the corridor.

"What did you call him?" I ask.

"I should have introduced you. He's Six. The Duchess has six personal guards." I must look confused because she frowns. "Didn't they number the Regimentals at your former palace?"

I straighten out my expression. "Yes, of course. I just . . . he looked like someone I used to know."

Maude's eyes twinkle. "A lover?"

"No," I say firmly.

"Good," she says. "The Duchess won't tolerate any of that nonsense here."

"She won't need to worry about that from me," I say.

Maude looks pleased. "Just watch out for William. Devilishly handsome footman. The Duchess has fired three girls because of him. Oh, and there's a companion here, so make sure you avoid all contact with him. Especially after the last one."

I wonder again if it would be safe to reveal myself to Rye. A companion, in the Jewel, on our side, could potentially be great help.

It's exactly what Ash wanted. He just wanted to do it himself. I feel a tiny stirring of guilt and squash it down. I am here and Ash isn't. I won't deny a possible ally.

We reach the end of the main corridor and Maude leads me up a set of steps, still doling out instructions.

"The Duke never gets up until after eleven and it's always best to avoid him," she is saying. "Terrible temper. The Duchess is very particular about her meals, they must be at certain times and always in the dining room. Unless she's attending a dinner party or luncheon. Garnet and Coral eat with her in the evenings, so you'll have to make sure Coral is dressed and ready, usually by eight."

I hope I can remember enough of what Annabelle used to do to pass as a proper lady-in-waiting. I should have asked someone back at the White Rose, but really, the only person who would know anything about how to properly dress for dinner would be Ash.

I wonder if he's still mad. I picture him, alone in our hayloft, stewing over where I am, if I'm all right, why I had to leave him. I think about how I would feel if the situation was reversed and then I don't because I'd be so upset with him. I've already made my choice so there's no point in regretting it now.

The door at the top of the stairs is wooden and doesn't have a knob—Maude slides it to the side, and we step out into a hallway I recognize. The hall of portraits. The eyes in the paintings stare at me as Maude slides a wooden panel back into place, concealing the door.

"Now, here is the concert hall—it hasn't been used since Garnet's engagement party but the Duchess likes to keep it clean."

I peek inside, the warm, rich air bringing another wave

of memories. This room holds so much meaning to me. It was where I used to play for Annabelle, just me and my cello onstage, a way to take myself away from the reality of my life.

It was where I kissed Ash for the first time.

It's also where I miscarried, bleeding so much that Lucien had to carry me off the stage and down to the medical room where he saved my life.

We're near my old chambers now, and Maude seems to have loosened up a bit, so I make another stab at finding Hazel.

"What's down there?" I ask.

"Those are the former surrogate chambers."

"The surrogate isn't staying there anymore?"

Maude hesitates. "The Duchess keeps her in the medical room day and night. As a precaution. She nearly died at Garnet's party. Bled all over the stage."

"Yes, I . . . remember hearing about that." It is so bizarre to talk about Hazel as though Hazel is me. I hate thinking of my sister locked up in that cold, sterile place.

Before I can ask anything else, Maude leads me away from the surrogate chambers to the east side of the palace. I remember Annabelle telling me that this is where the men's quarters are.

"Luckily, Lucien was there to save her. I don't think there's been a mind like his in the history of the ladies-in-waiting."

"Yes, I've heard he's very smart," I say.

"Brilliant, more like. Though he does have a bit of a temper. I suppose that's to be expected. The bigger the brain, the bigger the ego, the shorter the fuse. Ah, here we are."

She stops at the entrance to the east wing. It is carpeted in maroon, with portraits of previous Dukes of the Lake hanging on the walls. I wonder which one is the Duchess's father. From the way Sil talked about him, he seemed even crueler than the Duchess.

Sil was the Duchess's surrogate. The Duke forced her to focus all her Augury power on only one of his twin daughters before she gave birth to them. The Duchess is that daughter. Sil was strong enough to withstand the death that usually accompanies surrogate childbirth but only with the help of Paladin magic.

The hall we're on meets the men's quarters in a T shape, so we can only go left or right. Beside me, a staircase curves up and out of sight. The stairs are crafted out of mother-of-pearl, the banister a gleaming gold.

"The Duchess's private quarters," Maude whispers. "Never, under any circumstances, go up there."

I nod. I don't need telling twice.

"The Duke's chambers are down that way," she says, pointing to the right, "and he keeps several footmen tasked with the maintenance of his own personal quarters." Maude raises an eyebrow and adds, "He keeps the footmen *very* close, if you catch my meaning."

This palace is like a beehive of secrets and lies. Maude laughs at my shocked expression and beckons me to follow her. She knocks on the door and opens it with a "Hello? Miss Coral? Garnet? It's Maude. Your new lady-in-waiting has arrived."

Garnet and Coral's chambers are quite similar to the

ones I used to occupy in this palace. They have a drawing room, painted and decorated in shades of blue and gold, and a tea parlor with pink wallpaper and red-and-white trim. It doesn't look at all like Garnet.

"It's a bit much, isn't it?" Maude whispers. "Coral enjoys the color pink."

There are pink flowers in pink glass vases on the tables, and every chair and couch has been upholstered in varying shades of magenta, fuchsia, and rose. One entire wall is covered with glass-paned cabinets filled with miniature tea sets.

"Wow," I say, moving to get a closer look. "That's . . . a lot of china."

"Yes, Coral is rather particular about them. She won't let any of the maids touch them."

There are tiny cups and saucers and teapots in various colors and patterns—purple flowers and hummingbirds, horseshoes, glittery green vines, a golden sun and silver moon, stripes and solids and everything in between. I'm examining a blue cup with a bunch of grapes painted on its exterior when a door opens.

"Oh, hello, Maude, I thought I heard you," a girl's voice says.

I whirl around as Maude sinks into a low curtsy. Coral is frail and small, her blond hair curled and pinned in a very pretty fashion over one shoulder. I drop into a curtsy of my own.

"My apologies, Miss Coral," Maude says. "This is your new lady-in-waiting. She was merely admiring your collection."

"What?" Coral's whole expression brightens. "But I thought the Duchess dismissed my last candidate."

"It was Garnet, miss, who hired her."

"What a lovely surprise! Garnet is so busy, I didn't think . . . what is your name?" she asks me.

"She hasn't been given a lady-in-waiting name yet, miss," Maude says. "Cora is still out."

"Nonsense," Coral says. "I can name her just as easily as Cora. I've lived around ladies-in-waiting all my life. Besides, she's mine, isn't she?"

I forgot how awful it feels to be spoken about as if you're property.

A muscle in Maude's jaw twitches. "Of course, miss."

Coral cups my face in her hands, an uncomfortably intimate gesture given that we've only just met. She turns my head from side to side.

"Hmm . . . I think you'll be . . . Imogen," she says with a smile. "That was my grandmother's lady-in-waiting's name." She turns to Maude. "What do you think?"

"An excellent choice, miss."

"Coral, have you seen my cuff link—" Garnet enters the room and is brought up short at the sight of us.

"Maude," he says as she sinks into another curtsy. His eyes skim over me and I can see him working out if I am who I am, given that I look so different. "Is this her?"

Fortunately, Coral helps out. "My own personal lady-in-waiting at last!" she exclaims, running over to kiss his cheek. "Darling, how thoughtful."

Garnet shoots me the barest hint of a smile. "How do you like her, sweetling?"

"She's perfect."

He chuckles and turns to Maude. "See to it she has a room made up for her in the servant's quarters."

She curtsies again. "Of course, sir. I'll have it done right away."

"Excellent. That gives all of us some time to get acquainted before dinner."

Maude hurries out of the room.

"What should we do first?" Coral says, coming over to clasp my hands in hers. "Shall you do my hair? Or maybe we can choose a dress for dinner? Or you could read to me!"

"Darling, I'm going to need a moment to speak to . . ." Garnet's voice trails off, unsure of what exactly to call me.

"Imogen," Coral says. "I named her myself."

Garnet's smile looks so sincere. "Lovely. I need to speak to Imogen for a moment in private, just to make sure she's filled in on everything. Why don't you go out to the garden and I'll have her meet you there? I know how you love looking at the flowers."

"All right," Coral says. "Don't keep her too long."

"I won't."

Coral makes a big show of having me help her with her coat and pin a tiny hat into her curls. She pecks Garnet on the cheek and walks out, leaving the two of us blissfully alone.

Eight

As soon as the door closes behind his wife, Garnet's smile vanishes, replaced with a look of awe.

"Wow," he says. "Raven told me you looked different, but . . . wow."

"Thank you," I say, "for helping me get here. Lucien wasn't a huge fan of the idea."

"I know," Garnet says. "I think you might actually irritate him more than I do."

"But you're an upstanding citizen now," I remind him. "Regimental officer and everything."

"True. They're even promoting me to Master Sergeant in a few days. There'll be an official ceremony. Like I've done anything to warrant a promotion except turn a lot of Regimentals to our side." He cocks his head. "I'll have access to more information though. That's a bonus."

"Garnet, that's amazing," I say. "Really helpful. What else has been happening in the Jewel?"

"You'd think the bombings would have put a damper on all the parties and cotillions and whatnot, but people here are either ignoring it or assuming it's something that will never touch them, that will just go away on its own." He plops down onto a pink striped armchair. "I swear, the arrogance of some of them. . . . You know that barracks that got blown up in the Smoke two days ago?"

I think about the headline I saw on the train. "Yes."

Garnet's cheeks flush. "There were people on our side in there. And I get it, we have to make sacrifices, but to hear my royal friends talk, you'd think those Regimentals brought it on themselves. One of them even said to me, 'They just don't make them like they used to.' How did they *used* to *make* Regimentals? The more I work with the men in red, the more I see that most of them have been conscripted against their will or just need a job to feed their families. The ones in the Jewel are the worst. They're the real die-hards. That's what makes the Auction so tricky— it'll be all Jewel Regimentals guarding the Auction House. We really need the surrogates to bring that wall down. We need to get the people in here, to fight."

I swallow my doubts, and say, "We can do it. We've got so many girls willing to help already."

Garnet is lost in his own world. "You know, I can't even reach out to most of those Regimentals personally. It's too dangerous. I have to use other people, mostly privates and specialists and the like. No one will open up to a royal. I'm like the Lucien of Regimentals." He rubs his temple. "I sort of understand why he's so grumpy all the time."

Looking at him now, I can't believe this is the same man who wandered into my first dinner at the palace of the Lake, completely intoxicated, with no care other than where his next drink was coming from.

"I'm proud of you," I say shyly. "For whatever that's worth."

Garnet's face turns an even darker shade of red and he clears his throat. "Only a few more weeks to go, right?" he says. "Then we won't have to sneak around anymore. I'm tired of playing at being a royal."

"I'm tired of being treated like property again. Already," I grumble.

"Yeah, sorry about that. I can't really—"

I hold up a hand. "Like you said, a few more weeks and then this will be over, one way or another." An uneasiness settles over us as that thought sinks in. We could be dead in a month. "Is it true that your mother is keeping Hazel in the medical room?" I ask, changing the subject.

"My mother doesn't talk to me about the surrogate at all. Is that what Maude told you?"

"Yes."

Garnet scratches his chin. "Then it's probably true."

I take a step toward him. "And you haven't heard or seen anything that might make you think her life is in danger?"

"I haven't, but like I said, no one talks to me about surrogates." He frowns, as if he's just realized something. "You should be careful. You shouldn't speak around Mother or Cora, they could recognize your voice. Oh, and Carnelian."

Carnelian. I'd nearly forgotten her. The Duchess's niece, whom Ash was hired to escort. She found out about Ash and me, and told the Duchess. She got Ash thrown into a dungeon and nearly killed. Anger rises in my mouth, hot and bitter, like bile.

"This is so weird," Garnet says. "I know it's you, but you don't *look* like you. I mean, I know Violet's angry face and it's almost like . . . like seeing that expression on a stranger."

"That's a good thing, right?"

"Yeah. It's just . . . *weird*." He stands and glances toward the door. "You should probably be getting out to the garden."

"Right." I have no idea what to do, how to be a lady-in-waiting.

Garnet's expression softens. "Do whatever she says. Pick out dresses and stuff. And bring her breakfast if she wants it. That's all the job is. I'm sure you remember." I know he's talking about Annabelle. "Here," he says, heading over to a closet and handing me a soft, pink shawl. "Sorry about the color. Coral likes pink."

I give him a weak laugh. "You think?"

My hands tremble as I wrap the shawl around my shoulders.

"Hey, Violet?" Garnet says. "What you did was reckless and all that, but for what it's worth, I think your sister is lucky to have you."

"Thanks," I whisper, my throat tight. I point a finger at

him. "It's Imogen now. Don't forget. I might."

"Yes, ma'am," he says with a grin.

My legs tremble as I make my way back downstairs and out into the garden.

BEING CORAL'S LADY-IN-WAITING IS AN EXERCISE IN patience.

I hope Annabelle never felt this way about me. She prattles on about anything and everything, who's wearing a dress she wants or which old friend won't speak to her now that she's moved up in the Jewel. It's enough to make me want to jam my fingers in my ears. And on top of that, while we're in the garden I have to keep chasing after her. One second she'll be gushing over a particular flower and the next she'll see a bird and just *have* to run after it. Finally, she insists that she's exhausted and demands to be taken inside.

By the time dinner arrives, I'm tired and frazzled and haven't had even a second to spare to try and figure out a way to get into the medical room. When I was the Duchess's surrogate, I took a private elevator from the second floor straight down to the basement. I remember the route exactly; down the hall of the flowers, through the open gallery, then a right, then a left, then down a short hall paneled in oak. But thanks to Coral's incessant needs, I haven't had a chance to even attempt to get there. Besides the fact that Maude told me I mustn't be seen in the halls. Maybe there's a servant's entrance to the medical room? I try to remember if I noticed any other door during my doctor's appointments, but all I can recall is the sterilized feel, the clusters of bright lights, the tray of shiny silver instruments.

Dinner brings a brief respite (after Coral tries on and dismisses seven dresses and makes me redo her hair twice) and I'm grateful for it. Was Annabelle always this tired? My feet and calves ache, and the beginning of a headache is forming at my left temple. After I walk Coral to the dining room, I decide to try and find the kitchen again and get lost in the maze of underground servant tunnels. I'm too embarrassed to ask for directions. Everyone looks so busy. I pass a Regimental and can't help the way my chest seizes up, my pulse kicking into a sprint. He stops and introduces himself as Three, then very nicely points me in the right direction.

"So, you're serving Coral?"

I nod. After what Garnet said, I'm afraid to speak in front of anyone. Not that the Regimentals would remember my voice.

"What circle are you from?"

He's slim and brown-skinned, with big hazel eyes. He has the longest eyelashes I've ever seen on a boy. I've never really taken the time to look closely at the Regimentals before—they've always blurred together.

"The Farm," I lie.

"I'm from the Bank." I wonder if he is the son of the Cobbler, the man who Lucien sent to fetch me from Lily's house, the man who lost his son to the royalty to be trained as a Regimental. "What did they decide to call you?"

"Imogen."

"That's nice. I don't think I've heard that one before. I'm about the millionth Three to walk these halls. The Duchess fired most of her previous guard after that whole business with the companion. I've only been here a few months."

I smell the kitchen before I see it—the scent of ham and honey mixed with rosemary and thyme. My stomach growls and Three laughs.

"You'll eat soon. After Coral has retired for the night." He leans in. "Be nice to Zara. She's the fat cook. Well, the fattest cook. If she likes you, she'll let you snack."

The kitchen is a madhouse. Pots banging down on stovetops and large serving dishes being laden with food, footmen running around, cooks shouting at maids to add more of this or a pinch of that to various dishes.

"We need the second course now," one footman snaps.

"You'll have it when it's ready," the fat cook who gave me a tart earlier snaps back. One look around tells me she must be Zara. She squeezes half a lemon over an enormous whole dorado nestled among lemon slices and fluffy greens. A kitchen maid sprinkles a bit of seasoning on it, then Zara hands the tray to the grumpy footman. Her eyes land on me and light up. "The new girl! Did they give you a name yet?"

"Imogen," I say.

"I'm Zara," she says. "You must be starved. Help yourself to anything on that cutting board over there." Another kitchen maid drops a bowl of thick, white cream onto the floor and Zara starts shouting at her. I sneak off to the corner, desperate for food.

The board contains a hunk of blue-veined cheese and half a loaf of bread, a couple of small, firm tomatoes, a bowl of olives, half a dozen figs, some walnuts, and a few slices of cured meat. I shove as much of it as I can into my mouth, nearly choking on an olive pit.

The arcana in my bun begins to buzz and suddenly I'm desperate for a way out. I walk as quickly and casually as I can toward the door that leads to the garden, not wanting to attract attention. But everyone is so busy with dinner that no one notices me. I slip out into the cool April evening.

There is a large shrub, trimmed in the shape of a dancing bear, by the glass corridor to the east wing, and it's big enough to hide behind. I crouch down and carefully extract the arcana.

"Lucien?"

"Garnet told me you made it. How are you? He said you did a remarkable job with your disguise." The sound of his voice makes my insides melt with relief.

"I'm all right," I whisper. "I'm successfully situated as Coral's lady-in-waiting."

"You know, you are infuriatingly stubborn, but this might not have been the worst idea after all. Maybe we can even arrange a way for you to see the Auction House before the big day. Get yourself familiar with it in real life."

That's all well and good, but right now I only want my sister. "I need to see Hazel, Lucien. They're keeping her locked up in the medical room and I know where the elevator is but I'm not supposed to be seen walking through the halls and Coral always needs something from me and—"

"Calm down, honey. Take a breath. Every royal medical room has an underground entrance. You've seen the servants' tunnels by now, I imagine?"

"Yeah," I say. "It's really confusing."

"There are other tunnels as well, ones that are more private."

I pause. "Like the one I used to sneak into Ash's room?"

I can hear Lucien smile. "Yes. Look at that, your tryst had its uses." His tone is gently teasing.

"So one of those tunnels might lead to the medical room?"

"Definitely. Royals do not like wheeling pregnant surrogates through their gilded halls when they are ready to be sent to the birthing facility. Or dead surrogates to the morgue. They prefer a subtler exit. Many of these are close to the garages, so you might want to start there."

"Thank you, Lucien," I say fervently. "Any more news on . . . on the Electress's plans?"

"None, though if you recall before you so suddenly decided you had to come back here, I never had concrete proof. Only snippets of conversation between the Exetor and the Electress."

"What were they saying?"

"I distinctly remember the Exetor saying something about a wedding and the Electress laughing and saying a shroud might be more appropriate than a dress."

"That could be about anything," I say.

"Yes, but you don't live with the Electress. She despises the Duchess. She's constantly asking me to check up on the Duchess's surrogate, to find out how she's doing, the state of her pregnancy. The problem is, since the engagement has been officially announced, any attempt on Hazel's life would be seen as an attempt on the future Electress's. It would be considered treason."

"And you think the Electress would risk that?"

Lucien sighs. "I am not sure. She takes her situation entirely for granted. It would not surprise me to think that she holds herself above the law. But remember, she is not truly royal. There are many in this circle who would turn on her in an instant, who would clamor to replace her with a true royal." There's a pause. "The troubling issue is that she has not outwardly asked for my help. If anyone were to be able to accomplish a discreet surrogate killing . . ."

"Please," I say. "Don't finish that sentence."

"I would never do it, of course," Lucien says. "But she has asked me before. Why does she not seek my help now?"

"Maybe because you haven't done it in the past," I suggest.

"Maybe . . ."

A twig snaps near my hiding spot, followed by the sound of voices.

"Someone's coming," I hiss.

The arcana drops, silent and lifeless, into my open palm.

". . . don't even know where she came from," a girl is saying. "She just showed up."

"I thought for sure the Duchess would make you the new lady-in-waiting," a second voice says. I peer through the branches and see Mary, Carnelian's maid, with another servant.

"I know," Mary replies. "But it wasn't the Duchess who hired her. It was Garnet."

"Do you know what I bet it is?" the second girl says slyly.

"What?"

"She's really here for *him*. A little plaything for the royal son. I can't imagine Coral is all that exciting behind closed doors."

Mary stops and raises an eyebrow. "Oh yes." She giggles. "Elizabeth, I think you might be on to something."

Elizabeth shrugs. "So the Duchess will probably take care of her the same way she did the mute."

The two girls laugh, and it takes all my effort to remain rooted in my spot, not to join with Earth and have the ground open up beneath their feet or the trees tear them to pieces.

"Let's get inside," Mary says.

I wait a full minute before returning, head spinning, to the kitchen.

THE END OF DINNER IS SIGNALED BY MAUDE RUSHING into the kitchen and demanding to know where Imogen is.

For half a heartbeat, I look around for someone else before remembering that's me.

"Get upstairs," she hisses.

"Sorry!" I say, following her out into the stone halls. "I didn't realize dinner was over."

"You have about three minutes before it is," Maude says. "I rang the bell."

"I was in the garden. I needed some fresh air. It won't happen again," I say quickly, withering under her gaze.

"I certainly hope not. You are to escort Miss Coral upstairs, prepare her for bed, and then report to Cora. She will be your direct supervisor in this house."

"Y-yes," I stammer. "Of course."

We climb the set of stairs behind the tapestry and come out in the hall by the dining room. Cora is already waiting there. The sight of her brings back another flood of memories—a plate of grapes and soft cheese, the soothing feel of the ice ointment she applied after the Duchess hit me. Putting on my veil for Dahlia's funeral. The way the keys that hang from her belt would clink together. Her auburn topknot is exactly as I remember it, as are the crinkles around her eyes. She gives me a curt once-over.

"And Garnet hired her?" she asks Maude.

"Yes, ma'am."

I keep silent.

"Hmm." Cora's mouth turns down. "I heard Coral gave you a name."

I nod.

"Imogen," Maude says.

"Hmm," Cora says again. "You will report to my chambers after Coral has retired for the evening."

I drop into a curtsy just as the doors open. I look up and find myself face-to-face with the Duchess.

The panic that grips me is so complete, the fear so overwhelming, that for an instant it's like I no longer exist. My body is gone and my mind is blank and there is nothing left but terror.

I'd forgotten just how beautiful she is. Her caramel-honey skin, her ebony hair, the way her purple silk gown hangs perfectly off her thin frame, revealing her shoulders and collarbone. But it's her eyes that I remember the most. The way they used to study me, critical and impassive. How they could shift from vulnerable to cruel in an instant. The look in them when she ran the knife across Annabelle's throat, as easy as if she were slicing through a stick of butter.

The Duke is by her side. He looks drunk.

"Fabulous dinner, Maude," he roars. The Duchess winces. "You must send Zara my compliments."

"Yes, my lord," Maude says.

"What is this?" the Duchess asks, stopping short to look at me. It doesn't escape my notice that she says *what* instead of *who*. Sweat drips under my arms, and my knees shake, but I force myself to keep my gaze steady, my face neutral, the same way I did the very first time I met her, before she hit me.

It was harder then. I didn't know anything, about where I was or who I was or what I had the potential to be. I'm not that girl anymore.

"New lady-in-waiting, your ladyship," Maude replies.

At that moment, Garnet and Coral appear behind them.

"Mother, have you met Imogen?" Garnet says. He looks a bit intoxicated himself. "I got her for Coral. She must have a proper lady-in-waiting, right?"

The Duchess gives me a long, lingering look. Perhaps I'm imagining it, but she seems particularly focused on my eyes. Then the moment passes, and she turns to her son, an icy smile on her face.

"Why, darling, how marvelous. I never thought you capable of hiring help."

"Isn't she perfect?" Coral coos. "She looks just like me, doesn't she?"

I really wish she hadn't made that particular comparison. I don't need the Duchess looking at me any closer than she already is. I feel like she can see through this thin veil, my Auguried disguise.

"Yes," the Duchess says after a moment. "I suppose

she does." Her eyes flicker to mine one last time before she strides off down the hall in the direction of the main staircase. My entire body feels like it's deflating from the tension. Cora follows after her, their heads close together as the Duchess whispers something I can't hear.

"Sure you won't join me for a brandy?" the Duke says to his son.

"No, Father, I think I'll pass." Garnet barely hides his disdain as the Duke staggers off toward his smoking room.

"Come on, Imogen," Coral says. "It's time to get me ready for bed."

We retire to her chambers after Garnet makes some excuse about needing to use the library. I run a bath for Coral and find scented salts under the sink. Soon the air smells like lilac and freesia. I want to climb into this bathtub and never get out.

"Is it ready?" Coral says. She stands in the doorway wearing a thick white robe. As if it's nothing, she slips off the robe and hands it to me. She is completely naked. I don't know where to look, but Coral seems perfectly at ease.

"Shall I wait outside, miss?"

"Yes, that would be fine. Go arrange my best nightdress on the bed for me."

I curtsy and run out of the room. Coral has three closets, an armoire, and two dressers plus a vanity. I think Anna-belle kept all my nightclothes in a drawer, and sure enough, I find a wide variety of silky undergarments and sleepwear. As I sift through the contents, wondering what exactly her best nightdress might be, it occurs to me that I haven't seen any of Garnet's clothing in these closets.

"Imogen!" Coral shouts. "The water's gone cold, bring my towel now!"

What did she do before she had a lady-in-waiting? I wonder to myself.

After Coral has been dried off and her hair has been brushed out and her face and arms moisturized and the blankets have been tucked right up to her chin, I am finally released from my duties.

"Good night, Imogen," Coral says.

It wouldn't surprise me if Garnet has never spent a night in that bed.

"Good night," I say, closing the door behind me.

Now for the real challenge.

It's time to face Cora.

Nine

Cora's chambers are behind the first door in the east wing. Maude pointed them out earlier.

I take a steadying breath before knocking.

"Enter," she calls from within.

The parlor is lit with a soft glow—pretty sconces hang on the walls giving off a pinkish light. There is a fireplace and a large couch that curves in the shape of a smile and a thick gold rug. Oil paintings hang on the walls and golden curtains cover the windows.

It reminds me very much of Ash's old room in this palace, the parlor I used to sneak into when Carnelian was at her lessons.

Cora sits in a rocking chair by the window, a position

that is so reminiscent of Sil it makes my heart throb. She doesn't stand as I enter.

"Sit," she says, indicating the couch.

I do as she commands.

"When did Garnet hire you?"

I try to keep my voice low and husky, and answer as honestly and succinctly as possible. I don't need to get myself tangled up in any more lies than necessary. "Yesterday."

Her eyes narrow. "You will address me as ma'am. What House did you work for?"

It's like all the royal Houses have vanished from my brain. I can't think of a single one, but somehow, "The House of the Flame, ma'am," comes out. Cora nods as if that makes sense to her. I make a mental note to tell Garnet later, in case she asks him.

"He should have told me you were coming. This is a terrible time to be training new help, what with all the commotion in the lower circles, and the new Auction date, and the engagement, and Garnet's promotion . . ." Cora trails off and picks up a glass of water from the table beside her and takes a sip.

"Your primary function over the next few weeks will be preparing Coral for the Auction and making sure she stays out of the Duchess's way. It will be her first time attending and she is quite eager about it. Her ladyship does not have the time to waste on frivolous questions, so you must keep Coral occupied. As a lady-in-waiting, you should be able to manage this without issue."

She says this with such a conspiratorial smile, I respond in kind.

"Where were you trained?" she asks.

"I—beg your pardon?" I thought I'd already answered that.

"Who trained you?" Cora says, exaggerating the words.

"Lucien," I say, without thinking.

She raises an eyebrow. "Really. I didn't think he was instructing anymore."

"I was his last student," I say, hoping against all hope that that makes sense.

Cora takes another sip of water and puts the glass down. "Garnet is more competent than he seems, it would appear."

"He's certainly grown up a bit." As soon as the words are out, I clamp my mouth shut. What a foolish thing to say. Imogen the lady-in-waiting should not be talking about Garnet so casually.

Cora stares at me for a long moment before answering. "Yes," she says. "He has."

"I—I only meant he had quite the reputation, ma'am," I say.

"I know what you meant. What circle are you from?"

"The Farm, ma'am."

She taps her finger against the arm of the chair. "Very well. That will be all for tonight. You are dismissed."

I'm barely able to contain my relief as I hurry to the door.

"Oh, Violet?" Cora's voice stops me and I turn.

"Yes, ma'am?" It's only when I see a cruel smile twisting on her lips that I realize what I've done. My hand claps over my mouth as if that will help, as if I can change my own body's reactions.

"I knew it was you," she says, standing in one fluid

movement, "when you talked about Garnet. Your voice changed. Like you knew him. Because you did, didn't you?"

I can't move. Where would I go? Cora runs this house. She knows every inch of it. There is nowhere to hide and massive walls surround me on every side. Sure, I could call on Earth or Air, but that would give everything away and I'd still be stranded in the Jewel. I won't do that to all the Society members who are counting on the Paladin, who are waiting for Auction Day, for their chance at freedom.

I think of Hazel. I didn't even get to see my sister one last time. This whole plan has collapsed before it had a chance to begin.

Cora saunters over to me with all the confidence of someone who knows she has her prey trapped. When she is close enough, she grabs my face in her hand, much like the Duchess did the night she killed Annabelle.

"How did you do it?" she asks, turning my cheek to the side. "Your eyes, your hair, your *face* . . . was it the Auguries?"

I nod.

"It's very well done," she murmurs. "How did you get back here? Or have you been hiding in the Jewel this whole time?" My eyes widen and she laughs. "You think I don't know the Duchess is keeping your sister locked up in your place?"

"Please." The word is garbled through her grip.

"Please what? You came back here to save her, I assume."

I don't respond. Her fingers dig into my skin.

"I can help. I can help you save your sister."

That is not what I was expecting. Cora laughs at my expression. "For a price, of course."

"I'll do anything." The words sound fuzzy.

"I'm sorry? I didn't quite catch that." She releases her hold a fraction.

"I'll do anything," I mumble.

"I was hoping you would say that."

She lets me go and moves to sit on the couch. "Come here," she says, patting the spot beside her. I sit in a daze.

"I will not reveal your presence in this palace. I may even be able to help you get to your sister. But you must do one thing for me first."

I wait. She knows I have no other response to that than yes.

Cora's smile is terrifying. "I want you to kill the Duchess."

"*What?*" I gasp. "But . . . but . . . why?"

Her face goes very still. "Do you really need to ask? She murdered my daughter."

It takes me a second to wrap my head around this. "Annabelle? I never saw you treat her like anything but a servant."

"Just because I couldn't act like her mother doesn't mean I didn't love her," Cora snaps. She turns away, her gaze falling on a small portrait in an oval frame on the mantelpiece. "I remember the day the Duchess came to me and told me I had been authorized to have a child. I was so happy."

The word *authorized* makes my skin crawl.

"And when she came out she was so tiny and so . . . silent. At first I was terrified she was a stillbirth, but Dr. Blythe assured me she was perfectly healthy. She just . . . she would never speak a word." Cora brushes at something on her cheek. "I always wondered what her voice might sound like." She stands and walks to the mantel, picking up the picture. "Another House might have had her drowned for being defective. The Duchess cared for me, though. She let me keep her, let me train her. As long as she proved useful."

"She was more than that," I murmur.

Cora's head whips up. "You don't think I know that? I brought something *good* into this circle. I brought something pure and innocent and it was destroyed. I was powerless to do anything to stop it. She promised me. She *promised*. And then you came along and fell in love with that stupid companion and got her killed."

"I'm so sorry." The words feel hollow, meaningless. Feeling sorry won't bring Annabelle back. "I loved her too, you know."

"I know." Cora puts the picture back on the mantel. "That's why you will do this for me. For the love you bore her and the debt you owe me."

"Why do you need me to do it? Why not some other servant in this palace?"

"Because another servant would turn me in for money or higher status. You don't have that power. I could have you arrested right now. The Duchess could have your head cut off, or simply tie you up in the medical room with your sister. Either way, you're dead."

She makes a good point. "Why don't you do it yourself?"

Her expression is pained. "I can't. I have been with the Duchess since she was ten years old. No matter how much I might want to, I . . . I cannot kill her."

I might hate the Duchess, I may want revenge for

Annabelle, but cold-blooded murder is not something I can see myself doing either. But I see only one option here—to agree to Cora's plan. And if I can wait until Auction Day . . . I might not have to kill the Duchess at all.

"All right," I say. "I'll do it."

"Of course you will."

"And the Auction will be the perfect time," I say.

She frowns. "The Auction is a month away."

"Think about it. She'll be distracted then. Lots of commotion, dress shopping, dinners being planned . . ." I'm a little concerned at how convincing I sound, even to myself. "You've been waiting for months already, what's one more?"

Cora considers me for a moment. "I always thought you were a bit on the dim side," she says. "I'm glad I was mistaken."

"Thanks," I say, bristling.

"Of course," she says, taking a step toward me, "if you double-cross me in any way, or fail to complete this assignment, you will not live past the Auction. I may be unable to kill my mistress myself, but I have no qualms whatsoever about killing you."

"Understood," I say.

"Get some sleep," Cora says. "You'll need it. There's a bell by your bed that Coral will ring when she's ready. One rings in the kitchen too. You must always be up and ready before she is. She takes her breakfast in bed and then you'll need to pick out something for her to wear. Make sure she looks classy."

"I remember some things," I say. "From Annabelle. She always knew what to dress me in."

A muscle in Cora's jaw twitches. "Yes. She was very good at wardrobe." She sits back in the rocking chair, but her posture is tense, her back ramrod straight. "You're dismissed for tonight. Try not to speak in front of her ladyship; your voice is altogether too familiar."

"I will." I stop at the door. "Cora?"

"Yes?"

"Do you have any particular . . . way that you'd like me to kill her?"

Her eyes are black stones, dark and cold. "I want you to cut. Her. Throat."

I slip out the door, my mind racing.

"YOU'RE SUPPOSED TO DO *WHAT*?"

"Kill the Duchess," I whisper. "More specifically, cut her throat."

Raven makes a noise somewhere between a gasp and a cough. It's muffled through the arcana.

"Don't worry, I told her I'd do it at the Auction, which, if all goes according to plan, should negate any murder pact I've made."

It's after midnight. I know I should be sleeping, but I stayed up, hoping Raven would contact me. Sil has an arcana similar to Lucien's—meaning it can contact all other arcanas. Mine is only a receiver. Garnet's can only contact Lucien's and mine.

"So the servant is just as ruthless as the master," Sil says. "Doesn't surprise me."

"What's she like?" Raven asks. I know she means Coral.

"She's strange. Like an overgrown child. She's demanding

and babyish. I don't think Garnet likes her much."

"Oh," is Raven's only response, but I can hear the tiniest bit of relief in her voice.

"What about you girls? Are you all packed and ready for the final trip around the Marsh?" This day feels like it has lasted a week.

"We're more than ready." I can hear the smile in Sienna's voice.

"Sil is coming with us, to Westgate and the other facilities," Raven says.

"What?" I sit up.

"I'm not going to wait here with no idea what's going on," Sil says. "The Whistler can take care of things in this part of the Farm. I belong with the surrogates."

"You do," I say. "I feel better knowing you'll be there."

"You shouldn't," Sil says. "This whole plan is like a house of cards. We have to rely on the surrogates at the facilities keeping quiet. We have to rely on the royalty to stay stupid. We have to rely on who knows who to plant the key bombs the night before the Auction. We need to rely on *you* to send up the signal to set those bombs off. Then we have to cross our fingers and hope that eighty-odd surrogates can break down that wall and that the Society forces are already in place on the Bank side, ready and waiting to flood the Jewel. We could all be marching slowly to our deaths."

Seeing as Raven and I were already labeled to die being sold as surrogates, this idea doesn't bother me as much as it should. "It's like Ash said," I remind her. "I'd rather die fighting the royalty than serving them."

Sil snorts. "Brave words. Tell me that when bullets are flying through the air and people are dying around you."

"Is Ash there?" I was too cowardly to ask for him earlier, but I want to hear his voice. I want to know he's not still mad at me.

So I'm completely unprepared for the silence that follows.

"What?" I ask. My heart kicks into a sprint. "Did something happen to him?"

"Ash is gone," Raven says finally.

"What do you mean *gone*? Where did he go?"

"To the Bank," Sienna says as Sil mutters, "Damned fool."

It's like all the air has been sucked out of the room. The Bank. Ash has gone to the *Bank*.

"No," I gasp. "Raven . . . tell me it's not true. Please. He . . . he'll die there."

"He left a note," she says, and I can hear paper crinkle. Then she reads aloud. "Violet. I'm sorry but I had to try. I hope you can forgive me. I couldn't just abandon them. I need to be worthy of a place in this new world we are fighting for. I love you more than my own life. I will see you again. I will be there on Auction Day. Stay safe. Ash."

"Forgive him?" I spit. "Is he insane? I won't get the chance! He'll be dead before he makes it five feet in the Bank. He'll be—"

"Violet." Raven's voice is soft and steady. "He's gone and all the shouting in the world won't change that."

"But he . . . he . . ."

"Ran off without listening to you? Yeah. He did. You two are pretty well suited for each other, to be honest."

I fold my arms across my chest. "I had a plan. I have people helping me. What's he going to do, bang on doors and ask if any Society members are home? Walk up to Madame Curio's and ring the bell?"

"We already know he can get into the companion house without being seen," Raven says. "And as for the rest . . . well, he's not stupid. Why are you so sure he'll get caught?"

My shoulders slump. She's right. I'm refusing to believe Ash is capable of surviving on his own. "It's just . . . if I lose him now . . ."

"I know," she says gently. Then she sighs. "You should try and get some sleep. Sounds like you have a big day tomorrow."

"Yeah," I say, but my thoughts are far away, with Ash, wherever he is. Still in the Farm? On a train? In the Smoke already?

"We'll talk to you again soon," Indi says, clearly feeling it's safe enough to join the conversation.

"If you see the Countess of the Rose, stab her for me with a fork or something," Sienna says, referring to her former mistress.

"If you see the Lady of the Stream—"

"Good night," I say firmly, before Olive can get started.

"Good night," Sil says.

The arcana falls with a tiny thump onto the bed and I think of how fragile the connection to my friends is, this little silver tuning fork keeping us together.

"Be safe," I whisper. Then I settle down into the pillows, sleep taking me quicker than I would have thought, exhaustion overcoming my anger and fear for Ash.

Ten

A BELL IS RINGING SOMEWHERE NEAR MY HEAD.

I swat at it sleepily, wondering why Turnip's harness is making so much noise. My hand connects with metal and then falls onto something soft.

The bed. The palace. The Jewel.

I sit bolt upright. Coral's bell is ringing wildly. I scramble out of bed, throw on my lady-in-waiting dress, and shove my hair up into a hasty bun with the arcana inside. I scratch at the lace collar as I run down through the servant's quarters, slowing my pace when I reach the end of the glass corridor. The halls of the main palace are vacant. I slip behind the tapestry and run down the stone steps, finding my way to the kitchen much faster than I did yesterday.

Cora is leaving as I enter, carrying a tray laden with a cup and saucer, cutlery, and a covered dish.

"You're late," she says.

"Yes, ma'am," I say. She gives me the briefest once-over and leaves for the Duchess's chambers.

"Sleep late?" Zara says kindly. Her face is smudged with flour, her arms up to the elbows in a giant mound of dough.

"I forgot where I was," I say in a moment of blunt honesty.

Zara laughs at that.

There are breakfast trays laid out on a counter. I assume Coral's is the one with the pink cup on it. The nice Regimental, Three, and a footman are standing together by the door to the garden, reading the morning paper with identical frowns. For a moment, I panic. Has Ash been sighted? Caught already?

Three looks up as I pass. "Morning, Imogen."

"Bad news?" I ask casually.

"Those Black Keys killed a magistrate last night," he says. "One of the top ones, too, in the Smoke. The Exctor will have to replace him quickly."

"Oh," I say, grabbing the tray, grateful that Ash seems to have survived the night. It's only when I'm back in the stone corridor that I realize I don't know where I'm going. Two seconds later, Mary brushes past me with Carnelian's tray.

"This way," she says in a clipped, aggravated tone.

We climb back up the staircase to the tapestry but don't go through the woven fabric—instead I see that another set of stairs leads up to the second floor of the palace.

We emerge from behind a large pedestal holding a bust of one of the former Dukes of the Lake. I recognize the corridor to the men's quarters.

I get to the door and pause. Do I knock? I don't remember Annabelle knocking. Taking a deep breath, I balance the tray in one hand and open the door.

No one is in the blue-striped drawing room but I find Garnet sitting at the breakfast nook in the horrifically pink room. A handsome footman is laying a napkin in his lap.

Garnet gives me only a cursory glance. "Go on in, she's in bed."

Coral is still pulling on the fabric by her nightstand when I enter. Her whole face lights up when she sees me.

"Where would you like your breakfast, miss?" The tray is starting to hurt my wrists.

"On that table there. And pick me out a dress. I'm going to visit Mother today."

I put the tray down and head over to her closets, perusing the various colors and styles. I bet Ash would know exactly what to choose. I see a peach-colored dress that reminds me of one Annabelle put me in, so I grab that and lay it out on Coral's bed.

"So," Coral says, crossing her legs and looking at me over her cup of coffee. "What's the gossip?"

I blink. "I beg your pardon, miss?"

She puts the cup down and begins salting her fried eggs. "From downstairs. What's happening with the servants? Any trysts? Broken hearts? Fights among Regimentals? Tell me, I must know." She sighs. "I miss my old home sometimes. My maid would always fill me in over breakfast."

I busy myself by opening her curtains and tying them back. What sort of gossip am I meant to know about?

"A magistrate was killed last night," I say. "In the Smoke."

"Imogen, that's so depressing. Mother never let me read anything about the lower circles. She says they are dull and sad and nothing I need concern myself with."

Dull and sad? My hand clenches around the velvet curtain and I tie it extra tight.

"Oh! I forgot to ask Garnet if he'd come with me to Mother's today," she says, taking a bite of her eggs. "Will you—"

"I'll go ask him, miss."

Grateful for the excuse to leave, I slip out of Coral's bedroom, closing the door behind me, and find Garnet still at the breakfast nook.

"How long was she ringing that bell for?" he asks with a grin.

"Ages," I say.

"She's nothing if not persistent."

"She wanted me to ask you if you're coming with her to her mother's house today."

Garnet wipes his mouth and puts down his napkin. "Ah. No, I think I'll skip out on lunch with my mother-in-law. Society business and whatnot. But do let me know how the food is at lunch. The House of the Downs is famous for their poultry. I wonder if it will be duck this time." He winks.

"I'm not going," I say, taking a piece of toast off his plate. I have to find Hazel. Maybe I can sneak down to the medical room when the Duchess is eating her lunch. Or I could look for the secret passage Lucien told me about.

Garnet gives me an incredulous stare. "Violet, if she's going, you're going. What do you think being a lady-in-waiting is? You follow her around wherever she goes."

"But Annabelle never came with me anywhere when we left this palace."

"You were a surrogate. Coral's a royal." He stands up, takes the arcana out of his pocket, and rubs it affectionately with his thumb. "They haven't left yet, have they?"

I know he means Raven.

"No," I say, only half paying attention. "Tomorrow night. Did she tell you about Ash?" I add angrily.

He chuckles. "Yeah." Then he holds up his hands when he catches sight of the expression on my face. "Hey, I think he can do whatever he wants, and you know, he is sort of right."

"About running off to the Bank like an idiot?" I say.

"About getting the companions to our side. It's not like approaching factory workers or lower circle Regimentals. The companions are *smart*. They're well trained and perfectly placed—imagine if we could have a whole slew of companions in addition to Society members waiting on the other side of the wall when it comes down? And they won't listen to anyone but one of their own. Their lives revolve around secrets and lies. I'd be shocked if they even trusted one another all that much. So hey, this might actually be good for us."

I wish everyone would stop defending Ash, like he's done this great thing. They're not in love with him. They don't have to worry about their heart being smashed into a million pieces if he dies.

"Imogen!" Coral calls from the bedroom.

"Don't keep her waiting," he says.

I roll my eyes, then fix a pleasant smile on my face and head back to the bedroom to help Coral get dressed.

LUNCH AT THE PALACE OF THE DOWNS IS A TEDIOUS affair.

You'd think they didn't even know there was a whole city out there. Not once do they mention the bombings, the fighting, the Black Key. Coral and her mother prattle on about the Duchess and Garnet and what it's like being part of a Founding House. Coral is very excited about her first Auction. Lucien was right—it really is the event of the year, with every single married royal attending.

The only interesting part is when Hazel is mentioned, briefly.

"Did you know," the Lady of the Downs says, "the Electress has not seen the surrogate carrying her future daughter-in-law since she became pregnant? Her own physician has not even been allowed to examine her. The Duchess has not permitted it thus far."

"Oh, Mother, I can't believe it. How could the arrangement have been made otherwise?" Coral asks.

"It would seem the Exetor has met with the girl, but the Electress has . . . yet to be invited. If someone could arrange a meeting, I'm sure it would reflect favorably. On every House involved." She gives her daughter a significant look.

Coral nods eagerly. "I will speak to the Duchess."

Coral is probably the last person in the palace of the Lake who could convince the Duchess to do something like that. Even Carnelian would have a better shot.

We arrive home just as Carnelian herself is walking down the front steps to a waiting motorcar, Rye on her arm. I haven't seen her since that night in the dungeon when she helped set Ash free. She looks even more dour than usual. Rye is just as handsome as I remember, smooth dark skin and black curls. His eyes skim over me with no trace of recognition, his expression a mask of politeness, just the way Ash always used to look in this palace.

"Hello, Carnelian," Coral says. "Where are you off to?"

"Some stupid party," Carnelian grumbles. Her eyes land on me and I stiffen. "She finally got one for you, did she?"

"Garnet did," Coral replies, beaming. "I named her Imogen."

"How nice," Carnelian says sarcastically. Coral doesn't seem to notice, preoccupied by the Duchess, who is sweeping down the stairs, followed by Cora and the Duke.

"Come on, Carnelian, we don't want to be late," the Duchess snaps. I can't help how my heart stutters at the sight of her, how my legs seem to freeze up. "I'll never get you married and off my hands if you can't even show up to a simple party on time."

"Mother, I—" Coral begins, but the Duchess cuts her off.

"How many times have I asked you not to call me that?" the Duchess says as the driver opens the door for her. The door shuts before Coral has a chance to respond. Carnelian looks miserable as she gets in on the other side. Then the

motorcar is trundling down the drive and Coral watches it,
a frown on her face.

I couldn't be happier.

The Duchess is gone for the evening. This is the perfect
chance to find my sister.

Eleven

I SEIZE THE OPPORTUNITY TO SEARCH WHILE CORAL IS having her dinner.

The evening is cool when I slip out into the garden, a light breeze tickling the back of my neck. I skirt by the glass promenade and head to the garage. This is where Lucien said the secret passage to the medical room would let out. The problem with secret passages is that unless you know where they are, they're nearly impossible to find. I spent three months in this palace, never knowing about the maze of servant halls hidden within it.

After twenty minutes of examining rocks and shrubs, I give up and decide to try the one way I do know.

The palace is quiet so I chance the use of the main halls.

I hurry up to the second floor. Down the hall of the flowers, through the gallery . . . but when I find the oak-paneled hallway, my heart sinks.

The elevator with the golden grate has a new door on it, metal with a keypad installed beside it. I approach it anyway, pressing my palm against the cold surface. Hazel is right below me. I hear a noise from down the hall and jump, scurrying away and diving into the first secret passage I can find. I wander down to the first floor and emerge by the ballroom.

I have only one other option left to try—the passage in the library, the one I used with Ash.

The way to Ash's secret passage is as familiar as the house I grew up in. I walk down row upon row of books until I find the one I need—Cadmium Blake's *Essays on Cross-Pollination*. I pull it and the hidden door swings open. The corridor that stretches out before me brings another wave of memories. Ash's hand in mine. Sneaking down here late at night. Our entire relationship contained in this shadowy hall.

And I may never see him again.

No. I push Ash aside and close the bookshelf behind me. Just to be safe, I decide to make sure I'm really alone in here. Sil taught me this trick a month ago. I connect with Air and send it away from me, through the halls, then draw it back in a gust. It brings nothing but silence and the scent of stone and dust.

I slip down the hall toward Ash's former chambers. I remember that there were halls branching off this tunnel but I've never taken any of them. The first corridor I try leads me up a set of stairs and opens out into a second-floor study I haven't seen before. It's a comfortable room, with lots of bookshelves, a plush couch, and a small writing desk. A framed photograph catches my eye—a man, a woman, and two little girls, standing on the steps of what is unmistakably the palace of the Lake. I recognize one of the little girls as the Duchess immediately. The other one must be her sister. Even as a child, the Duchess has all the arrogance of her adult self—she stares into the camera with a haughty expression.

This room suddenly feels too private, almost dangerous. I put down the photograph exactly where I found it and leave.

I retrace my steps and take the next one. It's a dead end.

The third hallway proves much better. I can feel the floor sloping downward, and the air grows stale and cold. My palms itch and my breath quickens. I reach a set of polished stone stairs and creep down them, my footsteps sounding louder than they should in my ears. When I reach the bottom, a black door waits for me.

I know Hazel is behind it. I can feel it. The hairs on my arms prickle.

There's no knob, no handle, nothing to show the way to open it. I don't know what material it's made of but it feels unnaturally cold against my palms. I slide my hands along its outer edges and feel a slight indentation on the left side. Gripping it with my fingers, I pull and the door slides open.

A gust of antiseptic-tinged air washes over me as I enter. The medical room is just as I remember. The clustered, insect-like lights, the pristine white walls, the tray of silver instruments. The doctor is not here, though there are papers littered all over his desk.

But I only have eyes for the bed in the center of the room. There is a figure lying on it, covered up to her chin in a white sheet.

"Hazel?" My voice comes out like a croak. Then I'm running, but when the figure on the bed comes into view, I stop short and gasp.

She's different. They've done something to her. Altered her chin, made her nose pointier. And her hair is thicker, though it's still black and long and wavy, like mine. She's sleeping, her whole body covered with the sheet. I pull back the covers and a sob rises in my throat as I see the straps that hold her down, across her shoulders, her torso, her hips. Even her hands are strapped down at the wrists.

But her chest rises and falls. She is alive.

And even more important, her stomach is flat. There is no trace of a bump, like Raven's stomach when she was pregnant.

"Oh, Hazel," I murmur, putting my hand on her forehead and brushing a stray hair out of her face. She stirs, her eyelids fluttering open, and what I see makes my stomach turn.

Her eyes. Her beautiful, hazel eyes.

They're violet.

"What have they done to you?" I whisper.

Hazel's strange purple eyes widen and then she opens her mouth and lets out a bloodcurdling scream.

"Stop!" I cry, clamping my hand over her mouth, but she bites me hard.

"No more!" she screams. "No more, no more, no more!"

"Hazel, it's me! It's Violet!"

Hazel is thrashing around as much as she can against the straps. I hold her head between my hands to keep it still.

"Look at me," I say fiercely. "My hair is different and my eyes are different but it's me. Listen to my voice. It's Violet."

Hazel stares at me, panting, panicked.

"Listen to my voice," I say again.

"Violet?" she gasps.

A fat teardrop leaks from the corner of my eye and splashes onto her cheek.

"Yes," I say. "It's me."

And my sweet, strong little sister bursts into tears.

"You're here," she sobs. "You're real."

"I'm here," I say over and over as her chest heaves against the straps.

"Oh please," she says. "Get me out of here. They hurt me so much, Violet. Dr. Blythe and the Duchess, they . . . first they were putting something inside me every day and every day I would bleed and then they stopped but they started cutting into my face and they won't let me outside and I'm always so cold . . ."

"Shhhh," I say, smoothing back her hair.

"They took me because you left," she says. "That's what she said. She said I was your punishment."

Guilt clamps down on my heart. "I'm so sorry," I whisper.

"I want to go home," Hazel moans.

"Me too," I say, my voice cracking. I look for a way to

get the straps off her, but they are secured right into the medical bed.

"There's a button," Hazel says. "On the wall." She points to the left with her strapped-down hand. I hurry to the wall, slide back a silver white panel, and find a pad with six buttons. "It's the blue one," Hazel says. "I've watched the doctor do it."

As soon as the straps are off, I'm at her side again. She throws her arms around me, her whole body trembling.

"I've got you," I say. I wish I could whisk her out of here right now, fly her to the Marsh with my mother, or to the White Rose, somewhere the Duchess wouldn't be able to touch her.

"I need to ask you something," I say, my voice muffled by her hair. "Are you pregnant?"

Hazel's arms tense. She pulls away from me, her violet eyes dark. "No," she says. "They don't think . . . it's not working. They tried. They tried for . . . I think it was a month? Maybe more? I don't know. Time is so strange here . . ."

Tears fill her eyes and I brush an errant one away with my thumb. "It's all right," I say. "Take your time."

Hazel takes a deep, shuddering breath. "They came for me at night. Mother was—" She squeezes her eyes shut. "Mother was screaming and crying, but there were so many Regimentals. The doctor tested me on the train here. He said . . . he said I was a surrogate and if we were 'lucky' I'd be just like you. He told me about the Auguries. He told me I had to give the Duchess a baby, but fast, faster than I was supposed to."

Hazel's hand goes to her lower back, and dread fills my lungs. "He said I didn't have time to learn the Auguries," she whispers. "He said . . ."

Very gently, I lift up the back of my sister's nightdress. There is a welt at the base of her spine, the size of a walnut, a spiderweb of bluish-red veins radiating out from it.

The stimulant gun. Dr. Blythe must have been using it a lot, since Hazel never learned how to use the Auguries on her own.

"The Duchess was so mad," Hazel says, staring at her hands. "She screamed and threw things when Dr. Blythe told her I wouldn't . . . that I couldn't . . ."

"It's a good thing," I say. "Childbirth kills surrogates."

"*What?*"

"There's so much to explain. But for right now, can you tell me what she wants?" I ask. "If she isn't trying to get you pregnant anymore?"

Hazel shakes her head. "I don't know. The next time I saw her she was calm and said I had to be . . . changed. That's when the doctor started cutting my face." She probes her cheek and nose with one hand. "What do I look like?" she asks fearfully.

I try and put on a brave smile. "You look fine," I reassure her. "You . . . well, actually, you look like me."

Her eyebrows shoot up. "Really?"

"Everyone in the Jewel thinks you *are* me," I say.

"So . . . did you come back to take my place?"

She looks so eager and a guilt I wasn't prepared for rears up.

"Listen to me," I say, cupping her face in my hands. "If

staying down here meant that you could go back home to Mother, I would do it in a heartbeat. But . . ." The words burn as they leave my mouth. "I can't take you away, Hazel. Not yet."

"Wait, what? You're just going to . . . to leave me here?" she cries.

"I'm living in the palace," I say. "I'll be watching over you all the time, I promise. But if I let you go, they'll catch you and they'll know someone is helping you. And then we're both dead. There's so much going on in this city right now. I wish I could explain it all to you."

Hazel crumples, her head dropping into her hands. The seconds tick past in silence.

"So . . . you would have died here?" she whispers.

"Yes," I whisper back.

"Am I going to die here?" Her voice is so small and frightened. I wrap my arms around her.

"No," I say firmly. "I'm not going to let anything happen to you." I bite my lip, tears welling up again. "Remember those first few weeks after Father died?"

She nods against my chest.

"Remember how frightened you were, because Mother was barely speaking and Ochre kept getting into fights at school?"

Another nod. We don't talk about that time much. I haven't thought about it in years, because it's just too painful. But I need my sister to know that she is family, and I will never ever give up on her.

"What did we do together?"

"We lit a candle every night," Hazel says. "You said

Father could see us through the light. And you told me you could hear him. He would say that family is forever, and that we were always together, really, because he was watching me and he was proud. He would tell me he missed me and he loved me and . . . but, Violet, you made all that up, and I was a kid then, so I believed you."

"Who says I made it up?" I say. "Father did watch us through that candlelight. He does miss you and he loves you. He's watching over you right now. And so am I. Family is forever. I'm not going to let anything happen to you. And I *will* get you out of this place. I promise." A lump rises in my throat. "I let you believe I'd forgotten you once before. I told myself I'd never let you believe that again."

"I'm scared."

"Me too."

"Mother must be scared, too," Hazel says. "And sad. We're all gone now."

The lump in my throat gets bigger. "Father's watching over her as well," I say.

Finally, I know it's time to leave. I've stayed too long.

"I have to go," I say. "But I'll come back, I swear."

"Can you bring me food?" she begs. "They only feed me through tubes. I miss chocolate."

"My little sweet tooth," I say, giving her nose a teasing pinch. Hazel smiles at the old nickname Father used to call her, when she'd go searching through his pockets for a treat, a piece of licorice or a hard candy.

I help her lie down so I can put the straps back, pulling the covers up to her chin and kissing her on the forehead.

"Do you know," I say, "that I said good night to you

every night I was living in this palace? It always made me feel better."

"Really?"

"Really. And now I can say it to you in person. Good night, Hazel."

Hazel's answering smile is brittle. "Good night, Violet."

Then I turn and run as fast as I can out of the room before I lose my nerve and stay with her forever. I slide the door shut behind me, collapsing on the staircase, tears streaming down my cheeks.

What did they do to her face? To her eyes? And why? The Duchess clearly knows Hazel can't get pregnant, so there's no reason to keep her locked up in the medical room. There's no reason to keep her alive at all. And yet she's told the entire city Hazel already is pregnant.

So what is her endgame? I think as I pick myself up and make my way back to my room. *What is Hazel's role in her plans?*

Twelve

Over the next week, I adjust to life as a lady-in-waiting.

I sneak down to the medical room to see Hazel late at night. I bring her food when I can and fill her in on everything that's happening in the city outside the Jewel. I tell her about the White Rose, the Auguries and their true purpose, and all about the Society of the Black Key.

"Ochre used to talk about them," Hazel says, chewing on a pastry. "I didn't believe that it was a real thing. He told me he and Sable Tersing would draw keys on walls in the Farm."

"That's how the Society found him," I say.

"Is he okay?"

"Yeah. He's in the Farm. He's happy there."

Hazel smiles. "Good." She sighs. "Mother didn't believe him either. She probably wouldn't have let him out of the house if she knew he could get pulled into a secret society. She was always telling him to keep his head down." Hazel sniffs. "She needed the money he made so badly, especially after you were sold and we didn't get the surrogate compensation anymore."

Worry creeps into my stomach like a cramp. How is my mother surviving with all her children gone?

"Mother is strong," I say, more for myself than my sister. "And smart. I'm sure she'll figure something out."

"Yes," Hazel agrees, but without real enthusiasm. "Hey, do you think, when this is all over, we could live with you and Ochre in the Farm? I think I'd like the Farm. And Mother would, too."

I nudge her with my shoulder. "You would both love it. The White Rose especially."

I also tell Hazel about Ash. There's still no word from him. I am pulled back and forth between fear for his life and fury at his actions. Every time I see the paper I search for his face. I still remember the signs that hung in every circle of this city after he escaped.

Raven contacts me the night they leave Westgate, to let me know everything is going smoothly, except for Sil.

"We might have Sil wait outside for the rest of the facilities," she says. "You're a whole lot better with the 'let's be a team' thing than she is."

I grin. "Yeah, I can imagine. When do you get to Northgate?"

"A few days. We're testing the waters here, seeing if we can subtly rustle up some rebellious vibes." There's a pause. "And we're trying to help. With little things. We sneak around at night and make people's gardens grow bigger. We refill rain barrels and clean up streets a bit. If it's a cold night, we try and make sure people have fires."

My heart swells with pride. This revolution doesn't have to be all death and destruction. There can be kindness in it, too.

I talk to Lucien on the arcana most nights, before I see Hazel. Sometimes he's too busy to talk at all. I wonder if he ever sleeps.

"I have good news for you," he says one night. The Auction date is fast approaching. I am sitting in bed, brushing my hair, the arcana hovering near me.

"That's always refreshing to hear," I say.

"Ash made it to the Smoke."

I sit up straight, dropping the hairbrush. "What? When? How do you know?"

"I believe you remember my associate the Thief."

My heart warms at the memory of a young pickpocket with a soot-blackened face and a cavalier attitude. He helped us escape the Smoke. He helped Ash say good-bye to Cinder.

"He told me he made contact with Ash last night," Lucien continues. "Quite close to his old house."

"What?" I hiss, torn between relief that he is all right and anger that he's gone back to that awful place. "What is wrong with him? Why would he go back?"

"Yes, it can be quite frustrating when the people you care about, the people you have sacrificed so much to protect, act without caution or regard to that protection, isn't it?" I can picture the wry smile on his face. "But that is not all. Apparently, your brother is with him."

"Ochre?" I gasp. "What . . . what's he doing with Ash?"

"From what I gather, he discovered Ash leaving the Farm and insisted on accompanying him. It appears that acting without caution runs in your family."

"Ugh!" I run my hands through my hair, yanking a few strands out in my frustration. "What is he playing at?"

"The same thing you and I and every Society member are. Freedom. Choice."

"But you'll help them, right? You can't just leave them out there on their own."

"Do you expect me to magically appear in the Smoke and offer Ash and Ochre sanctuary? I do have one or two things going on at the moment." I open my mouth but he speaks again before I can say anything. "Of course they will be helped, Violet, they are Society members. For now, do your best not to worry too much about them. Your job is here. Watch over your sister. And when the time comes, bring down the wall."

"You make it sound so easy," I say. But the news that Ash is safe seeps into my chest, a knot of fear dissolving. Part of me is furious that Ochre is now at risk, too, but another part of me is grateful that Ash isn't alone, that he has someone with him. I fall asleep that night feeling lighter than I have since I returned to this circle.

THE NEXT DAY, THOUGH, THE PALACE IS IN TURMOIL.

The kitchen is always bustling but this morning it's a madhouse. Maids scrambling everywhere, steam issuing from pots, pans sizzling, dough being rolled out. Zara is shouting orders like a drill sergeant.

"Is this because of Garnet's party?" I ask Mary, because she's the only one who doesn't look too frazzled to talk to me. I know today is the day of Garnet's promotion ceremony.

"Yes. The Duchess just told Maude that the party for Garnet will probably be bigger than she expected. 'Probably,' she said. Zara and Maude don't know what that means." Mary looks worried. "The Duchess always gives exact numbers for events. She's quite particular about it."

I chew on this bit of information as I head up the stairs. I pass Three and One, a bulky Regimental with a shaved head, in close conversation with each other. I hear Three say, ". . . posted at all entrances, so at least twelve extra men," before they disappear down another hallway.

"The kitchen is going crazy," I say to Coral when I arrive, because she likes it when I fill her in every morning. "The Duchess is planning quite the party for your husband."

"I know, it will be even bigger now," she says, taking a sip of orange juice. "Is Elizabeth still mooning over William?"

"Why will the party be bigger now, miss?" I ask, sensing there's more to that comment.

Coral gives me a conspiratorial smile and I lean toward her, eager in the way I know she likes when she is telling a secret. "I spoke to the Duchess last night before dinner and I said, wouldn't it be just *so* lovely if the Jewel could see the surrogate again? I mean, she is carrying the future Electress of this city, after all. It would be such a boost to morale, what with everything happening in the lower circles. And the Duchess said it was very thoughtful of me and of course, it seems so cruel to deprive this city of celebrating the next generation of its leaders. So the surrogate is coming to the party after the ceremony! Isn't that exciting!" She gives me her most serious look. "I wasn't supposed to tell anyone, but you'll keep this a secret, won't you, Imogen? Promise me."

I can't breathe. I can't think. Why? Why now, after keeping Hazel locked up all this time? She's not even pregnant—won't people notice that? Coral's pleas had nothing to do with it, I'm certain. The Duchess suddenly *wants* Hazel in public. There is a threat there, a very real, potent one and I can't *see* it, I can't understand it.

All I can do is force out a lie to the girl looking up at me earnestly.

"Yes," I say. "I promise."

~ Thirteen ~

THE CEREMONY IS HELD ON THE LAWN OUTSIDE THE REG-
imental headquarters in the Jewel.

The day is unseasonably hot, and the ladies-in-waiting
have to stand way in the back, so I can't really hear or see
anything. My mind is consumed with thoughts of the party
and why, after all this time, the Duchess would allow Hazel
out in public.

Once the ceremony ends, there is a small reception, but
the Duchess sweeps over to Cora, her family trailing behind
her. "We're leaving," she says. "Now."

I ride back in the motorcar in silence with Coral, Garnet, Carnelian, and Rye. When we arrive, the front doors to
the palace are open and the halls are bustling with servants.

Coral drags me to the ballroom and gasps in delight.

The garden has been transformed.

Little colored lanterns have been strung up in the trees. There is a fountain of chocolate with piles of plump red strawberries beside it, trays of canapés waiting to be served, and bottles of champagne cooling in silver ice buckets. A string quartet is warming up off to one side. My heart squeezes at the sight of the woman tuning her cello. There are extra Regimentals stationed everywhere. The entire back wall of the ballroom is made of many little glass doors, so that the parquet floor leads right out to the garden. Several drinks tables have been set up around the room, clearly meant to serve as a first stop on the way to where the main party will take place.

After rushing around to get a look at every decoration, Coral whisks me away to change her clothes. I choose a shimmery, sea-green gown with capped sleeves, though she can barely stand still as I lace her into it.

"The garden is gorgeous," Coral gushes. "How does the Duchess do it all, and so quickly? Her taste is impeccable. And my hair looks fabulous today, you are simply the best. Have I told you you are the best, Imogen? Because you are!"

I can't help smiling through my nerves. "Thank you, miss."

She continues to babble on until I pronounce her finished; then we walk back down the main staircase to the ballroom.

My eyes are immediately searching for Hazel, but only Garnet and his father are in the ballroom. The guests have yet to arrive.

The Duke is well into a glass of whiskey. Garnet looks relieved to see us.

"Coral, you are an absolute vision," he says.

She beams. "Where is the Duchess?"

"You know Mother. She loves to make an entrance."

"Look who's talking," Carnelian says as she joins us, Rye by her side. He is dashing in his tux. I'm reminded so much of Ash, of the parties he used to attend on Carnelian's arm.

"Now, Cousin, you know I haven't made a big entrance in at least five days," Garnet says with a wink.

Rye laughs. "Quite the achievement."

"What I want to know is," Carnelian says, "where's the surrogate?"

It occurs to me then that Carnelian knows I am not the surrogate. Does she think the Duchess just stole a random, unsuspecting girl to fill my place? Or does she know what Hazel means to me? I can't see how, unless Garnet told her. And why would he do that?

Just then several royal couples arrive, ushered into the ballroom by one of the footmen. Garnet offers his arm to Coral to go and greet them.

"Come on," Carnelian says to Rye. "I need a drink."

They walk off toward one of the many tables laden with champagne and wine and whiskey. I'm left to stand awkwardly against a wall.

Soon, though, the guests begin to arrive and I'm joined by other ladies-in-waiting. Many of them know one another—they cluster together and whisper while their mistresses chat and sip champagne. The string quartet plays softly in a corner. The open back wall lets in a warm April breeze, scented with jasmine and honeysuckle.

"Hello," a young male lady-in-waiting says to me. He has dark skin and blue eyes, a striking contrast, and he can't be more than a few years older than I am. His smile is warm and genuine. "I don't believe we've met. I'm Emile."

Emile! This is Raven's lady-in-waiting, the kind one who took care of her. He helped her keep as much of her mind for as long as he possibly could. Which means . . . now I see the Countess of the Stone, her large figure cutting a wide path through the partygoers in the ballroom as she makes her way over to Garnet and Coral. Hate curls in my stomach like a fist. This woman tortured my friend.

"Where's Frederic?" I ask bluntly. Frederic is the Countess's lady-in-waiting, and even more of a sadist than the Countess herself. Raven told me about the wall of torture equipment in the dungeon where the Countess kept her, and how Frederic crafted each instrument himself.

Emile chuckles. "I see my House precedes me. Frederic is ill. Spring cold. The Countess abhors germs. He's been quarantined in the medical room until it passes. So that leaves me." He gives a little bow.

I wish I could tell him how grateful I am that he helped Raven. I wish I could let him know she's still alive.

"It's a pleasure to meet you," I say. "I'm Imogen, Coral's new lady-in-waiting."

His blue eyes brighten. "Oh, lovely. She seems like a sweet girl. Easy to care for."

"She is," I say, looking over to where she stands by the open glass doors beside Garnet, chattering away while the

Countess of the Stone looms over her, a fake smile plastered on her face. "I don't believe your mistress is enjoying the party much."

"The Countess has eccentric tastes," he replies. "I don't think most people would quite understand what she truly enjoys."

I know exactly what he means, but I just nod politely.

"Really, she's here to see the surrogate," Emile says, leaning toward me. "As most of them are."

"Ah. Right."

"Have you seen her recently?" he asks.

"No," I lie. "The Duchess keeps her locked up."

There is a sudden burst of laughter, the Duke and a few other royal men guffawing about something and slapping each other on the backs. I note the Lord of the Glass, the Duke's brother-in-law, among them. The Duke is laughing so hard he spills his drink and a footman rushes over with a fresh one, while a waiter cleans up the mess. One of the Regimentals by the ballroom door watches the Duke warily.

Emile sighs. "He really does know how to make a scene. Probably where Garnet gets it from."

"At least Garnet is funny," I say.

He laughs.

Just then there is the wailing cry of a baby and the Exetor and Electress's arrival is announced. A nurse accompanies them, carrying little Larimar, wearing a child-size suit. He is bigger than when I saw him at the Exetor's Ball, all chubby cheeks and dark curls. He's actually quite adorable. He squirms in the nurse's arms, rubbing his eye with a fat little hand. Lucien trails behind them, a shadow in white.

They make their way to the front of the reception line to congratulate Garnet. The Electress's voice is so high and loud, I can hear her easily.

"Why, I haven't been here since your engagement party," she exclaims. "How are you two finding married life?"

"It's wonderful, Your Grace," Coral gushes. "I adore being married."

The Electress laughs her chirpy laugh. "So do I."

Larimar spits up a little and the nurse wipes his chin with a cloth.

"Isn't he just the most precious thing you've ever seen?" Coral coos.

"Yes, darling," Garnet says.

"I'm eager to see the girl carrying his future wife," the Electress says, glancing around. Subtlety is not her strong suit.

"I'm sure we will shortly, my dear," the Exetor says. Unlike his wife, he does not sound particularly eager to see Hazel. "Where is your mother, Garnet? I'm surprised she's not in the thick of things as she usually is."

"She's probably in the kitchen shouting at the cook," Garnet says lazily. "It's her second favorite pastime. Aside from shouting at me, of course." He grins and the Electress and Coral giggle.

"You will be attending the Auction this year," the Electress says. "Are you excited?"

"I can hardly wait, Your Grace," Coral gushes. "I'm having a dress specially made for it."

"Where are you getting it done?"

"Miss Mayfield's."

"Oh! She's one of the best."

"That's what everyone says."

"Darling," the Electress says, pressing herself against the Exetor, "we must have Coral and Garnet over for dinner. They are a couple in their own right now; it only seems appropriate that we dine with the future Duke and Duchess of the Lake, don't you think?"

Coral's smile widens even more.

"Yes, of course," the Exetor says. His gaze drifts around the room and I wonder if maybe he is interested in seeing Hazel after all.

"You are too kind," Garnet says. "We would love to."

Trumpets blare from out in the garden. The Duchess enters the ballroom wearing a beautiful gown of silver, diamonds stitched into the bodice and skirt so that she sparkles when she moves. She stops just inside the door. Those who have made their way out into the garden begin to crowd back toward the palace, necks craning, everyone eager to see the surrogate.

It's disgusting. I remember the way they stared at me at the Exetor's Ball when I was forced to play the cello. I hate that Hazel has to experience that.

"My friends," she says, spreading her arms out wide. I notice a silver bangle on her wrist that makes my heart sink. "I am so pleased to present to you once again, after quite the whirlwind few months, my surrogate."

She jerks the wrist wearing the bangle and Hazel shuffles into view. She is attached to the Duchess by a thin chain that is fastened to an ornate collar around her neck. Tension rolls over me in waves. Hazel is on a *leash*.

But even worse, her stomach protrudes from under her dress, a round curve that clearly shows she's pregnant.

But she's not. She can't be. I saw her two days ago. And they've stopped trying to impregnate her.

My thoughts are snarled up, and then, from across the room, my sister's eyes find mine and she gives me the slightest shake of her head. Reassuring me. Whatever is under her dress, it isn't real.

It is disconcerting, though, how easily she is able to pull off being me. The Duchess was very clever. Hazel must be in heels to match my height. They've padded the bodice of her dress so her chest looks like mine. She wears the exact same dress I wore to my first dinner in this palace—pale purple, with an empire waist. Her hair has been curled and pinned just how Annabelle used to do mine.

The only new addition, besides the pregnant stomach, is a veil. A shimmering layer of white gauze covers Hazel's face from the bridge of her nose to just below her chin. It is translucent, so her features are still partly discernible. Maybe the Duchess wanted a precaution against anyone realizing she isn't me. Or maybe it's just some new surrogate fashion.

Hazel's purple eyes are wide with a mixture of fear and wonder at the scene spreading out before her—I realize she's never actually seen this palace, or any other royal, before. Her gaze travels over the glittering fabrics to the glossy instruments of the string quartet and finally lands on the tables of food laid out in the garden, before returning to me.

The royals are watching her with interest, too. Their eyes all flicker between the Duchess and Hazel's stomach.

"She has been through a terrible ordeal," the Duchess is saying. "So please, keep your distance. We don't want to overwhelm her too much."

The Electress has already crossed the ballroom to stand in front of Hazel. The Duke makes his way unsteadily to stand beside the Duchess and they bow and curtsy as the Exetor joins them, the nurse trailing behind. The room watches with bated breath as the Electress looks Hazel up and down.

"She seems . . . thinner," the Electress says.

"She is perfectly healthy, I assure you, Your Grace. The doctor visits her every day."

The Electress opens her mouth, but the Exetor puts a hand on her shoulder and turns her to face the waiting crowd. He gestures for the nurse to hand Larimar to the Electress so that they are grouped together, the Duke and Duchess, Hazel, Larimar, and the Electress and Exetor, in a bizarre mockery of a family photograph.

"Ladies and gentlemen," he says. "I present to you the future of the Lone City!"

The crowd erupts in cheers. The Countess of the Stone, I notice, claps unenthusiastically. The Electress's smile looks forced. Larimar begins to cry, reaching out for his nurse. I spot the gray-haired Countess of the Rose in the crowd, Sienna's former mistress. She watches the scene with a smug expression.

"Now let's celebrate with a drink!" Garnet says. The cheers turn to laughs, and the string quartet starts up again. Hazel is immediately surrounded by royal women who are clearly dying to get as close to her as possible without inciting the wrath of the Duchess.

It makes me furious. Hazel looks terrified, all these unfamiliar ladies gawking at her, talking about her to the Duchess like she's not standing right there, a leash fastened around her neck.

Lucien glides over to where we are standing. "Emile," he says. "Is Frederic still sick?"

"He is."

"Do send him my best wishes for a speedy recovery."

"I will."

Lucien ignores me completely.

"The Electress must be very happy to see the surrogate," Emile says.

"Indeed," he replies. "I don't think she's going to let the girl out of her sight all evening."

It does seem as though the Electress has glued herself to Hazel's side. Her closeness hasn't escaped the Duchess's notice either. Cora hovers behind them. When our eyes meet, she gives me a curt nod.

I feel better knowing that I'm not the only person looking out for Hazel tonight.

The party moves into the garden as the sun begins to set, decorating the sky with streaks of pink and orange. The ladies-in-waiting keep on the fringes, and I find myself enjoying this party more than any of the ones I attended as a surrogate. Probably because no one is staring at me or talking about me like I don't exist. I watch Rye feed Carnelian a chocolate-covered strawberry and my heart aches thinking of Ash again. And Ochre now, too. I hope they're all right, wherever they are. The only consolation I have is that, if Ash had been caught, I surely would have heard by now. The Duchess would be ecstatic.

I spend quite a bit of time with Emile and find myself enjoying his company immensely. He is kind, and smart, and has a quick wit. I feel bad that he has to live in that horrible palace. I can't wait to tell Raven I met him.

The Duke gets staggeringly drunk. He keeps making elaborate toasts that no one wants to listen to. The Duchess tries to stay as far away from him as possible, Hazel by her side. Hazel and I have exchanged a few glances, but there's simply no way to talk to her here. The Electress keeps petting the top of her head, like she's a dog.

"Ladies and gentlemen!" the Duke says, raising his glass for the third time. "I would like to make a t—"

Suddenly a loud voice booms out over the music.

"The House of the Lake is a poison to this city!"

A Regimental stands in the middle of the crowd. He's smaller than most of the other ones I've seen, with a haggard face. There is a moment of shocked silence among the partygoers.

"Their blood shall never sit on the throne!" he shouts. Then he draws his pistol and points it straight at Hazel.

And with a loud pop, the shooting begins.

Fourteen

Hazel.

That's all I can think.

I have to get to Hazel.

After the first shot rings out, chaos erupts. More shots are fired and it seems like they're coming from everywhere. Someone yanks me to the ground and I realize it's Lucien.

"Stay down," he growls in my ear, before rushing into the fray. I'm on my feet as soon as he's gone. Rye runs past me with Carnelian, her face pressed against his chest, his arms wrapped protectively around her.

Hazel. I have to find Hazel. That man was pointing the gun right at her.

As I shove through the crowds fighting for the exit, I

stumble on something and fall to the ground, scraping my palms.

The Duke's eyes stare up at me, unblinking, a red spot in the center of his chest growing bigger and bigger. I scoot backward and see One and another Regimental standing over the body of the haggard man beside another dead Regimental—his accomplice I would guess, judging by the way One is glaring at him.

"Search them," One spits. "Then get them out of here."

The garden is emptying out now. The Exetor and Electress are nowhere to be seen—they must have been the first ones the Regimentals protected when the shooting started. Then I see a fine silver chain in the grass, its end broken off the wrist it was once attached to. I crawl on the ground toward it, and find a pair of little feet poking out from underneath a white-clad body.

Cora is prostrate over Hazel. I grab her arm and pull her off my sister. She moans.

Blood has seeped through her dress, staining her shoulder bright red. Hazel coughs and sits up.

"She . . . she pulled me down," she says, staring wide-eyed at Cora, who has sunk into unconsciousness.

"Protect my surrogate, you fools!" the Duchess shrieks, crawling out from behind a table. Three comes bounding out of nowhere, scoops Hazel up, and disappears with her.

It takes every ounce of self-control I have not to scream after her.

"Cora!" the Duchess cries, seeing her cradled in my arms. She runs over and sinks to her knees, her dress billowing out in sparkling waves around her. "Give her to me," she snaps, grabbing Cora's limp figure from my grasp and holding her to her own chest. "Oh, Cora, Cora, what did they do to you . . ."

I've never seen the Duchess look like this before. Tears spill down her cheeks as she rocks her lady-in-waiting back and forth, blood dripping through her fingers.

"Help me!" she screams, and more Regimentals swarm her. I get up and stumble backward as they lift Cora up and carry her, I presume, to the medical room. I bump right into Garnet, who is staring down at the body of his father.

"What's happening?" I ask numbly.

"I . . . he . . ." Garnet looks confused, as if the scene before him doesn't make any sense. "Will you help me carry him inside?"

The ballroom is empty. Broken glass, puddles of wine, and overturned food platters litter the parquet floor. We lay the Duke out by the doors. I grab a clean linen tablecloth and drape it over him.

"Thanks," Garnet says, but there's no emotion behind the word. "I think a footman got shot as well."

We find the footman slumped over a shrub. He is young, with copper skin and a large nose. I'm pretty sure his name was George. Garnet and I carry him inside to lay him out beside the Duke. Maids and footmen have begun to tentatively inch back into the ballroom.

"Start cleaning this up," Garnet says. I've never heard him sound so commanding. He looks like he's aged ten years tonight.

"Garnet—" But before I can continue, there is a commotion in the hall and then we hear a voice cry, "For the

Exetor's sake, Five, it's me, let me through!"

A few seconds later, Dr. Blythe hurries through the ball-room door. He stops short and gasps at the scene before him. He hasn't changed a bit—though maybe there are a few more streaks of gray in his thick black hair. His green eyes grow sad as he lifts the corner of the tablecloth cover-ing the Duke.

"Where is your mother?" he asks, looking up at Garnet, who points out to the garden.

Dr. Blythe hurries off, and I hear a wail, followed by, "Cora, attend to Cora, you idiot!"

A second later, he's back and out the door. I realize someone's missing.

"Garnet," I say quietly. "Where's Coral?"

Garnet blinks and looks around. "I don't know." He stares blankly out the door for a second, then says, "I'm . . . I'll be back."

He wanders out of the ballroom like a man in a trance.

I head out into the halls, searching for Coral. After a few minutes, I find her crying on one of the smaller stair-cases. I sit down and wrap my arms around her as she falls into my chest.

"Oh, Imogen," she sobs.

"Shhh," I say automatically, holding her tight as much for my own sake as for hers. Hazel nearly died tonight. I was right there and powerless to stop it. I came here to keep her safe and I failed. If Cora hadn't . . . I squeeze my eyes shut because I can't think about that.

I finally get Coral up to bed and settled. Then I walk in a daze back down the stairs and through the halls, not caring about using the servants' tunnels. I pass the ball-room, where Mary and the other maids are cleaning the floors, while footmen pick up the shattered bottles and bro-ken tables. I should join them. I should help. But my feet keep moving.

As I walk past the Duke's smoking room, I hear a quiet noise, like a sob. The door is slightly ajar and I peek in and see Garnet, sitting in an armchair, head in his hands.

I don't know what to do. I'm about to turn and leave when he looks up.

"Oh," he says, quickly rubbing the tears from his cheeks.

"Are you all right?" I ask, slipping inside and shutting the door behind me. It's a stupid question. Of course he's not. "Do . . . do you know what that was? I mean, was it planned? Was it a Society action?"

"No," Garnet says grimly. "Definitely not."

"Then—"

"I don't know, Violet." His tone is sharp and he seems to realize it. He sighs and leans back in the chair. "I hate it in here," he says. "Always have. Stinks. I never understood why my father liked cigars so much." His voice cracks the tiniest bit on the word *father*.

I perch myself on the edge of a leather-covered ottoman. "I'm sorry," I whisper.

Garnet's face grows red and he looks away. "I didn't even like him all that much," he says. "He was so embar-rassing. Boring. Always drunk. But I didn't . . . I didn't want him to . . ." He rubs at his eyes again.

"When my father died, I felt so guilty," I say quietly, keeping my gaze focused on a crystal ashtray. "I thought

I should have been able to do something, I thought . . ." I clear my throat. Talking to Hazel about this is one thing—it's hard for me to share these memories with someone else. But Garnet needs this right now. "Then I got angry. Which only made me feel more guilty."

"I don't feel guilty," Garnet snaps.

I pause. "Don't you?"

A vein in his neck throbs. Then he crumples, the sobs heaving in his chest. I kneel beside him and take his hand in mine.

"It's not your fault," I whisper.

Garnet's head falls onto my shoulder, and I let his tears soak my dress for a while, until we hear voices outside. Regimental boots are marching up and down the corridors. Garnet sits up and wipes his nose on his sleeve.

"You should go," he says. "We shouldn't be in here together."

I stand. Then I kiss him on the forehead. He gives me a watery smile, before I slip back into the halls. I'm so tired. I want my bed.

I'm almost at the glass promenade when I run into Dr. Blythe. All my exhaustion disappears in a flood of adrenaline. He looks drained, mopping his brow with a handkerchief.

"Good evening," he says, then frowns. "I'm sorry, I don't believe we've met."

My heart leaps into my throat. He'll know my voice.

"I'm Imogen," I say, grateful that I'm already so full of emotion, the words come out thick and muddled. "Coral's new lady-in-waiting."

"Ah." He sighs and puts the handkerchief back in his pocket. "You didn't suffer any injuries, did you? I'd be happy to examine you."

That would be a terrible idea, since nothing about my body has changed. I shake my head vigorously.

"The surrogate?" I ask. "Is she all right?"

One of his eyebrows curves up, curious. "She is fine. I'd thought you'd be more concerned with Cora."

"Yes, I—how is Cora?" I can feel my cheeks turning pink and I try to will the color away.

Dr. Blythe studies me for a moment. "She's fine. The bullet grazed her shoulder. She saved the surrogate's life." He rubs his temple. "I'm sorry, have we met before? You seem familiar somehow."

"I don't think so," I say, looking down. "Please excuse me, I'm very tired. It's good to hear that Cora is all right. Good night, Doctor."

Stop talking, Violet, I scream at myself inwardly. Without waiting for a response from Dr. Blythe, I hurry down the glass corridor, not stopping or looking up until I've reached my room and closed and locked the door. I collapse on the bed and the weight of the whole evening crashes down on me.

A tear leaks from the corner of my eye and leaves a warm trail down my cheek. So many tears being spilled tonight.

I feel like such a fool. I can't protect Hazel here. Ash was right. And who am I to tell anyone what to do, how much to risk and for whom?

I wish desperately for our hayloft. I want to sink down on the woolen blanket and feel his arms around me, his breath stirring my hair as I let out all my fears and frustrations. I want to feel as though I am loved, no matter what decisions or mistakes I've made.

Because I love him for all of his.

My arcana begins to buzz. I yank it from my hair and my bun comes loose, blond waves falling around my shoulders.

"What happened?" I demand, before Lucien has a chance to say anything. "What was that?"

"I don't know." I've never heard him sound like this before. Confused. Almost frightened. "I cannot believe the Electress would orchestrate something like this on her own but . . . if she did, it's a very bad sign."

"How?"

"It would mean she no longer trusts me, and that is something we cannot afford."

"So do you think she planned it or not?" I say.

"She was by Hazel's side all night, until right before the shooting began, when she insisted on going inside because it was cold, even though this night was quite pleasant. She and the Exetor were whisked away immediately and she insisted I come with them, even though she knew I could help with the injured. After all, I have saved your life before. Perhaps she did not want me to repeat the performance."

"We've got to keep her away from Hazel," I say.

"I have no power to do that," he says gently.

"Then what's the point of all this?" I say. "Why am I here at all? Why did I come? I can't help. I can't . . ."

There's a pause. I can feel Lucien gathering his thoughts.

"Do you remember," he says, "when you asked me

about Raven, back when you were still the Duchess's surrogate? When you wanted to know where she lived?"

That feels like a million years ago. "Yes."

"I thought it was so foolish of you. A complete waste of time. I was actually quite upset to realize she lived next door to you. I saw her as a distraction. A weakness." He sighs. "But she was not a weakness. She is one of your greatest strengths. So is Ash. So is Hazel. The people you love make you strong, Violet. They make you brave and fearless. I wish there were some way I could make you see that."

"But I'm not brave," I say. "Not like you."

Lucien chuckles. "No," he says. "You are infinitely braver."

I wish I could believe him. I have to try. Because this night has shown me that Lucien cannot solve all my problems for me.

I let his words form a shell around my heart, tough and sinewy. I must be strong. For my friends, for my sister, for this city. The only way to truly save Hazel is to destroy the royalty and surrogacy once and for all.

I am not a mere surrogate, bought and leashed and paraded around anymore. In the end, the royalty will know that.

And they will fear me.

Fifteen

THE DUKE IS BURIED TWO DAYS AFTER THE SHOOTING.

I sit on a stool in the kitchen the afternoon of the funeral, nibbling on a raspberry scone. The funeral is for family only, so I have an entire afternoon to myself.

I pick up the paper someone left on the table. "Tragedy Strikes Again!" the headline reads. "House Plagued by Misfortune." And underneath, the very telling question, "Duchess's Surrogate the Target?" The article doesn't outright blame the Electress for the events of the party, but rumors are flying and this reporter is clearly aware of them. He strongly suggests that someone "influential and with a reason to want the surrogate dead" must have been behind the shooting. That goes in line with what everyone in the

Jewel seems to be thinking.

I want to go see Hazel, but the doctor has moved back into the palace, like he did after I miscarried. Which makes the medical room extra dangerous to visit. I don't know when I'll get to see her again.

I turn the page and the next headline jumps out at me, along with a very familiar photograph, making me feel as if the floor has just dropped out from under my feet.

"Ash Lockwood Sighted?"

Ash's face, the same one on the wanted posters from January, stares at me, the hint of a smile on his face, his hair smoothed back instead of tangled. Quickly, I read the article.

"Ash Lockwood, once one of the most highly sought-after companions in the Jewel, now a notorious fugitive, may have been sighted near his former companion house late last night. A man matching Lockwood's description was seen lurking around the park near Madame Curio's Companion House a little after midnight. The witness, a Mr. J. R. Rush, claims to have seen Lockwood while walking his dog. No doubt the Regimentals will be looking into the matter thoroughly. Lockwood is believed to be one of the leaders of the infamous Black Key Society, a band of rebels intent on vandalism and destruction, who have been linked to several bombings in the Bank and the Smoke and, most recently, the assassination of Magistrate Awl. He escaped the Jewel after raping the surrogate belonging to the Duchess of the Lake. Anyone with information on his whereabouts should contact their local law enforcement office immediately. The public is warned, however, that this individual is considered extremely dangerous."

Ash has made it to the Bank! I want to stand up and whoop with joy. Maybe he's already made contact with some companions. But it says nothing about Ochre. Have they been separated? Perhaps Ash left him someplace safe when he went to visit his old companion house. He'd never risk Ochre's safety, I'm sure of that. Though Ochre may have a different definition of *safe* than Ash does. Worry and pride war inside me.

"Imogen, hand me that rosemary, will you?" Zara says, breaking into my thoughts. The mood in the palace is subdued. Even the normally bustling kitchen is quiet and mostly empty. A scullery maid name Clara scrubs pots in the sink and William rolls a cigarette by one of the stoves.

"Awful," Zara mutters as I hand her the herb. She crunches the rosemary in her meaty fist and rubs it onto a roast. "He was a good man."

"I didn't know you knew the Duke so well," I say.

"Not the Duke," she snaps. "George, the footman. But no one cares that he's dead, do they? No, it's all weeping and sorrow over an alcoholic waste of space."

"He wasn't that bad, Zara," William says. "Better than *her*, that's for sure."

"Oh, shut up, William, he always gave you special favors, that's why you liked him," Zara says, wiping her nose on her sleeve.

"Did they ever find out who those men were?" I ask. "Who they worked for?"

William adopts a bored expression. "The Electress, isn't it obvious? She's hated the Duchess for as long as she's been married to the Exetor. And if her son marries the Duchess's daughter, they'll be stuck with each other for life. Wouldn't be the first time that sort of thing happened. I heard the Exetor's sister's death wasn't really an accident."

"She fell off a horse," I say. "How do you fake that?"

"Did she?" William shrugs.

"Rumor and conspiracy theories," Zara says. She glares at William. "And don't even think of lighting that up in my kitchen."

He is heading out the door to the garden when a small figure comes flying into the kitchen, screaming.

"Help! Help me, please!"

Hazel's face is streaked with tears and there are scratches on her wrists and arms. She's still wearing the fake stomach under a white, torn nightdress. Without the heels and the padded dress, she looks so much younger than she did at the party.

Zara gasps. I feel my mouth hanging open. I want to run to her, I want to shout her name, but I'm frozen with shock. How did she get here? How did she get *out*?

"Stop her!" another voice cries, and suddenly Cora runs into the room, her arm in a sling, two Regimentals on her heels. Hazel pelts in my direction, and my arms instinctively reach for her, but William grabs her around the chest.

"Let me go!" Hazel cries. Her eyes lock on mine. "She's trying to kill me. She's trying to kill me!"

"Five, Three, take her back to the medical room *right now*," Cora commands. Hazel is struggling against William's grasp.

I stand there, wide-eyed, feeling paralyzed and helpless.

What do I do? Who is trying to kill her? Is she talking about the Electress?

The two Regimentals wrangle my sister out of William's grasp. She bites Five's hand and he swears.

"Calm down," Cora says. "No one's going to hurt you."

Hazel spits in her face as they drag her away, wrenching her head around to meet my gaze one more time.

"She's trying to kill me," she says, her eyes flickering back to Cora. I hear her scream it one more time, her voice echoing over the stone floors, before it fades. Then she's gone.

The four of us left in the kitchen are stunned into stillness.

Zara clears her throat. "I'd suggest we all forget what we just saw here," she says.

Clara goes back to scrubbing pots with renewed fervor and William hurries out the door to smoke. I continue to stand stock-still, dumbstruck. Hazel was right here and I did nothing. I've never felt so useless.

She's trying to kill me. And she looked at Cora when she said it.

Is Cora trying to hurt my sister? Then why save her life at the party?

"Imogen?"

I start. One of the footmen hovers in the doorway, looking nervous.

"Yes?"

He holds out a letter.

"This just came for Coral. From the Royal Palace."

I numbly take the cream-colored envelope from him.

Coral's name is written in elegant script, in golden ink.

I bring it to her chambers in a daze, not seeing where I'm going, not focusing on anything but the image of my sister's tearstained face, her last words still echoing in my ears.

When Coral arrives home hours later from the funeral, I give it to her and she rips it open eagerly.

"'My dearest Coral,'" she reads aloud. "'We would love to have you and your husband over for lunch in three days' time at two o'clock. My deepest sympathies again on the loss of your father-in-law. We must all remain strong in these troubling times. Please send your reply back as soon as possible. All the very best, The Electress.'" She presses the letter to her heart. "How wonderful! We must respond right away, as she says. I've never received a personal invitation to the Royal Palace before!"

She quickly writes a response and gives me the letter to post. I find one bright spot in this situation—a trip to the Royal Palace means I get to see Lucien. I need his advice and guidance more than ever.

~ Sixteen ~

CORA SEEMS TO BE AVOIDING ME OVER THE NEXT FEW days.

She's always with the Duchess, who has been looking tired, almost haggard, since Hazel's escape. She never seems to be in her room when I've tried seeing her before bedtime. I finally manage to corner her by waiting outside her room the morning of Coral and Garnet's luncheon at the Royal Palace.

"What's going on?" I demand, and she jumps at the sight of me.

"Everything is fine," she says, glancing up and down the empty hallway. "She got out when the doctor was distracted. She's safe in the medical room now."

"*Safe?*" I hiss. "She said you were trying to kill her!"

"Why would I do that?" Cora takes a step forward so my back is pressed against the wall. "The doctor gave her something to calm her down after the shooting. It was still in her system. She was confused. Disoriented. No one in this palace would want to hurt her."

"But—"

"Look, I made a promise and I'm going to keep it," Cora says through clenched teeth. "Just don't forget to hold up your end of the bargain."

Then she turns on her heel and storms off. I lean my head against the wall and close my eyes. I want to believe her. I want to believe that Hazel is safe.

But she isn't. None of us are.

I make my way back up to Coral's chambers, to prepare her for the luncheon.

Maybe Lucien can help me sort all of this out.

THE ROYAL PALACE IS JUST AS GRAND AS I REMEMBER IT.

Our motorcar winds its way up through the thick forest and past the topiary, which showcases birds and beasts crafted impeccably out of ten-foot-high hedges. We emerge into a large square with a fountain in its center, four boys blowing trumpets, water pouring out of their horns in thin arches.

The palace itself is crafted out of a burnished metal that glows like liquid gold. It climbs into the sky in turrets and spires and towers, its gleaming surface making me squint in the bright sunlight.

"I can't believe the Duchess tried to advise us not to

come," Coral says as the chauffeur opens the door for her. "How could we refuse an invitation from the Royal Palace?"

The Duchess was not thrilled when she heard about this luncheon.

"You know what they're saying, darling," Garnet says with a casual glance in my direction. "Mother is simply trying to keep us safe."

"Well, of course we'll be safe," Coral says, her chest swelling with pride. "Doesn't she know my husband is a Master Sergeant in the Regimentals?"

Garnet's expression softens and I feel my heart soften, too. Coral might be a royal, but she's a sweet girl, really.

We walk up the low steps to the front doors, opened by footmen clad in blue and red, shiny brass buttons on their coats.

Lucien is waiting for us in the immense, circular foyer.

"Garnet, Coral, welcome," he says warmly. "Their Royal Graces are eager to see you. Lunch will be served in the Lotus Garden. Please, follow me."

He leads the way, Coral and Garnet arm in arm behind him, while I bring up the rear. I've been to the Royal Palace twice before, once for the Exetor's Ball and again for the celebration of the Longest Night. But clearly, I haven't even seen a fraction of it. Lucien leads us down wide halls lined with huge oil paintings, others with richly detailed murals. One hall's floor seems to be crafted out of pure diamond. Another has lights that shift their color as you pass, changing from mauve to lavender to pale green.

We end up in front of a set of glass double doors. Lucien

opens them and bows, gesturing Coral and Garnet outside. I stop in the doorway and can't help the way my breath catches in my throat.

The Lotus Garden has no discernible walls, just lush greenery in a wide circle. And instead of rows of flowers or neatly cut grass, all around us is water. Crystal-clear water filled with lotus blossoms and lily pads. The soft white flowers float lazily, as frogs and fish dart around them. There is a flagstone walkway out to a large stone island in the center of the garden, where a white table and chairs sit underneath a wide umbrella, plates and cutlery laid out, a bottle of white wine chilling in a silver bucket in its center.

The Exetor and Electress are already sitting. The Electress waves.

"Garnet, Coral, you've arrived!" she calls out. "Wonderful. The chef is making lobster thermidor. I do hope that's all right. Lucien, leave us. Show Coral's lady-in-waiting to the green room, she can wait there until we're finished."

"Yes, my lady," Lucien says with a bow, and we leave Garnet and Coral to their lunch.

As soon as we're out of sight and alone, Lucien whirls around and envelops me in a hug.

"There's so—" I'm about to tell him about Hazel's escape when he interrupts.

"I wish to show you something. And we don't have much time. This way."

He glides down the hall and turns left, stopping at a large, gilt-framed mirror to pull on its right-hand side. It opens with a click, revealing a small landing with a stone staircase branching off it in both directions. We climb through the hole and walk up until we reach another hall-way. Left, right, up a set of stairs, left, more stairs . . . I quickly lose track of where we are except that we are climb-ing high up within the palace. The halls are bustling with servants, and everyone bobs a curtsy or nods to Lucien as he passes.

We reach a simple wooden door—it's locked, but Lucien takes out his key ring. A spiral staircase curls up, and when we come to its end, there is only another wooden door. This one has no lock.

Lucien opens it and I find myself staring at a bedroom. It's plain, almost austere, and reminds me of my room at Southgate. A neatly made bed, a dresser, a small armchair by the window. There is a watercolor painting hanging on the wall, a meadow of blue flowers. A closet door is slightly ajar.

"Is this . . ."

"My room," Lucien says, and he doesn't look at me. I feel embarrassed. This is so personal. Why did Lucien take me here?

Then he crosses the room to the closet, pulls aside the row of hanging lady-in-waiting dresses, and reveals a hid-den door.

It is made of metal and has no discernible handle. Luc-ien takes his arcana off his key ring and inserts it into a depression in the center of the door. The tuning fork begins to buzz, then the door clicks open. Lucien holds out his hand and the arcana drops into his palm. Once it is secured safely back on its ring, he pushes the door wide.

"Yours will open it as well," he says. "As will Garnet's and Sil's."

I leave the bedroom behind and walk into the secret room. The door swings shut, plunging us into darkness for a moment before lights begin to switch on one by one.

"What is this place?" I ask.

"My workshop," Lucien says.

Bookshelves line the wall behind me and the one opposite, books crammed in wherever there is space. Where there isn't, stacks of books pile up on tables or under chairs. The wall to my left is plastered with maps and illustrations and scraps of paper with hastily scribbled notes. There is a large drawing table with three glowglobes hovering over it like miniature suns. An easel is set up in a corner, a collection of paint tubes on a nearby table, their guts spilling out in shades of magenta and lavender and lemon yellow. A large screen, like the one Dr. Blythe used when giving me Augury tests but larger, is mounted on the wall among the papers, glowing faintly.

The center of the room is dominated by a long wooden table, covered in strange equipment. There are glass beakers in every shape and size, some filled with bubbling liquids, others smoking in hues of gray and gold, some with flames burning underneath, some that emit faint humming sounds, like a faraway arcana. There is a mortar and pestle filled with crushed leaves that give off a minty scent and another one with black things inside that look like peppercorns. Thin copper coils twist out of several beakers and into others.

The wall to my right is entirely filled with clocks. Large and small, some fancy, some plain, some made of intricately wrought metals, others just simple white faces with wooden frames.

I see a familiar-looking object, lying half-buried under a sheaf of papers on the drawing desk. I pick the slate up in trembling hands.

"Yes," Lucien says softly, and I jump. "I made Annabelle's slate. That was a prototype."

My fingers tighten around it briefly before I set it back down on the table.

"Why are you showing me this?" I ask.

"I felt it was time. The Auction draws closer every day. No one has ever seen this place. Besides, you are so opportunely available now." Lucien moves a pile of books off of an armchair and indicates that I should sit. He pulls up a stool from in front of the easel. I notice that there are the beginnings of a drawing on it—the rough outline of a girl's face with long hair. I would be willing to bet it's Azalea.

"It's incredible," I say.

Two pink spots appear on Lucien's cheeks. "Thank you."

"I doubt I could ever understand what you're doing here." I glance at a beaker filled with bright emerald liquid.

"I'm sure you could work a few things out," he says, eyes twinkling. He glances around the room. "This place has been precious to me for so long."

"The Electress doesn't know about it?"

He chuckles. "Oh no. Neither the Electress nor the Exetor know about this room. There are many secrets in this palace that they are unaware of. That is what happens when you do not look below the surface of things, when you only focus on what is right in front of you."

He picks a copper spring up off the floor and twists it around in his hands.

"Why so many clocks?" I ask.

"I told you a bit about my childhood," he says. I cringe inwardly, remembering the horrific tale of how Lucien was castrated against his will by his own father as his mother and sister watched. "I loved taking the one clock in our house apart and putting it back together. I suppose old habits die hard, as they say." He glances at the wall of timepieces behind him. "Some of them feel like very old friends."

It occurs to me then how little I truly know about Lucien.

"How long have you been collecting them?"

He slowly begins to unroll the coil in his hands. "Since I was twelve. This is the seventh iteration of my wall of clocks. Some I've kept. Most are new. The clockmakers in the Bank adore me. Fortunately, neither the Electress nor the Exetor seem to notice or care that we order so many new ones each year." He sighs. "They would not understand if I ever had to explain it to them. These clocks comfort me. They remind me of someone I used to be. That would sound foolish to them."

"It doesn't to me," I say.

"I know, honey." The coil has entirely unrolled into a thin line of copper. Lucien bends it in half and tosses it aside on the table. "I remember the first time I heard you play the cello. At the Exetor's Ball. The intensity of your playing, the simplicity of the music, the expression on your face . . . I remember thinking, I know that feeling."

"That seems like ages ago," I say.

"Yes, I imagine it does to you."

"And not to you?"

Lucien shrugs. "I have lived in this circle a very long time. I suppose I've become used to the way time passes here. It ages you. It changes you."

Silence falls, broken only by the bubbling of beakers and the ticking of the clocks on the wall.

"Hazel escaped," I say. "She somehow got out of the medical room and ran up to the kitchen. She said . . . someone is trying to kill her. I think she meant Cora. But that can't be right, can it? And Cora denied it, said Hazel was drugged or something."

"She escaped the medical room?" Lucien says, raising an eyebrow. "Impressive."

"She said someone was trying to *kill her*," I say again. I'm not feeling like he's grasping the severity of the situation.

"We know someone is trying to kill her, Violet," he says patiently. "That's why you came back to the Jewel in the first place."

"So what do I do?" I ask, slamming my fist down on the arm of the chair. "She was right there, Lucien, right in front of me begging for help, and I . . . I couldn't do anything."

He purses his lips. "I fear there is nothing for us to do now except let this whole thing play out. I imagine the Duchess has increased security around her, after the shooting. That is the best we can hope for—*all* we can hope for, really. The plans of this Society will come together on Auction Day, or they will not. Time will tell."

"Do you think the Electress was behind the shooting?" I ask.

"It is certainly the most popular theory." I give him a look. "Yes," he admits. "I do."

I shudder. "It's so strange," I say. "That palace . . . it's gone completely back to normal. Like the Duke never existed."

"He was not well loved, I'm afraid." He smacks his hand against his chest. "I forgot to tell you! Ash has made contact with a group of his former colleagues. They are eager and willing to join our side. What a boon! A group of highly trained young men with access in and out of the Jewel. I could not have planned it better myself."

"He's all right?" I ask, jumping to my feet. "What else did he say? Is Ochre okay? When did you speak to him?"

"He is fine, as is your brother. I have not spoken with either of them myself. They made contact with another one of my sources two days ago—I believe you met the man during your time in the Bank. The Cobbler, he is called."

"Yes, I remember him." I sit back down, my heart beating fast. Ochre and Ash are still together. They are all right.

"He is attempting to coordinate as many companions as he can—both inside the Jewel and out. I believe he's created some sort of code. He will lead those in the Bank, joining the Society members by the wall near the Auction House on the day of the Auction."

I remember what Ash's note to me said. *I will be there on Auction Day.* He's keeping his promise.

Lucien is still talking. "Anyone on our side will wear a piece of white fabric tied around their left arm, to identify them." He pats my knee. "That was Ash's idea, and quite a smart one. I will spread it to the rest of the Society. It will make it easier for us to identify our friends."

"Won't it make us easier to be identified by the Regimentals?"

"I do not believe the Regimentals who are against us will care much if they shoot a member of the Society or a random shop owner. And for those Regimentals who are with us, it will be extremely helpful for them to see who they can trust."

"I'm surprised he didn't choose black fabric. For the Black Key and all."

"I believe it is meant to symbolize the White Rose," Lucien says. "Which has been just as important, if not quite as well known, as the Black Key."

"Yes," I murmur. "That's nice."

Another silence falls, a peaceful one. I think about that last conversation Ash and I had in the hayloft, about our future together. For a moment, I allow myself to believe it could be real.

"What do you want for this city, Lucien?" I ask.

He smiles lazily. "No walls. No separation. A united city. A ruling body chosen based on the quality of minds and the depth of compassion, not bloodlines and Houses. People from every circle represented. I want the people of this city to have a legitimate say in how they live their lives."

"Yes," I agree. "No more walls. I want everyone to see one another as people, not companions or surrogates or servants." I take a deep breath, inhaling the scent of wood varnish, and books, and paint. "I really like it here."

Lucien looks overcome for a moment, his eyes brimming with emotion.

"Thank you," he says finally. "You do not know how

much that means to me. And how much it pains me to ask this one favor of you."

"Anything," I say.

"If the time comes . . . the Auction . . . and we lose—"

"Let's not think ab—"

He holds up a hand. "Should things start to look bad for us . . . I want you to destroy this place."

I gasp. "What? Why?"

Lucien takes in the beakers, the clocks, the unfinished portrait of Azalea. "I will not let this fall into their hands. And you are the only one who can destroy it."

Even as he says it, I sense the air around me pricking, charging. Air and I could tear this place apart easily. Even if it would break my heart to do so.

He looks at me with eyes so desperate, so pleading. "Please, Violet. Do not let them take this last piece of me."

I have no choice but to agree. "All right," I say. "But only as a last resort." I reach out and place my hand on top of his. "Azalea would be so proud of you."

Lucien lets out a quiet sob, then pulls himself together. "I truly hope so." He takes my hand in both of his and kisses my knuckles gently. "I did not know how you would change me. I didn't realize my own prejudices, my own shortsightedness. I thought I knew everything; I thought I had a plan and the execution would be simple. I was wrong."

"Haven't we all been wrong about this at some point?" I say. "I mean, isn't that how we learn to be right?"

"You are a good person, Violet Lasting. I hope that never changes."

"*You* are a good person, Cobalt Rosling." Lucien starts

at my use of his true name. "I hope we both make it out of this. This city needs you." The mood has grown too somber. I try to break it. "And I'm sick of being called Imogen. How do you handle it?"

Lucien crosses his legs and leans back. "You know, I don't even mind it anymore. I've assumed ownership over the name, I suppose. There hasn't been a Lucien in over a hundred years. Do you know, the Exetor named me himself? Since there was no Electress when I was purchased by the Royal Palace." His eyes glaze over a bit with the memory. "I was so scared I was shaking. There was an ancient woman named Gemma who trained me. And the Exetor came into the dining room while I was learning the finer points of service. He is an avid hunter, and I knew that. He asked me about all the different types of prey that are groomed for the Royal Forest, and the best methods to track each one. He asked me about royal lineages. He gave me a gun in pieces and watched as I put it together, while a footman timed me. He gave me a list of taxes collected from some royal holdings in the Farm and asked me to predict the percentage increase over the following ten years. I had just turned eleven. By the end, I was sweating. I remember the Exetor rolling up several sheets of parchment, handing them to Gemma, and saying, 'Most impressive. His name will be Lucien.' And that was it. I wasn't Cobalt anymore."

"You still are," I insist.

"I suppose." He scratches his elbow. "For all their preening and airs, the royalty are still just people. Twisted, yes, but people all the same. The Exetor was very lonely. I think that's why he married the Electress. Because I have always suspected that he is still in love with the Duchess."

"Then why was their engagement broken?" I wonder aloud.

"As far as that goes," Lucien says, standing, "your guess is as good as mine. Come. We have lingered here long enough."

As we leave the secret chamber, climb down the spiral stair, and emerge back into the bustling servant halls of the palace, I feel like I have just left a dream and entered the real world again. Lucien's workshop feels like a part of some other place, a piece of him made tangible.

I truly hope I don't have to destroy it.

~ Seventeen ~

ONE WEEK.

That's all we have left. Seven days until the world changes, for better or for worse. Raven and Sil should be leaving for Southgate tomorrow. And the next train they take will be to the Auction House.

I'm carrying a basket of Coral's laundry down to be washed, lost in thoughts of the surrogates, of the Auction, of the impending deadline that moves closer each day.

Lucien's workshop keeps popping up in my head, too—the bubbling beakers, the unfinished painting, the wall of clocks that symbolize his childhood. I hate the promise I made to him, but I know I'll keep it. Lucien is right. That place should never fall into royal hands.

I'm barely paying attention to where I'm going, so when

I round a corner and run straight into Dr. Blythe, I drop the laundry, and some of Coral's undergarments spill onto the stone floor.

"Oh!" I cry, stooping quickly to pick them up.

"I'm terribly sorry." Dr. Blythe reaches down to lend a hand but I wave him off.

"No, no, it's all right, I wasn't paying attention to where I was going." I take my time, stuffing a silk chemise into the basket, hoping he'll be on his way.

"You are just the person I was looking for." Dr. Blythe seems delighted to see me. The feeling is not mutual. "Please remind Coral she needs to schedule an appointment with me before the Auction, so that we may go over the protocol for creating an embryo, compatibility with a surrogate, all that sort of thing."

"Y-yes," I stammer, standing up. "Of course."

"How would six o'clock this evening be?"

I keep my eyes trained down at the basket in my hands. "That should be fine. She will be in the Bank for her final dress fitting at two but I can have her back by six."

"Excellent." The doctor claps his hands together and gives me a polite nod. "Good afternoon."

I drop into a quick curtsy and make my way down the hall, handing the laundry off to a red-faced washerwoman. I take the stairs back up to the second floor by the east wing. Just as I've emerged from behind the bust of the old Duke, I run into another familiar face.

Rye is impeccably dressed, as usual. I haven't really seen him in this palace without Carnelian, but he's alone now. And looking at me strangely. I curtsy again, for lack of a better idea. He glances behind him at the empty hall, then turns back to me.

"Violet?" he says quietly.

My eyes widen. "How—"

But before I can say another word, he pulls me into a small room across the hall. Butterflies in glass cases line the walls.

Rye grips my wrist, my pulse humming against his fingers.

"Ash sends his regards. To both of us."

"Is he all right?" I ask. "Where is he? Have you spoken to him?"

"No, but someone else has. A mutual friend."

I assume he means another companion.

"Who? When?"

He chuckles lazily and I wonder if he's on drugs. "No one you know. And yesterday."

"Did he say anything about my brother?"

"Your what? No." Rye looks me up and down and whistles. "He said you looked different, but . . . wow. You surrogates are full of surprises."

"I'm not a surrogate anymore," I say.

"Right," he says. "Anyway, I wanted to tell you earlier but it's hard getting away from Carnelian."

"I bet," I mutter.

He grins. "Yeah, she's pretty obsessed with Ash. Can't stop asking me questions about him. The Duchess, too. At first, at least. She stopped after a while. Not Carnelian though."

"Terrific," I say dryly, switching the subject to more important matters. "Has he spoken to any other companions? Are they willing to help us?"

"Help the Black Key, you mean? Sure." He shrugs. "It's

not like our lives can get any worse."

I bite my lip.

"I'm staying in Ash's old rooms," he says. "I'm sure you can remember the way there." He winks. "Meet me tonight and we'll talk."

I wait a few seconds after he leaves, then hurry down the hall to Coral's room. I'm so distracted by this new development while I'm dressing her for the trip to the Bank, I end up putting her high heels on the wrong feet.

"Is something wrong?" she asks.

"Nothing, miss. I'm sorry," I mumble, correcting the mistake.

Miss Mayfield's is one of the top dressmakers in the Lone City, with a waiting list a mile long, and Coral cannot stop chattering about how fabulous her dress will be.

"I chose pink, obviously," she says, looking up as I apply her eyeliner. "My mother always wore blue or silver to the Auction." She sniffs. "Pink suits me better."

"Yes, miss." I suddenly remember I haven't told her about the doctor's appointment. "Dr. Blythe would like to see you this evening, after your fitting. He said—"

"My very first surrogate appointment!" Coral studies her reflection in the mirror as I finish with the eyeliner. "Of course. We'll be back well before then, won't we?"

I've learned over the past few weeks that "our" whole schedule is entirely in Coral's hands. She doesn't want to do something? It doesn't happen. Yet she always insists on asking me anyway.

"Yes, miss," I say. "Will Garnet be accompanying us this afternoon?"

I haven't seen much of Garnet since his father's death.

He's thrown himself into his role as a Regimental, making more trips to the lower circles than he had before.

Coral giggles. "Boys don't come to dress fittings." She scrunches her nose. "Carnelian will be coming though. She's always so dull and serious."

"Is Carnelian going to the Auction?"

"Of course not, Imogen, she isn't married. But there will be lots of festivities the day after, the dinners of course, and some other parties, so she must look nice for those, even if she can't come to the event itself."

Coral fusses with a curl by her left ear.

"My mother has been telling me stories about the Auction since I was little and I can't believe I finally get to go. It sounds so wonderful. There are rooms for entertainment, and games on the lawns. It starts in the afternoon and lasts the whole day! And there are distractions for the women waiting to buy surrogates and then things to do once you've bought yours. I've never been inside the amphitheater before, but I've heard it's just lovely." I *have* been inside that amphitheater and *lovely* is not a word I'd ever use to describe it. "There will be food and drinks and games to watch and musicians and jugglers and all sorts of fun things!"

She looks so excited. As if the Auction isn't about a bunch of girls being carted off to a strange place, drugged, dressed up, and then paraded onto a stage. As if all that fear, all that anxiety and worry, all that abuse, is merely entertainment.

But this Auction isn't going to be like the others.

I'm going to make sure of that.

Eighteen

I SIT IN THE MOTORCAR OPPOSITE CORAL AND CARNE-
lian as we drive to the north train station. Miss Mayfield's
is in the North Quarter of the Bank.

"This is so stupid," Carnelian grumbles. "After all those
bombings and riots and stuff. I can't believe she's sending
us out there."

"Nonsense," Coral replies. "There hasn't been a bombing in a week."

"Not in the Bank, maybe," Carnelian says. "But the
Smoke and the Farm are getting pretty dangerous. Don't
you read the papers?"

I'm impressed Carnelian is following the Society's movements. Though I do remember, at a dinner so many months
ago, the Duchess mocking her for working on her father's

printing press. Maybe she's always read the papers and I just never noticed.

And privately, I agree with her. With the Auction almost here, it's unsafe for royals to be in the lower circles. But of course, they don't know that.

"The Smoke has always been rather rough around the edges, though, hasn't it?" Coral says. "The Bank is lovely. It will be nice to have a change of scenery."

"I still don't see why I couldn't have brought Rye," Carnelian says.

"Yes, he's very funny, isn't he?" Coral says. "I remember when he was my companion. He used to do impressions of the servants that made me laugh for days."

I'd forgotten Rye worked for the House of the Downs. It seems wrong to me, unnatural that she and Coral would share a companion, but I suppose it must happen all the time.

"Don't remind me," Carnelian mumbles.

"And he's a good deal nicer than that awful Ash Lockwood," Coral continues, oblivious to Carnelian's murderous expression. "I remember how jealous I was when the Duchess procured him for you! My mother was dying to get her hands on him. But I suppose that worked out for the best."

"Don't talk about him like you know him," Carnelian snaps. "Because you don't."

"Well, neither did you, really," Coral points out.

Carnelian stares out the window and fumes for the rest of the drive.

Our motorcar pulls into a station that is even smaller than the one I arrived at when I was pretending to be Lily.

There is no little house beside it. It's nestled in a copse of trees, their buds just beginning to blossom. The train is only one car, gleaming black with copper detail. The conductor jumps to attention when we arrive, doffing his hat and opening the train door for us.

The interior of the car looks very similar to a royal parlor. There are two couches, one upholstered in silver with a pretty snowflake pattern, the other gold embossed with leaves, as well as two armchairs. Lamps decorate the various tables, their shades in muted tones of peach and beige. A miniature chandelier hangs from the ceiling. There is a marble statue of a woman in a long dress, a bird perched on her outstretched hand. A glass cabinet filled with liquor bottles sits beside a very large, very realistic portrait of the Exetor.

Carnelian and Coral take seats on opposite couches. I've learned by now that my job is to stand quietly in the corner and pretend I don't exist. Today's paper sits on a small side table and Carnelian picks it up and flips through it as the train rumbles forward.

"I *do* read the papers, by the way," Coral says. "There was an editorial by the Lady of the Dell about the inequity of pre-birth engagements."

Carnelian snorts. "Please. That was a veiled attempt by the Electress to discredit the Duchess. Everyone knows she doesn't want the Duchess's daughter marrying her son. Probably why she sent those men to kill the surrogate at Garnet's party."

"The Electress wouldn't do that," Coral says. "It's treason. People are just jealous."

"You don't really believe that, do you?"

Coral very studiously ignores the question.

Carnelian groans. "You act like you haven't lived in this circle your whole life. You know how ruthless it is."

"That's such a cruel word." Coral adjusts her hat. "People just have very strong feelings about things here, that's all."

Carnelian laughs at that, and I'm glad she can, since I can't.

"You're a joke, Coral."

"At least I'm pretty and happy," she responds with a shrug. "Maybe if you tried smiling more, someone in this circle will want to marry you."

"I don't think it's my lack of smiles that's preventing any House from making a match with me," Carnelian says. "Besides, there are more important things than finding a husband and buying a surrogate."

It's Coral's turn to laugh. "Like what?"

Carnelian brandishes the paper at her. "The city is falling apart out there."

At that moment, the iron door between the Bank and the Jewel groans open. The train moves forward slowly, chugging through the darkness until we finally emerge on the other side, reminding me unpleasantly again of just how big this wall is.

But I won't be alone. It won't just be me trying to take it down, as Lucien once planned. I think of Indi and Sienna and even Olive, waiting in the Marsh, ready to ride into the Jewel with the girls being sold. I think about Raven and Sil hiding out near Southgate. I wonder how Ginger, and Tawny, and Henna are doing. I hope they'll be ready, that Amber and Scarlet and the other girls have helped them practice with the elements. I hope they learn from one another, strengthen one another.

As light filters back into the train, Coral smiles smugly. "How is anyone ever going to get through that wall, Carnelian? We are perfectly safe in the Jewel. And I'm sure this whole business will blow over soon enough. These ruffians will be caught and punished." She sniffs, smoothing out her skirts. "Can't they be thankful that we provide them with jobs, put clothes on their backs and food in their bellies? It seems so ungrateful of them to be throwing these tantrums."

Once again, Carnelian speaks my mind for me.

"Coral, you have absolutely *no* idea what you're talking about. What you know about the lower circles could fit inside one of your stupid miniature teacups."

The train slows and we pull up to the Bank station before the fight can continue.

It is as private as the one in the Jewel, if not more. There are trees that hide it within the confines of a brick wall. A motorcar waits for us just inside the golden gate that leads to the rest of the circle.

I've only ever been to the South Quarter of the Bank, for that brief time I spent with Lily and then at the warehouse. Everything was pink stone and immaculate gardening. The North Quarter is wilder. All the trees here are evergreens. The buildings are made from materials in silvery gray and pale blue, so they gleam among the dark green. Lots of them have white tiles for their roofs, giving the impression of newly fallen snow.

We reach a street that is twice as wide as any other

we've been on so far. It's filled with shops of every kind, and the chauffeur pulls over to let us out. We pass a store with boarded-up windows and scorch marks on its walls. A sign on the door reads, "Closed for Renovations." A black key is scrawled over the words.

"Ungrateful," Coral mutters. Carnelian rolls her eyes, but she glances back at the building several times until it fades from view.

She catches me watching her and quickly faces forward.

I look away, too. I don't need Carnelian studying me too closely.

One or two other stores have broken windows and "Closed" notices and I catch sight of more spray-painted keys.

The shops that remain untouched have large ornate signs, like the ones in the South Quarter. One proudly boasts "The best milliner in the North Quarter!" over a display of brilliantly colored hats. Another proclaims "Fine linens: make your house look like a royal palace!"

We finally stop outside a bright red building, a sharp contrast to all the iron and brass that makes up most of this quarter. There is an imposing branch of the Royal Bank to the left and a furniture store on the right. The sign over the red building's entrance says, "Miss Mayfield's Ladies Emporium: Purveyor of Fine Evening Wear." A girl no older than me in a smartly cut black pencil skirt and blazer greets us at the door.

"Coral of the House of the Lake," she says warmly. "We've been expecting you. And Miss Carnelian as well. Come in, come in."

Coral soaks up the attention like a sponge. We walk into the store and two other girls in similar garb are immediately called over. Coffee is poured, fresh fruit is offered, as well as a seat on a plush velvet sofa. Once again, I hover in the background, not needed except when Coral removes her hat and hands it to me. Dresses surround us, modeled on wooden mannequins or hanging on racks arranged by color. The ceiling is so high that there are tiers of gowns accessible only by a sliding ladder on the wall, like the one in the Duchess's library. The floor is carpeted in a deep crimson, and the light fixture that hangs from the ceiling is wrought out of copper in the shape of many antlers, each point fixed with a glowglobe, so that the room is bathed in a warm light.

"Miss Mayfield will be right with you," the head girl assures Coral. "You'll love it when you see it, it's absolutely stunning. She was up all night finishing it."

Coral looks pleased.

"What about my dress?" Carnelian asks. She sits on a small pouf with her cup of coffee, looking disgruntled.

"Oh, yours is lovely, too!" the assistant chirps.

"You must be thrilled," another assistant, who's nearly as tall as Indi, says. "To have your aunt commission a dress like this just for you."

"Yes, I'm ecstatic," Carnelian replies dryly.

"We both are," Coral says, smiling enough for the two of them.

"Have you seen the lists for the Auction yet?" the head girl asks.

"No, they never arrive until a few days before, do they?

I can't wait to see what sort of surrogates are on the docket this year."

"Not nearly as many as last time, though, are there?" the third assistant, a girl with bushy hair and a lot of freckles, asks.

"No," Coral says. "But it's really about quality, not quantity, isn't it?"

"Besides, no one's fighting for Larimar's hand in marriage anymore," Carnelian points out.

"We were so sorry to hear about that awful shooting," the head girl says. I notice she speaks only to Coral. "Is it true they were after the surrogate?"

"Yes," Coral replies in a hushed voice.

"Everyone is saying it was the Electress," the freckled girl interjects, as if hoping to get confirmation of this from Coral, but the head girl silences her with a sharp look.

"No one knows who was behind it," she says curtly. "The Duchess must be so worried for her surrogate's safety."

My stomach lurches, Hazel's frantic pleas ringing in my ears.

"She keeps her secure in the palace," Coral says.

"And no more parties until the little bundle of joy is born," Carnelian says.

The tall girl titters nervously, as if she's unsure whether or not Carnelian is making a joke, and if so, whether she is supposed to think it's funny.

"Is she showing yet?" the head assistant asks.

"Yes, she's gotten quite big." Coral puts down her china cup.

"So remarkable that the Duchess managed to orchestrate

the engagement before the sweet little girl is even born," the tall girl says, moving closer to be a part of the gossip. "How ever did she manage it?"

"You know the Duchess," Coral says airily. "If she wants something, she will do whatever it takes to get it. She wanted me for her son and look how that turned out!"

All the assistants laugh.

"Now, girls, give the ladies some air." The woman who enters from the back of the shop is style personified. She wears a floor-length, plum-colored gown that hugs her curves perfectly, accentuating her hips and breasts. The detail is astounding—beads are sewn into the bodice and skirt in a wave pattern, taking up one whole side of the dress like an ocean of blue and silver and lilac. A simple shawl is draped around her shoulders, giving the effect that she just threw this outfit on without really thinking about it. Her hair is a vibrant red, at sharp contrast with her midnight-black skin. Like the Duchess, this is a woman with the power to silence a room.

The three attendants hush and back away.

"Coral, how delightful to see you again," Miss Mayfield says, swooping down to kiss both of Coral's cheeks. "And, Carnelian, you're looking lovely." Her gaze lands on me. "Ah, did you get a lady-in-waiting at last?"

"She's mine," Coral interjects before Carnelian can respond. "Garnet bought her for me."

Miss Mayfield gives her a feline smile. "Your husband is a good man. Though I do wish he could help with our little Key problem here in the Bank. I've had to repaint the walls of my shop twice already."

"Vandals," the head assistant agrees.

"He's doing his very best," Coral says, and I can't hide my smirk at that. Fortunately, no one except Carnelian sees me, her face turning curious. I quickly smooth out my expression.

Miss Mayfield nods. "Well, let's not drag ourselves down with depressing matters. We have gowns to see!"

She claps her hands and her assistants scatter like well-trained mice. The tall one opens up a set of wooden doors and the bushy-haired one wheels out a mannequin in a blue dress, the head assistant following behind her with a pink one.

"It's beautiful!" Coral gasps, reaching out to touch the soft fabric.

"I thought mine was going to be red and black," Carnelian says, looking disdainfully at the blue chiffon as it's wheeled in front of her.

"Yes, darling, but unfortunately, the Duchess pays the bill and she felt your chosen color scheme was a bit too . . . intense." Miss Mayfield pats Carnelian's shoulder. "Don't worry," she says in a low voice, "it's going to fit you like a glove."

That was the exact phrase Lucien used when he allowed me to choose my own dress for the Auction. For a moment, I'm back there in the prep room, staring at my face for the first time in four years.

A bell tinkles as the front door opens. A Bank woman and her daughter enter. The little girl can't be older than five or six, with thick black plaits in her hair and a cute little hat with a yellow ribbon.

"I'm so terribly sorry, Mrs. Linten," Miss Mayfield says. "But we are closed for the afternoon."

Mrs. Linten looks miffed before she sees Coral and Carnelian.

"Your Ladyships," she says, making a little curtsy and nudging for her daughter to do the same. "I did not . . . I am so sorry. Of course, Miss Mayfield, we will come back tomorrow."

She wheels out of the shop, dragging her daughter with her. I guess Carnelian counts as a ladyship in the Bank, even if she doesn't in the Jewel. Miss Mayfield turns a sharp eye on the head assistant, who in turn glares at the freckled girl, who runs over to lock the door and hang a "Closed" sign in the window, pulling a shade down over it.

"Now," Miss Mayfield says, "where were we?"

Quickly, the three assistants strip the royal girls of their gowns, leaving them in only their slips. Miss Mayfield helps Coral into the stunning pink number, a gown with a sweetheart neckline and a subtle skirt bolstered by a layer of tulle. The only ornamentation is around the waist, tiny flowers made of diamonds and rubies.

"What do you think, Imogen?" she asks, twirling for me.

"It's perfect, miss," I say. And it is. She really does look lovely. All three assistants scatter once more and return, each carrying a full-length mirror. They move this way and that in perfect unison, almost like a dance, so that Coral can see every inch of herself.

"I love it," she says, and Miss Mayfield looks pleased.

Carnelian is next. As she steps into the blue gown, Miss Mayfield herself fastens the dress up.

"Oh!" Coral gasps. "Carnelian, you look . . . beautiful."

She sounds jealous and I don't blame her. The gown Miss Mayfield has fashioned for Carnelian is unlike any ball gown I've ever seen. The skirt is made of chiffon, pretty layers that float to the ground like clouds. But the bodice is carefully cut out in satin ribbons that form a crisscross pattern, navy-blue silk layered over baby-blue lace, so that her ivory skin peeks through. It cuts off in a tight circle at the base of her neck and right at her shoulders, leaving her arms bare.

It makes Carnelian look like a woman in her own right, someone who could turn heads at a ball.

"What do you think?" Miss Mayfield asks.

"It's perfect," she whispers. Then she whirls and embraces the dressmaker. The assistants look away, embarrassed.

"Well, let's make sure everything is as it should be." Miss Mayfield snaps her fingers and the mirrors disappear. She takes out a pair of strange eyeglasses and a measuring tape and begins to examine every seam and hem.

"Loose thread here," she mutters, peering at Carnelian's left shoulder. The tall girl makes a note. "And let's take—"

But whatever she was going to say next gets lost, as the wall opposite me suddenly explodes in a deafening burst of heat and plaster and dust.

~ Nineteen ~

I AM FLYING THROUGH THE AIR, THROWN BACKWARD into a rack of dresses.

Some deep protective instinct causes me to join with Air, so that the rubble and debris shooting toward me are deflected in a gust of wind. The dresses soften the blow as my back slams into the wall, my connection with Air broken. Sparks explode in front of my eyes, my ears ringing. For several seconds, or maybe minutes, I lie there, half-hidden by layers of satin and wool and brocade. My chest heaves as I struggle to breathe. My head feels like it's been stuffed with cotton. Everything is dull, muted. Slowly, my hearing returns.

The first thing I notice is the screaming. One long sustained scream. I sit up, rubbing my left ear, and see the head attendant standing in the midst of the ruined shop, staring at her arm. Something sharp and white is poking out of her skin, thick lines of red dripping down her forearm into her hand. I swallow back the bile that rises in my throat as I realize it's her bone. Her arm is shattered.

Miss Mayfield's dress is torn down one whole side and there is a large bruise blossoming under one eye. She is crouched on the floor, tending to the tall girl, pressing a green lace ball gown against a gash on her forehead. I don't know where the freckled girl is.

Diamantes are littered all around us, glittering in the rubble like stars. My brain is slow to respond, my head fuzzy. Where did all this money come from?

Where are Coral and Carnelian?

The picture forms in front of me like a jigsaw puzzle with some pieces missing. There's a giant hole in the wall opposite me. Through it I can see broken tiles and melted hunks of copper, splintered wood and huge chunks of concrete. A man's shoe. A broken lamp. And fire. Fire everywhere.

The bank. The Royal Bank next door.

Those are the targets the Society is hitting.

I scramble to my feet as the girl with the broken arm shrieks louder. The fire burning through the bank has caught on the carpet of the shop. I can feel its delicious heat from across the room. But it's headed straight for Miss Mayfield and her charge, devouring every scrap of silk and lace in its path.

In the distance, I hear the faint wail of sirens. They'll never make it here in time.

I join with Fire—an excruciating burst of heat

accompanies the element. My skin boils, a pain that is unbearable and welcoming at the same time. Fire always makes me feel equal parts alive and frightened.

For a second, the flames flare higher, but I am in control now, and I calm it, slowly and steadily, focusing on my heart beating in my chest, forcing the fire to recede. It shrinks down to half its size, then a quarter, then it is nothing more than a few wisps of smoke wafting up from the remains of a charred carpet. A crackle of its heat echoes over my skin as I release my hold on the element.

I come back to myself and immediately search for the two royal girls. When I see the high heel hanging from a limp foot, my heart turns from fire to lead. Coral is pinned beneath a large hunk of plaster. Blood seeps out in a dark puddle from underneath her.

"Coral!" I cry. I try and lift the plaster but it's too heavy. The sirens in the distance get louder. "Coral, no, no . . ."

I shake her shoulders. Her head bobs around, lifeless. Her eyes are closed, almost as if I've just tucked her into bed, except it's concrete instead of blanket on top of her and she'll never open her eyes again. I sit back on my heels, pressing my palms against my own eyes as if I can rub this horrible sight from my brain.

I hear a small moan from behind an overturned sofa. Forcing myself to move, I stand and leave the corpse of Garnet's wife behind to find Carnelian trapped beneath the sofa, alive.

"I can't . . . breathe . . ." she croaks.

"Just hold on," I say. "I'm going to get this off of you."

I connect with Air again—the initial swooping sensation

in my stomach that accompanies the element doesn't give me
the same thrill it usually does. Instantly the air around me
is ready, waiting. As I push my fingers underneath the edge
of the sofa I can feel its entire weight, not just the smooth
mahogany frame that I'm touching. I am aware of all of it.
I am the air underneath it and around it and nestled in its
cushions. I am everywhere.

Lift, I think. As I stand, Air pulls with me and the sofa
is thrown into a mannequin with such force that its head
comes off its body. Carnelian rolls onto her back, gasping
for breath.

"Are you all right? Can you move? Are you hurt?" My
hands flutter around her uselessly, afraid to touch her.

"My . . . ribs . . ." She clutches her side.

"Stay still. Help is coming." The sirens wail again. I
grab the remains of an indigo gown, balling it up and gently
lifting Carnelian's head to rest it on the makeshift pillow.
"You're going to be okay," I say again, more for myself
than for her. Her breathing is shallow and there's a deep
cut on her shoulder. I press another gown to it to stanch the
bleeding.

"Is she . . . is she . . ." Carnelian stares past me, to where
I know Coral's body lies.

"Yes," I whisper, and the guilt is agony, a hot knife twisting in my gut, a punch in the chest that leaves me breathless.

All those bombings. I knew it was violent. Of course.
But this . . .

Carnelian begins to cry, tears rolling down her cheeks.

"Shhhhh," I say, taking her hand in mine. "It's okay,
we're okay . . ."

"I don't want to die," she whimpers.

She looks so frightened, so young. I might not like Carnelian, but in this moment, we are the same. We're just two scared girls.

"You're not going to die," I say. "Help is coming. You're going to be fine." I squeeze her hand. "I'm right here. I won't leave you."

She looks at me with an unfocused gaze.

"I—I know your voice," she says. Her brows knit together for a moment before her eyes widen. "*You*," she gasps.

I nod. I don't even consider lying.

Carnelian's lips part, she lets out a little huff, then her eyes roll back in her head and she sinks into unconsciousness.

Minutes later, Regimentals run into the ruined shop. One immediately heads for the screaming girl while two more move to help Miss Mayfield and her charge.

"Help the royals, help the royals!" Miss Mayfield cries, pointing to where I sit by Carnelian. A young Regimental rushes over.

"Are you hurt, miss?" he says.

"No," I say. "But she is. Her ribs, I think, and her shoulder."

"Medic!" he calls, and a man in a gray coat with a black bag comes over to look at Carnelian. The head girl is taken away, cradling her broken arm. Four Regimentals manage to get the hunk of plaster off Coral. The entire lower half of her body has been crushed.

I close my eyes and hate myself for my cowardice. I

should watch this. I deserve to see what the Society of the Black Key is doing. I gather my courage and open them again. Coral is being put in a black bag, like the one they put Raven in when they sent her to the morgue. Two Regimentals carry her out of the store.

Carnelian has been put on a stretcher.

"She's from the House of the Lake, isn't she?" the young Regimental asks. I nod.

"She'll be all right," the medic says. "I'd guess a couple of broken ribs and that laceration on her shoulder will need stitches. Best get her back to the Jewel. She'll be safest there." He glances at the sofa smashed against the wall. "Was she underneath that?" I nod again. "And you lifted it off her?"

I stare at him blankly. Of course I did. He looks impressed but I don't feel very impressive right now. I feel hollow.

"Come, miss," the Regimental says, putting a gentle hand on my shoulder. "Let's get you out of here."

He leads me to an ambulance waiting outside. Carnelian is slid in after me, along with the medic and another Regimental.

Right away, he starts asking me questions. Did I see anyone suspicious near the bank when we arrived? Did anything seem off? Do I think Miss Mayfield could have had something to do with it? Or one of her assistants?

I answer no to everything as the ambulance tears through the streets.

"Where's Coral?" I ask.

"She's well taken care of, don't you worry." The Regimental pats my knee.

The conductor is shocked when we pull up at the station.

"Get this train ready to leave now!" the medic yells at him. "And let the Jewel know. Carnelian of the House of the Lake has been injured in a Black Key bombing."

"Where is Miss Coral?" he asks, but the Regimentals blow past him with Carnelian and he pales at the sight of her unconscious form. He jumps into the driver's seat and I rush into the carriage behind everyone. The train lurches forward as I stumble into the statue of the woman with the bird. The Regimentals have moved aside one of the couches so that Carnelian's stretcher lies out on the floor.

I can't believe she and Coral were in this train car, snapping at each other, only an hour ago. It doesn't seem real.

When we arrive in the Jewel, there is a glamorous motorcar waiting, with an extra-large backseat. A chauffer opens the back of it and the Regimentals slide Carnelian inside.

"Just . . . just the one?" the chauffeur asks.

The medic nods, and repeats what he told me about Carnelian's condition.

I ride in the front with the driver as he peels through the streets of the Jewel. Gravel flies from under the tires as he pulls up to the palace of the Lake. The doctor is waiting by the garage with One and Six.

"This way, this way," he says as they rush to get Carnelian out of the car. He pulls down on the branch of a shrub that I thought was real, but instead slides aside to reveal a dark tunnel and a set of stone stairs. The secret passage to the medical room I couldn't find. They vanish down into the darkness and the shrub glides into its original place.

The chauffeur goes to park the car in the garage and I find myself alone.

I don't know where to go, what to do. Everything feels like a dream. My feet take me wherever they want and I end up in the kitchen. The servants are huddled together in groups, talking worriedly. Even Rye is there.

The silence that falls as I enter is abrupt, like someone pulling the needle from a gramophone. Maude is the first to spring into action.

"Imogen!" She rushes over. "Are you all right? Are you hurt? What happened?"

"She's in shock," Rye says, and then Zara is by my side, a bowl of broth in one hand and the end of a baguette in the other.

"Sit down," she says gently, and I realize there's a stool beside me. I wonder if it's been there this whole time or if I only just noticed it.

"Clara, bring a wet washcloth," Zara commands. Mary and Elizabeth gaze at me with fearful eyes, as if I'm something unreal and dangerous. I clutch the baguette like a lifeline. It's still warm, and the scent reminds me of my mother. Hot tears fill my eyes.

"You're all right, child," Zara says, wiping my face with the cloth. "Be still now. You're safe."

I didn't realize how badly I was shaking.

"Back up, back up," Maude says. "Give the poor girl some room to breathe."

All the room in the world won't make breathing any easier. I look down at my dress and for the first time have some idea of what I must look like.

The white fabric has turned a mottled brownish gray, covered with dust and bits of rubble. There is a large tear in one sleeve, and blood on the other. My hands are crusted with dirt and more blood.

Coral's blood on my hands.

When I'm finally calm enough to breathe normally, Zara begins spoon-feeding me a bit of the broth. I'm surprised at how quickly it helps steady me and clear my muddled head.

"Now," she says, taking my hands in hers. "Tell us what happened. All we know is that there was an explosion in the Bank." I nod. "And Coral and Carnelian were injured." I close my eyes.

"Dead?" Rye gasps.

"Just Coral," I croak. There are more gasps and murmurs.

"Was it the Black Key?"

"Yes," I say. "There was a Royal Bank next door. I don't think they intended to hurt . . . I don't think . . ."

I don't know what I think. The fact is, the Society *did* intend to hurt people. I just never thought about it being people I knew personally.

"Poor Garnet," Maude says. "First his father, now his wife . . ."

I hadn't even thought about Garnet. I wonder how he'll feel. Probably the same way I do. He might not have been in love with Coral, but he didn't hate her.

Suddenly, a bell begins to ring in the kitchen, a tiny golden bell that I've never seen ring before. All the servants stare at it, dumbstruck. Then Cora appears in the doorway.

"The Duchess wishes to see everyone in the ballroom. Immediately."

Her gaze lingers on me for a moment. Then she turns and we all traipse after her, Mary and Elizabeth whispering together, Maude's face wary, William looking more ruffled than I've ever seen him.

We file into the ballroom, where the Duchess stands waiting for us, resplendent in black satin with long gloves that come up over her elbows.

"As you may have heard," she says without preamble, "there has been another vicious attack on our House. This time, from the Society that calls itself the Black Key. They have killed our beloved daughter-in-law, Coral, and severely injured our niece. This will not stand. The Regimentals are doing everything in their power to stop these rebels. But we will not let them dampen our spirits. We will stay strong and unified in the face of our aggressors. I have sent an emergency petition to speak with the Exetor. I am hopeful he will be able to make time to see me tomorrow. I want everything spotless. I want smiles on faces and pep in your steps. I want to see you proud to serve this House that helped found our great city. Do I make myself clear?"

Everyone nods in unison.

"You." The Duchess points a finger directly at me. "Come with me. The rest of you are dismissed."

Twenty

I'M SURPRISINGLY CALM AS I FOLLOW THE DUCHESS OUT of the ballroom.

Maybe there's simply nothing left in me to feel. After the day's events, I wonder if I'll ever be able to muster up any strong emotion again. I should be terrified right now. I should be worried the Duchess could discover me, could recognize my voice. Could kill me.

But as she opens the door to a small study, a grim determination sets in. Hazel is still in danger. So are Ash and Ochre. Raven, Sil, Sienna, Indi, Olive, all the girls in the holding facilities are counting on me, on this plan, on the fact that this year, at this Auction, they will not be sold as slaves. They will declare themselves free citizens of the Lone City. I hate that Coral died but she is not the first person who's died because of this cause. And she certainly won't be the last.

The Duchess sits in a leather armchair and studies me over steepled fingers. "You have done an adequate job as Coral's lady-in-waiting," she says.

I curtsy.

"And I like that you don't prattle on like so many other maids in this house. You will stay here, as Carnelian's lady-in-waiting. She should like that, she's been asking for one for long enough." She smirks. "And that way you can't run off and sell your story to the papers or another House. I'll have your tongue ripped out if you try."

I hadn't considered that I'd be dismissed from service. Coral hasn't even been dead two hours.

"Yes, my lady," I say huskily. "Thank you, my lady."

The Duchess sighs and rubs her temple. She glances at the clock on the mantel and I realize I've been in this room before. The first time I ever wandered around the palace alone. The day I met Ash. There was a picture of the Duchess on a rolltop desk, a small, lifelike painting. In a moment of rebellion, I used the first Augury, Color, to change her skin from smooth caramel to garish green.

She nearly broke my hand because of that.

"You're dismissed," the Duchess says sharply. I curtsy again and rush out the door, heading in the direction of the servants quarters.

Cora is waiting for me outside the dining room. The halls are empty.

"Did she make you Carnelian's lady-in-waiting?" she asks.

"Yes."

"Good. She was going to dismiss you. I tried very hard to convince her otherwise. Without tipping my hand, of course." Cora fingers the keys on her belt. "I hope you have a plan for Auction Day." I don't miss the note of warning in her voice.

"I do," I say. It's not entirely a lie.

"The doctor is still seeing to Carnelian at the moment. You will attend to her in her room this evening."

"Yes, ma'am."

She looks me up and down. "You could use a bath and a change of clothes."

I look down at my ruined dress. "Yes."

"You may use my private powder room if you wish. Oh and, Violet . . ." She leans in close to me so I can see the wrinkles around her eyes. "If you do not keep up your end of our agreement, then I promise you—your sister *will* be in very real danger. And not from the Electress."

A chill runs down my spine.

She turns to leave and calls back over her shoulder. "The Exetor will be here tomorrow morning at eleven. Be ready and in the foyer at ten forty-five. Sharp."

I LOOK IN ON GARNET THAT NIGHT AFTER I BATHE, BEFORE attending to Carnelian.

I find him taking Coral's miniature tea sets out of their glass display case, wrapping them in brown paper, and putting them in a box.

"Hey," I say. "Are you okay?"

He looks down at the saucer in his hand, a looping pattern of silver and gold etched around its edge. "I wasn't really sure what to do with all these. But she loved them so much. I didn't want Mother to get her hands on them. She'd probably have a good old time smashing them against a wall or something."

"That's really nice," I say. "Coral would appreciate it, I'm sure."

Garnet wraps the saucer up and places it in the box. "Are you all right? You weren't hurt, were you?"

"No," I say, remembering the way my instincts took over, joining with Air to protect me from the worst of the debris. "I'm fine."

"She didn't . . . I mean . . ." He clears his throat. "Did she suffer?"

"No," I say quietly. "It was . . . instant."

He nods.

"I'm so sorry, Garnet," I say. "First your father, and now . . ."

"It's . . . I'll be all right." He sounds dazed. "Everything is getting real, isn't it? It's not just a vague plan back at the White Rose anymore."

"It isn't," I agree.

"Ash must be losing his mind."

I frown. "Why do you say that?"

Garnet's eyebrows shoot up. "Violet, he knows you are—sorry, you were . . . Coral's lady-in-waiting. You can bet the entire Bank knows about the bombing and her death. He understands how the Jewel works—he'd know you'd have been with her at that fitting."

"Oh no," I gasp, my hand flying to my mouth.

"Lucien will find a way to tell him," Garnet says.

"Or Rye," I add.

"Rye?"

"He knows." I fill Garnet in on what happened earlier.

"That's really great," he says. "He could be helpful at the Auction House."

I know he means it but the sentiment comes out half-hearted. I understand the feeling. I'm so exhausted, all I want to do is curl up under the covers of my bed and not come out for a day.

But I have to face Carnelian and then meet Rye tonight in Ash's old chambers. I give Garnet's arm a squeeze and he smiles wanly. I leave him with the tea sets and head to Carnelian's room.

I've never been inside it before. Maude only showed it to me in passing on my first day as a lady-in-waiting.

I knock. "Come in," Carnelian says from within.

Carnelian does not have chambers like I did when I was a surrogate. Her one room is large and airy, with a view of the garden. It contains a four-poster bed, a round mahogany table with two chairs, a vanity, and a chaise lounge by the window. One wall is lined with bookshelves. Another has a pretty painting of a farmhouse that reminds me of the White Rose.

She lies in bed, the bandage on her shoulder poking out from beneath her nightdress. Her arms rest at her sides, but her face is alert. From the way she's looking at me, it's clear she hasn't forgotten the moment she recognized me earlier, before she slipped into unconsciousness.

"So," she says as I close the door behind me. "You came back."

I swallow. "I came back."

My heart thumps in my chest. Now that I'm face-to-face with her, with the threat of dying removed, I don't know what she'll do. She could call for the Regimentals at any time.

"Why?" she demands. "Ash is safe." Her eyes widen. "He *is* safe, isn't he? I read in the paper he was sighted in the Bank, but I didn't think it could be true."

"He is safe," I say. Then I add, "And it is true."

"How could you let him do that?" Carnelian snaps. "He could get caught. She still wants to find him, to kill him!"

"I didn't have a choice," I say. "He left without telling me."

"Because he doesn't trust you?" she asks hopefully.

"Because I wasn't there," I say. "Because . . . because I left him to come here."

Carnelian chews on her lip. "Why? Is it revenge? Against the Duchess?"

My jaw clenches and she smiles smugly. "Good. I hope you get her before the Black Keys burn this city to the ground." She cocks her head. "It's something more, though, isn't it? Not just revenge . . ." She pauses, studying me. Then she gasps. "Of course. The surrogate. Whoever the Duchess stole to replace you. You're here for her, aren't you? Is she a friend of yours?"

"Something like that," I say. Then I blurt out the question that's burning in my throat. "If you knew the surrogate wasn't me, why didn't you tell anyone?"

"Oh, don't think I didn't try," Carnelian says. "It was the perfect trump card to hold over her. But the Duchess plays dirty. She threatened to have me committed to an asylum if I so much as breathed a word." Her mouth sets in a hard line. "I hope that whatever you're planning, you make her suffer the way she deserves."

"Aren't you frightened?" I say. "You were nearly killed today."

Carnelian's laugh is hollow. "Even if I had died, no one would care. The Duchess would probably throw a parade." She stares out the window. The sour mask she usually wears falls away, replaced with an expression of utter hopelessness. "It doesn't matter to anyone whether I live or die."

I remember what Ash said to me, when we were waiting in the morgue for Lucien to come. He told me Carnelian was sad, and that that sadness had been twisted into bitterness and anger. All the time I lived here, I saw her only as a nuisance. I saw the sullenness and ignored the grief and pain beneath it.

Because she's right. No one in this palace would care if she had died today.

All the hatred and resentment I've held on to against Carnelian melts away. I see a girl who's been put down and mistreated for so long. I see the girl Ash saw, the one I ignored because I was busy being jealous and petty. A girl who misses her mother. A girl who wants to be loved.

I make the decision then, to be brave, where once I was timid. To be a different person, a better person.

I move toward her and sit on the bed. She rolls her eyes.

"What, are we going to be best friends now?"

"No," I say. "But we *are* on the same side."

"What side is that?"

"We both hate the royalty, right?"

She narrows her eyes at me and waits.

"And we both love the same boy," I say. I hold out my hands, palms up, as a peace offering. "You want to turn me in, do it. Ring the bell, call the Regimentals. My life is in your hands. You can end it right now."

Carnelian hesitates. I can see the desire to cry out, to have me handcuffed and executed for treason. I know the danger I've put myself in. But I look into her brown eyes and sense the war going on inside. Who does she hate more, me or the Duchess? The seconds stretch into minutes. I won't break the silence.

"Your name is Violet, right?" she says, finally.

"Yes."

"Well. I guess I should thank you. For saving my life."

"Ash never would have forgiven me if I didn't try."

The yearning in Carnelian's face is a palpable thing. "Does he ever . . . talk about me?"

I take a breath and give her the honest answer. "Right before I left, he told me to be careful around you. That you are sharper than I gave you credit for."

A tiny smile lights on her face. "He said that?"

I nod. She leans her head against the pillow and stares up at the ceiling.

"Can I get you anything?" I ask.

"No. I want to be alone."

I stop at the door and turn. "He cares about you, you know. I hate it, but he does. He's been defending you ever since we escaped—since before then, really. I know it's not what you want, but . . ." I sigh. "He cares."

Carnelian does not look at me. She very deliberately

closes her eyes. "Go away," she whispers, and just as I close the door, I see a tear tumble down her cheek.

EVERY BONE IN MY BODY ACHES. MY EYELIDS ARE DRY and my mind is numb. It has been a long day, but still, I have to see Rye.

I take a servant staircase down to the first floor and pause when I reach the hall where the library is. Joining with Air, I push it out from me in a gust, then pull it back.

I smell boot polish and hear the even steps of a Regimental. I slip back into the secret passage, behind a sliding panel of wall, and wait. The footsteps draw closer. Then they pass. I count to thirty, then sneak out into the hall and run as quickly and quietly as I can to the library.

As soon as I enter the tunnel, my arcana starts buzzing. I pull it out of my hair and talk as I walk.

"Are you all right?" Lucien is distraught. "Were you hurt in any way?"

"No," I say dully. "Coral's dead."

"I know. I'm so sorry you had to experience that."

"Why?" The word comes out sharp and pointed. "This is what a revolution looks like, isn't it? It's about time I saw it, acknowledged it. You got me into this. Don't apologize now."

I can feel it in the silence emanating from the tuning fork. I know I've hurt him. I stop walking and press my forehead against the cool stone wall.

"Sorry," I mumble. "I didn't mean to —"

"To what, be honest? Never apologize for that, Violet. You are right. This is what a revolution looks like."

"What are we going to do with them, Lucien?" I ask. "The royalty. Are we just going to . . . to kill them all?"

"There are many in the Society who wish for that. Blood for blood."

"What do you think?"

"I think there has been enough death already. I think we should set them to work. See how the others in this city have lived for so long. Make them tear down the Great Wall with their own bare hands." He sighs. "How I would love to see that. And see the ocean beyond. This city has been isolated for ages. It would be nice to know what is out there."

The ocean. I'd like to see that, too.

"I'm going to see Rye now," I say. "Ash got a message to him. He knows about me."

"That is excellent news! And he will be at the Auction. Tell Garnet. I'm sure he can find a use for Rye and the other companions who will be at the Auction House."

"I already told him," I say. "Oh, and I've been reassigned as Carnelian's lady-in-waiting. She knows about me, too. She recognized my voice." I hear a sharp intake of breath on his end. "She won't tell. I gave her the chance. Even told her to go ahead and do it. But she hates the royalty more than she hates me."

"Well. Hasn't this day just been full of surprises."

"It's all really happening, isn't it?"

"Yes, honey. It is."

"I have to go," I say. I want this night to be over. I want to sleep, to lose myself in blissful oblivion.

"Of course."

I hold my hand out for the arcana to drop, but it stays hovering in the air.

"Violet?" Lucien says, and his voice is timid.

"Yes?"

"I am so very proud of you."

The arcana falls into my hand and I clench my fist around it, squeezing it tight before setting off down the cold, quiet hall.

Twenty-One

IT IS SO STRANGE, BEING BACK IN THIS PARLOR.

I open the secret door, behind the oil painting of the man in the green hunting jacket with the dog at his side, and find Rye standing by the window, waiting for me. The room is dark, the only light coming from the moon outside.

"I didn't know if you'd come," he says as I shut the painting behind me. "After what happened today."

"I told you I would," I say. "And there isn't much time left, anyway."

"No," he agrees. "There isn't."

We stand in awkward silence for a moment.

I'm almost afraid to ask about Ash, even though he's

why I'm here. Rye moves to sit on the sofa. I take the arm-chair by the window.

"Ash managed to contact one of our friends who wasn't working at the time, a guy named Trac. Found him on the Row. You've seen the Row, right?"

I nod, remembering the sleazy strip in the Bank filled with cheap taverns and brothels.

"Trac's been in pretty bad shape for a while. He drinks too much and cuts himself. He was probably gonna get Marked soon."

Ash explained to me about Marking—if a companion fails to be perfect in every way, they are tattooed with a black X on their right cheek and kicked out of the companion house with only the clothes on their backs. All their earnings revert back to their madam.

"So," Rye continues, "Ash told him all about you, and the Society, and the rebellion, and how things could change . . . how they already were changing. He offered Trac the chance at a new life, painted a picture of what was possible. He gave him—"

"Hope," I say softly, my throat swelling up. "He gave Trac hope."

Why was it so hard for me to see it back then, at the White Rose, when I brushed aside his desire to help the companions because it was too dangerous?

"Yeah, and it caught on like wildfire. There are tons of companions who hate their lives, as I'm sure he's told you. And I include myself in that category." Rye tugs at his curls. "I was killing myself with blue. Now, at least if I die, it might actually mean something. I won't just be another anonymous companion overdose."

I'm glad to hear he's not using anymore.

"Then Trac got assigned to the House of the Light and I saw him at one of the thousand parties I've gone to with Carnelian." Rye smiles, his teeth a flash of white in the darkness. "Ash told him to look out for me. He told him I should contact Coral's lady-in-waiting. I didn't get it at first, until I overheard you talking to Zara. It wasn't even the sound of your voice so much as the way you spoke." He throws his arm over the back of the sofa. "I guess you made an impression on me at Madame Curio's."

"I'm flattered."

"We've been making contact with other companions in the Jewel, too. Ash is famous now."

"I know," I say, smiling myself this time.

"So it all goes down at the Auction, right?"

"Yes. You should talk to Garnet. He'll be able to give you some advice about what to do."

"Garnet?" Rye says incredulously. "Garnet-of-the-House-of-the-Lake Garnet?"

I nod.

He whistles. "This thing is deeper than I realized."

"I'm surprised Ash didn't tell you."

"I'm not. He didn't talk to me directly, remember?"

"Right." I gaze out the window. The moonlight sparkles off the surface of the lake in front of the palace. "This room was where he told me what he did, what being a companion was really all about. This was where we fell in love."

It's such a personal sentiment, and I immediately regret saying it out loud.

"Sorry," I say, blushing. "You don't need to hear that."

There's a pause. I look at Rye and see his posture has changed. He leans forward, staring down at his hands. "Yeah," he says quietly. "I do."

I'm not sure what to say.

"We are unloved," he continues after a moment, "and unlovable. That's what they train us to think. We are objects of sexual and monetary value. Who could love someone as filthy as a companion? We are made to look pretty, but we are rotten on the inside. I don't think you understand just how important you are to him. I don't think you understand the value of your love. Because let me tell you." He looks me right in the eyes. "It is priceless."

I'm about to say "I know," when I realize I don't. Being a surrogate never made me feel unlovable. It made me feel cheap and used and angry. But I had Raven and Lily, I had my mother and Hazel and Ochre. Ash had Cinder and then nothing. And even Cinder wasn't enough to stop him from hating himself.

I remember his words the night we fought before I came back to the Jewel.

And what do I have, Violet? You. Just you.

I'd thought it was an exaggeration at the time. I never thought Ash would find it difficult not just to love but to *be* loved as well.

"And now he's passed that hope to us," Rye continues. "That we might actually be able to live a life of our choosing, with someone who wishes to be with us, not someone who pays for the pleasure of our bodies. Companions are smart. We are well trained, and extremely disciplined. Give us a purpose, a single-minded focus, a cause that unifies us . . . well." Another flash of teeth in the night. "We're a force to be reckoned with."

"Yes," I say. "You are."

"What's your role in this whole thing?"

"I'm going to bring down the wall that separates the Bank and the Jewel. I'm going to let the people into this circle once and for all." The words come out easily, with a confidence I haven't heard in my voice before.

Rye's mouth falls open. "By yourself?"

"No," I say. "I'll have some help."

"Who—"

I hold up a hand. "I'll explain another time." I can't muster the energy to tell him about the surrogates and the Paladin tonight.

"Of course. It's late. You must be exhausted." Rye stands as I do, ever the gentleman. I walk over and wrap my arms around him. He hesitates at first, then returns the hug.

"You deserve to be loved," I say. "You all do."

He doesn't say anything, just squeezes me once, and I release him.

By the time I make it back to my chambers, I barely have the energy to slip my dress off over my head before I collapse onto the bed and fall into a dreamless sleep.

WHEN I WAKE THE NEXT MORNING, THERE'S A CRICK IN my shoulder from sleeping on it wrong.

I groan and roll onto my back, sunlight streaming through my open windows.

I gasp and sit up. The clock on the wall says it's nine forty-five.

"Crap!" I yelp, throwing on my spare lady-in-waiting gown and shoving my hair into a bun. The Exetor is coming today. I need to have Carnelian dressed and ready in an hour.

I skip the kitchen, figuring I can bring her something after she's dressed, and dive through the tapestry of the Duchess by the dining room. I pound my way up the stairs, slowing my pace when I enter into the main halls, and knock three times on her door.

"You're late," she calls, and I take that as permission to come in. She sits up in bed, a tray of half-eaten waffles beside her. "Mary brought me breakfast. My bell doesn't connect with your room." She smirks. "Mary *hates* you, by the way."

I bristle. "She hates you, too."

Carnelian flushes, then shrugs. "Everybody hates me."

I don't have time to feel bad, or even argue with her, right now. "Come on," I say. "Get up. You can boss me around all you like today. That's got to count for something."

A broad smile spreads across her face. I have to help her out of bed because her chest is taped up. The doctor gave her pain medication so her ribs and shoulder don't hurt, but the tape makes maneuvering her into a dress take longer than usual.

Somehow, we manage to make it to the foyer by 10:42. Ryc meets us at the top of the main staircase, all in black. He doesn't even glance at me, smiling at Carnelian and offering his arm.

"How are you feeling?" he asks as they descend the stairs. Carnelian leans on him heavily.

"I'm all right," she says. "Whatever the doctor gave me is working. I don't want to go to any parties tonight, though."

"As far as I know, our schedule is completely clear. We can do whatever you wish."

We reach the foot of the stairs and I slink into line beside Cora. Rye and Carnelian stand with Garnet and the Duchess, who are already waiting at the front doors. The fountain twinkles merrily, surrounded by black-clad servants and maids. Even Zara is in attendance, looking strange out of her apron. The red coats of the Regimentals and the white dresses that Cora and I wear are the only splashes of color.

The minutes tick past. At eleven o'clock on the dot, an opulent motorcar pulls up. Little flags whip in the wind from their perches above the headlights—the Royal Crest is emblazoned on them, as well as on the motorcar's doors.

The Exetor emerges from the car and climbs the steps to the palace, trailed by two members of his private guard. The entire foyer bows and curtsies as he enters.

"Pearl," he says, in a commanding voice. "I am deeply sorry for your loss. As you said in your letter, it is truly a tragic time for the House of the Lake."

"Thank you, Your Grace," the Duchess replies. "I am honored you took the time to visit me here."

The Exetor smiles. It's a surprisingly nice smile. His beard is close-cropped and streaked with hints of gray, but you can see the strong jaw underneath.

"You wished to meet with me," he says.

"Yes," the Duchess replies. "If you will accompany me to my private study, we can speak there. Cora can bring us refreshments."

"That won't be necessary," the Exetor says, stopping Cora in her tracks.

"As you wish." The Duchess curtsies again. I've never seen her be so deferential. "Please follow me."

They begin to ascend the staircase. The Exetor's guards shadow him, but he waves them off with a hand. "You will wait for me here."

They reach the second floor and disappear.

It's like everyone in the foyer was holding a collective breath. The Regimentals break ranks, One and Two moving to stand by the main stairs, Four and Five going over to greet the Exetor's guards. Zara claps her hands and all the scullery maids follow her down to the kitchen. Garnet turns to Rye and Carnelian.

"I'm off to the library. We'll have to be back here soon enough when he leaves."

"I'll come with you," Carnelian says. "I need to get a new book." She glances at me with a smug smile. "Come along, *Imogen*."

I bob my head and try to look docile.

"Are you sad?" Carnelian asks Garnet as we walk through the halls. "About Coral?"

"Of course."

"But you didn't love her."

"That doesn't mean I wanted her to die." We pass the dining room and make a right. "I'm glad you're all right," Garnet adds.

"Thanks."

This whole quartet is so strange. I know about everyone. Garnet knows about Rye but not Carnelian and vice versa. Carnelian knows about me but not Garnet and Rye.

Is this how Lucien feels all the time?

"What do you think they're talking about?" Carnelian asks.

Garnet shrugs. "Not a clue. Mother is probably angling to use Coral's death"—he stumbles over the word—"to some advantage or another."

When we reach the library, Garnet spreads out onto one of the leather couches and throws an arm over his eyes. Carnelian peruses one of the shelves with Rye.

"Imogen, it's hot in here and I forgot my fan," she complains. "Go get it for me from my room."

I can tell she's enjoying her position of power.

"Yes, miss," I say with a strained curtsy.

I turn to leave, passing the table with all the crests on it and then a family portrait of Garnet with his father and mother, when an idea occurs to me.

The Duchess said she was going to her private study. When I was first looking for Hazel, I discovered a hidden staircase that led me to a study with a photograph of the Duchess's family in it. It was a place that felt intensely personal. What if she and the Exetor are there now?

I pretend I'm leaving the library, then make a sharp left and dart behind the shelves. Silent as a ghost, I make my way to Cadmium Blake's *Essays on Cross-Pollination* and slip down the tunnel. I find the staircase and climb it quickly. Murmured voices tell me my suspicions were right.

I reach the door to the study and am shocked into stillness by a sudden burst of laughter.

"Oh, Onyx," the Duchess says. There's a silence, and then the unmistakable sounds of kissing.

The Duchess. Is kissing. The Exetor. I knew they were engaged once, but . . .

"I'm tired of this charade," she says.

"I know," the Exetor replies. "So am I."

"Did you bring it?"

There is a rustling and then the sound of something clattering onto a tabletop. "From her personal library," he says.

"And no one saw?"

"Not a soul. Not even Lucien. I think he believes she is behind the shooting. At least, he doesn't suspect you or me."

"That is excellent news."

I'm trying to make sense of what she's saying. The Duchess and the Exetor were the ones who planned the attack on Hazel. But why?

"It really is a beautiful piece," the Duchess says with a sigh.

"I gave it to her for the Longest Night two years ago. Very publicly." There is a pause. "I don't think she appreciated it."

"She is too pedestrian to understand it."

The Exetor laughs. "She doesn't have your love of history. Or your passion for fine weaponry."

Weaponry? My heart sinks lower in my chest. What is happening here?

"It was your great-grandfather's, wasn't it?" the Duchess asks.

"What an excellent memory you have." I can hear the smile in the Exetor's voice.

"I remember everything about us," she says. I've never heard her sound so vulnerable. "Every single second. I first saw this when I was thirteen and we broke into that old chest your father kept in one of his studies."

"We got in quite a bit of trouble for that."

The Duchess's laugh is gentle, and full of memory. "We did, didn't we? My father kept me locked in my room for a week."

"And I arrived two days into that week and demanded he release you."

"Yes, I'm sure you were very intimidating."

"I'm surprised he didn't box my ears."

"So am I."

It's the Exetor's turn to laugh. "I'm certain he wanted to. But I don't think my father would have been so forgiving of one of his subjects accosting his own son."

"What do you think our fathers would make of us now?" the Duchess asks.

There is a long pause. "I don't think I care, to be honest. After what they did . . . after . . . it was our lives, Pearl, *our* lives, and they—"

"I know," she says softly.

I hear a stopper being popped off and liquid poured into glasses. "I'm worried, Onyx. What if we fail? What if people don't believe it was her? We need the royalty to love this engagement. We need them to be so attached to the joining of our Houses that there is an outrage when the surrogate is murdered."

She's trying to kill me. Hazel's words come back to me with full force. Someone in this palace *is* trying to kill her. I was just wrong about who.

"Yes, I've thought on this quite a bit," the Exetor says. "Your House has garnered so much sympathy recently. What if we were to make use of all that goodwill?"

"In what way?"

"We make the Auction double serve as an engagement party for Larimar. A grand affair, not like Garnet's little promotion celebration. We will make it the event of the century. And we will open the invitation to every member of the royalty."

"Of course," the Duchess says. "The royals will love it, especially the unmarried ones who wouldn't be able to come otherwise. A party on top of a party."

"We appear as a united front. No one will doubt the validity of this engagement. Then, when the surrogate is murdered with the Electress's dagger, this circle will turn on her like a pack of wild wolves."

"Oh, my darling," the Duchess says. She murmurs something too low for me to hear.

"I could have been better," the Exetor says, his voice straining with emotion. "I should have been. With you by my side."

"We can't change the past."

"I should never have let—"

"Shhh." There are some more muffled movements. "Soon. After the Electress is hanged for treason. This will all die down in a year or so."

"That seems so far away."

"We've been waiting twenty-eight years," the Duchess says. "I think we can wait one or two more."

I don't understand. If they love each other so much, why did the engagement break off in the first place?

There is a silence and then he asks her something in a whisper, too soft for me to make out.

"I don't know," she replies, and she sounds like she's in pain. "I never knew. It was too early to tell."

Too early to tell what? I want to shout.

"I am so sorry," he says.

"I know, my love," she murmurs. "I know you are."

One last bit of kissing and then the Exetor says, "I should be getting back. The announcement needs to be made."

"Yes, of course." She chuckles. "It's going to send this circle into a tizzy."

There's the sound of footsteps and then a door closes.

I slide down the wall and perch on the edge of a stair, my heart thrumming in my chest.

This whole thing has been one elaborate scheme to get the Exetor and the Duchess back together. At the cost of my sister's life.

~ Twenty-Two ~

THE ANNOUNCEMENT THAT THE AUCTION WILL SERVE AS an engagement party as well throws the circle into gleeful chaos, as the Duchess and the Exetor predicted.

Invites come pouring in, for cocktail parties and luncheons and wine tastings. Everyone wants the Duchess's attention. The loss of Coral and the Duke mixed with the ironclad promise of a union between the Royal Palace and the House of the Lake makes the Duchess the Jewel's most wanted woman. And with only one day left until the Auction, the palace is buzzing with excitement.

I haven't spoken to Lucien since the Exetor's visit. But tonight is the annual pre-Auction dinner party for the Founding Houses at the Royal Palace, and fortunately,

Carnelian was invited. Which means I'll get to see him one last time before the city changes, for better or worse.

This development also means Carnelian will be attending the Auction, a huge relief since Coral's death meant I would not have had a reason to attend myself.

The lower circles have been bubbling with discontent. Fires, lootings, more bombings . . . the Farm is in turmoil now, too. The factory workers in the Smoke have been striking. I haven't spoken to Rye privately again. But I manage to get a moment alone with Garnet before I prepare Carnelian for the big dinner. He tells me Rye reached out to him. He's very excited to have the companions on board.

"They're really good with strategy," he says, adjusting his bow tie. "And they already know how to fight. When you Paladin start causing all that chaos, we're going to be ready. It's like the royalty trained the perfect weapons for us!"

I quickly fill Garnet in about the conversation I overheard between his mother and the Exetor.

He whistles. "Well, I can't say I'm entirely surprised. She's been in love with him for years. You didn't hear what broke off the engagement, did you?"

"No, but that's not the point," I say. "Hazel is the *target*."

"Yeah, at the *Auction*. Mother won't have a chance. Everyone will be too busy fighting the Society."

I hope he's right.

THE ROYAL PALACE IS LIT UP LIKE A GIANT CANDLE, IN anticipation of the Auction tomorrow.

I caught a miraculous glimpse of Hazel for the first time

since she escaped. Leashed and veiled, she was led to the motorcar by the Duchess, but it was enough to make my heart soar. I have time. She is alive and I'm going to make sure no one threatens her life again.

We arrive at the same time as the Countess of the Rose. Her hair is piled up on her head and dotted with real roses. The Count leans heavily on a cane as he walks up the front stairs beside her. Her lady-in-waiting is an older woman with a topknot as gray as the Countess's own hair.

"You are the talk of the circle, Pearl," the Countess says with admiration. I listen attentively but keep my eyes on my sister. She glances back at me, and I give her the tiniest shake of my head. She gives me a minuscule nod and keeps her eyes forward. "Just what you've always wanted."

"That is where you are wrong, my dear Ametrine," the Duchess replies, her gaze fixed on the front doors of the palace. "There has only ever been one thing I truly wanted. And it wasn't winning the Jewel's popularity contest."

As soon as we step inside, footmen take cloaks and hats and lead the royals away to the dining room. I keep my eyes on Hazel's retreating form for as long as I can. Just as they are about to turn a corner, she looks back at me one more time. Then she's gone.

"Come along, Imogen," Cora says. I turn and catch a glimpse of the Countess of the Stone making her way up the stairs with a short, frail man by her side. The Count, I assume. I wonder if Emile will be here tonight.

I follow Cora and the older lady-in-waiting (both of whom clearly know where they're going) to a room with colorful couches in shades of peach, turquoise, emerald, and lilac. Several tables have been laid out with all sorts of food and glass pitchers of water. There is one lady-in-waiting already here—he must serve the Duchess of the Scales. She's the only Founding House I haven't seen yet.

"Olivier," Cora says, coming over to greet him. "How lovely to see you. Have you met Imogen?"

Olivier is plump and cheery, with a carrot-orange top-knot.

"You were hired for Coral, yes?" he says, shaking my hand. His are unnaturally soft.

"Yes," I say. "But I serve Carnelian now."

"Such a shame," he says with a sigh, then directs his attention back to Cora. "Your House has been hit hard these past few weeks. Turning the Auction into an engagement party was a brilliant idea of the Exetor's. Just the thing this circle needs to lift its spirits."

"I'm surprised the Duchess brought her surrogate here at all," the gray-haired lady-in-waiting says, coming to join us with a plate of cheese and fruit. "Isn't she worried about the Electress?"

"Come now, Eloise," Olivier says. "The Electress would never attempt to harm the surrogate in her own house."

"I wouldn't put it past her," a thin, dry voice says from the doorway.

I know him, even without ever really having seen him before. Raven told me all about Frederic—his voice, his bloody gums, his beady eyes, his beaked nose. He glides into the room, plucking a grape off a bunch in a silver bowl.

"Eloise. Olivier." He acknowledges them with a nod.

"Glad to see you're up and about," Cora says dryly. "We

missed you at Garnet's party."

"I was sorry not to be there," Frederic says with a distinct lack of sincerity. "Though I do like my soirees to come with a little less violence."

"Really," Cora shoots back. "I was under the impression it was quite the opposite."

Eloise and Olivier look uncomfortable. But Frederic merely smiles at her, and I see them, the bloodred gums Raven told me about. It is a hideous smile, one that clearly wishes the receiver harm. Frederic pops the grape into his mouth and chews it slowly.

"Will the Countess be buying another surrogate this year?" Olivier says in a blatant attempt to diffuse the tension.

"Of course," Frederic says. "Such a shame about the last one. It was truly . . . unique."

Raven told me they used to call her "it." Knowing it is one thing, but hearing him say it out loud . . . I ball my hands into fists, the desire to join with Air and throw him across the room potent inside me.

"Ah, good, you are all here."

I turn and see Lucien. "Welcome, my friends. Another year, another Auction. Though this year seems to be shaping up a little differently than the previous ones."

In more ways than one, I think, and his gaze lands on me for half a second, but in that time, I know his thoughts are in line with mine.

"Indeed," Olivier agrees, bouncing on the balls of his feet. "An engagement party *and* an Auction? The entire Jewel attending?"

"No doubt the Duchess will be thrilled by the attention," Frederic says.

"And the Countess is known for her humility?" Cora retorts.

"We must be in top form," Lucien says, ignoring the snipes between the two. "And keep close eyes on your mistresses. With all the violence and the distress in the lower circles, we must be on high alert."

If I didn't know better, I'd think he was sincerely concerned with the well-being of the royal women. He snaps a finger at me.

"You," he says. "Carnelian requires you. Come with me."

My heart in my throat, I follow him out the door. I expect him to lead me far from the room with the other ladies-in-waiting, or maybe back to his secret workshop, but instead he takes me only one room over.

"Do you know how to get to this room from the front doors?" he asks.

"Yes," I say, surprised. "It's just down the hall to the left, right?"

"Correct." The room is a small antechamber, nothing in it except for a round, blue rug and a painting of a white fluffy dog sitting on a plush stool. Lucien pulls back the painting to reveal a hole in the wall, large enough for me to climb through. I can see stone stairs on the opposite side.

"This will take you to my room," he says. "I left markings for you to follow. I wanted to make sure you could find it. If . . . if the time comes."

My chest is tight. Lucien replaces the painting so nothing looks out of place.

"This is it," I say.

"This is it," he echoes in reply. He puts his hands on my shoulders. "Whatever happens tomorrow, whatever the day brings . . . at least we tried. We tried to do something bold and brave."

"We tried to change the world," I say.

He smiles gently. "Or our own little corner of it, at least."

I smile back. He has meant so much to me, and I don't know how to express my thanks for everything he has done. He seems to sense my feelings, though, and envelops me in a freesia-scented hug.

As we walk back out into the hall, a footman rushes up. "Lucien, come quick. Arabelle has burned the venison pot pies and Robert and Duncan are at each other's throats again. The kitchen is a nightmare."

Lucien pinches the bridge of his nose. "Of all the nights," he mutters, and the two hurry down the hall, disappearing behind a tapestry.

I'm left alone. I turn to reenter the chamber where the food and ladies-in-waiting are, when a dancing glint of light catches my eye.

A door across the hall with a golden handle is slightly ajar. Curiosity gets the better of me and I push it open, slipping inside.

The room is larger than I expected. And full of . . . me.

Mirrors hang on every wall, reflecting my startled face back at me. Except that it's not my face, not really. It's the face of a blond girl with a high forehead and wide green eyes. It's the face of a stranger.

I make a circuit of the room, my stranger's face appearing in an oval mirror inlaid with mother-of-pearl, a square-shaped one with golden roses fixed on its four points, and a long rectangle with pearls dotting its edge.

I stop at one that sets my heart pounding. It's a simple square mirror with a silver frame, but etched lightly in its center is a tree that looks exactly like the lemon tree that grows in the backyard of my house in the Marsh. The one that never produced a lemon until I used the third Augury, Growth, on it when I visited my family on Reckoning Day. I grew a lemon for Hazel, to remember me by.

And now she's sitting in a glitzy dining room, on a leash, next to a woman who is planning to murder her tomorrow.

I take one step back from the golden tree. Then another, and another, until I'm standing in the center of the room. My reflection stares out at me with a hundred pairs of eyes.

This is not who I am, this blond-haired girl in lady-in-waiting garb. I am Violet Lasting. I am one of the Paladin and I could destroy this room if I wanted to.

And I do want to. Desperately.

I join with the element effortlessly, sweeping all the Air in here to me, calling on it to do as I command. I feel it swirl around me, restless, waiting and eager.

Break, I think, and my focus is so sharp, so intense, the image of what I desire strong and specific, like I'm conjuring an Augury. But the elements are stronger than any Augury. I shoot the air away from me, and it hits the center of each mirror perfectly. I feel as if I am flying in a hundred different directions, as if I am reaching out with my own hands to imprint the pattern on each and every mirror in this room.

All but one.

I release the hold on the element to the sound of tinkling bits of glass clattering to the floor. The lemon tree mirror is as it was, perfectly smooth and reflective.

In the center of every single other mirror, the glass has cracked to form a very well-known, very specific shape.

A skeleton key.

I look around the room in awe. Keys surround me, fragmenting my face in grotesque fashions. I've never been so proud of myself, so sure of the power I possess.

I have marked this room for the Society. And tomorrow, the royalty will feel the weight of our fury.

~ Twenty-Three ~

The morning of the Auction is crisp and clear.

The sky is a perfect, robin's-egg blue and the garden looks even lusher than usual. My fingers tremble as I lace up the back of Carnelian's dress, careful not to hurt her shoulder or ribs. I have to remind myself to breathe.

"Are you all right?" she asks, when I fumble with the laces for the third time.

"I'm fine," I say. "I just . . . I don't like the Auction."

"Right." Carnelian grimaces. I finish getting her dressed in silence.

Rye is waiting outside her room. He takes her arm with a strained smile.

"What's wrong?" she asks.

"There were some whispers in the kitchen," he says, his eyes flashing to me for half a second. The hairs on the back of my neck prickle. "Something's happened, I don't know what. Everyone stopped talking when I came in."

"Something happened with my aunt?" Carnelian asks.

Something happened with my sister? I want to demand.

Rye shrugs. "I'm not sure." Then his whole demeanor shifts, like a light being turned on. "Are you excited to attend your first Auction?"

They chat as we walk to the foyer. I trail behind them, heart hammering, and when I see the Duchess's gleeful face, it pounds even faster. Anything that makes her look this happy can't be good.

Whatever it is, Hazel appears to be safe for the time being. The Duchess has her on the leash, but she's dressed in an extravagant gown, blue and silver silk stitched with pearls and sapphires. Her face is veiled and there is a delicate crown on her head, strands of gold woven with diamonds. Her purple eyes meet mine and the look in them is fierce. She knows what this day means, even if she isn't aware of the plot for her murder.

We take two motorcars to the Auction House. Ours is thick with tension. Garnet is in his Regimental uniform, and his leg won't stop jiggling. Rye's posture is a bit too forced to look casual. I stare out the window at the palaces flashing by, my mouth so dry it's uncomfortable to swallow. I wish I knew why the servants were worried, why the Duchess looked so excited. But I have to stay focused. I have to get to the train station underground. I waited all night for the arcana to buzz, to hear Raven's voice, or Sil's, or

Lucien's. But it stayed frustratingly silent.

When we arrive at the Auction House, there is a small platform set up on the lawn in front of it with a smooth block of marble in its center, inlaid with gold and rubies. I don't know what that's for. Rye and Carnelian seem confused by it, and Garnet looks perplexed as well. Perplexed and . . . frightened?

The crowd is tense, none of the cheerful laughter and conversation I was expecting. The royals huddle together on the sprawling grass that surrounds the pink domed building, muttering urgently to one another. As we get out of the car, I catch snippets of what they're saying.

"Never could have imagined it . . ."

"I'm having my lady-in-waiting interrogated the second I get home."

"And he was so helpful in securing me an invitation to the Longest Night Ball last year!"

My pounding heart jumps to my throat and stays there, choking me. A feeling of dread creeps up my spine. Something is very wrong.

We make our way through the crowd and the royals fall silent at our approach, bowing and curtsying to the Duchess as she passes. When we are only a few yards from the marble block, the Countess of the Rose swoops over.

"Did you hear?" she says, fanning herself with a pink feathered fan. "They found him. The leader of that horrid Black Key society."

The second before she says the name stretches out to eternity. I wait in it, unable to blink or breathe, my body a living vessel of terror.

"It's *Lucien*," the Countess of the Rose says.

The ground shifts beneath my feet. I think I might be falling. A strong hand reaches out to steady me. It's Garnet.

His face is barely masking his fear and I realize we've got to do better. My world may have stopped turning in this moment, but there are so many worlds to consider on this day. We have to be strong. We have to be brave.

I've almost convinced myself I can do it. Until the executioner walks up the steps to the platform. He wears a black mask and carries a silver ax slung in his belt. I can't take my eyes off it, its sharp edge catching the light. My mind can't wrap my head around its purpose.

"Lucien?" the Duchess is asking incredulously. "I heard they caught the leader but . . . *Lucien?* He always seemed so . . ."

"Obedient?" The Countess of the Stone looms over the Duchess, her large breasts spilling out of her bronze-colored dress. "It's always the ones you trust the most, isn't it?"

"How did they know?" the Duchess asks.

"Apparently he wanted to leave his mark in the Royal Palace itself. Smashed all the mirrors in the Room of Reflection with imprints of that key."

The keys. *My* keys. Lucien must have taken the blame when they were discovered.

I thought the world stopped spinning when I heard Lucien had been caught.

It is nothing compared to knowing that he was caught because of *me*. The Auction House swims in my vision. My lungs have shrunk to half their normal size. I can't get enough air.

My fault, my fault, my fault . . .

The royals keep talking but all sounds have faded to a dull buzz. What was I thinking? Why did I do that? It was reckless and foolish. Lucien is neither of those things. He is careful and cautious. He is kind and generous. He saved my life, he showed me who I was and what I was capable of. He has watched over me like a brother, like a father.

And I failed him. I ruined everything in one moment of arrogant idiocy.

Trumpets blare, piercing through the fog of my mind. The Exetor and Electress step onto the platform, decked in crimson and black and gold, matching the crests pinned on their chests. The Electress looks shell-shocked. The Exetor is somber. His eyes rest on the Duchess for a moment before he holds up a hand and the last remaining whispers fall silent.

"My fellow royalty," he says in his rich tenor. "We have discovered a traitor among us." He turns to someone standing off to the side where I can't see. "Bring him out!"

Garnet's hand moves to his pistol, but there's nothing either of us can do. It takes every ounce of self-control I have not to scream, to cry out to him, as Lucien is paraded onto the platform.

One eye is bruised and swollen. There is a gash on his forehead and he walks with a limp. Instead of his lady-in-waiting garb, he wears a burlap sack, tied around his waist with a length of rope. His feet are bare and dirty. His hands are bound and he is flanked by two Regimentals. One of them prods him in the back and he stumbles, nearly losing his balance. The crowd laughs and jeers.

They've shaved his head completely, his beautiful chestnut topknot gone. He looks so much younger without it. The Regimentals march him to the marble block and the Exetor speaks again.

"This man, formerly known as Lucien of the Royal Palace, has been charged with treason and sedition. He has been discovered as the leader of the rebel society that calls itself the Black Key. He is responsible for all acts of violence committed in the lower circles, attacks against royal outposts, which is tantamount to an attack on the Jewel itself. He has been found guilty of these crimes. The sentence is death."

I feel nauseous, my stomach churning as they force Lucien to his knees. My heart slams against my ribs, each thud sending the same word repeating over and over in my head.

No, no, no, no . . .

The Exetor turns to his former servant, a look of disgust on his face. "Do you have any last words before your sentence is carried out?"

Lucien's deep blue eyes scan the crowd. They light on Garnet for an instant before they find me. Relief flickers across his face, as if he is glad I am here.

"This is no one's fault but my own," he says, choosing his words carefully. "I take full responsibility for my actions. I will not apologize for my crimes. They were done for love of my city, for the love I bear to all the people in it. The lower circles have been mistreated for too long. The royalty have taken our sons and daughters, forced them into servitude, destroyed hopes and dreams and lives purely for their own greed. It was time they paid the price. I am not ashamed of what I have done." His eyes land on me again. "This is *no one's* fault but my own."

I'm shaking my head, because it is, it is *my* fault, and the guilt is searing, blistering. It claws at my lungs, it shreds my heart to pieces. It should be me up there, not him. The city needs him. I need him.

He gives me the softest smile and I see the forgiveness in his eyes and I hate myself more than I ever thought possible. I hate myself more than I hate the Duchess or the Auction or this evil, glittering circle.

When Lucien speaks again, it is as if we are alone, as if he is speaking just to me, the way he did the first day I met him in the prep room, the day my life changed.

"This is how it begins," he says, echoing the words his sister spoke, so many months ago, in front of the walls of Southgate. A tiny smile lights on his lips. "I am not afraid."

Then he gently lays his head on the block as if it were a pillow. I can't stop the tears that fill my eyes. They are hot and shameful and I don't deserve to cry them.

The ax makes a shimmering, whistling sound as it cuts through the air. Blood stains the white stone red, dripping over rubies and golden swirls.

My whole body is paralyzed. The crowd around me starts making noise again but I can't make sense of anything. I watch Regimentals carry Lucien's body off the platform. Another one follows behind with a basket. The marble block is removed and the Exetor claps his hands and announces something but all the sound has been sucked out of this place. The crowd swells forward, past the platform, toward the Auction House, and I am swept up with them, walking woodenly on legs that don't remember how to work, that can't seem to understand the rules of a world without Lucien in it.

I feel a soft pressure on my arm and blink up at Garnet. His eyes are filled with tears and I realize I'm crying, too. The Duchess leads Hazel in front of us on the leash, Rye and Carnelian right behind them. They seem stunned, confused, but their worlds have not been shattered like mine.

Garnet nods toward the open doors of the Auction House and fixes me with a fervent look. "For him," he whispers.

I thought I'd lost the power of speech, but my mouth works independently of my brain.

"For him," I whisper back. Garnet blinks and rubs his eyes, releasing his hold on my elbow. I wipe my face with my hands. There will be time to mourn for Lucien, to punish myself for the role I played in his death. But I will not fail him now, at what could be the end of everything.

The foyer of the Auction House is massive. The top of the dome is made of glass, light pouring down and spilling over the mosaic of tiles that decorate the floor. In the center is a huge fountain, water spurting from the outstretched arms of a statue of Diamante the Great, the Electress who started the first Auction. Waiters skirt the crowds with glasses of pink and blue cocktails. The royals mingle, discussing the execution as if it were entertainment.

I can't help but think of my own Auction experience. This is what was happening while Lucien was prepping me, while I was in the Waiting Room with Dahlia.

The Duchess sits on a raised dais off to one side, the

Exetor in the center, the Electress on his right. Hazel stands behind the Duchess, her eyes fixed on me, the collar shining in a cruel mockery of a necklace around her neck. I'm grateful that Larimar does not seem to be invited to his own engagement party. Perhaps the royals thought children would be in the way.

Half an orchestra is playing and there are jugglers and acrobats darting and dancing through the crowds, just like Coral had described.

"The Regimentals that pick the surrogates up won't be down there for ten more minutes," Garnet murmurs to me, his back turned so it doesn't look like we're talking. "I had someone change the clocks so they think they've still got time. The trains should be pulling up any moment. You'd better hurry."

"Hazel," I say, glancing toward my sister. I know I need to go, but I don't want to leave her here. What if she is murdered before this whole thing starts?

"I'll keep an eye on her as long as I can," Garnet says. "Go."

My grief is melting away in the face of fear. This is really happening.

Carnelian is engaged in conversation with Rye and the Countess of the Rose, and I take the opportunity to slip away.

The train station is on the very lowest level of the Auction House. I locate the door I need, the one I remember clearly from the blueprints. Facing south, third door on the left. It leads me to an antechamber that I cross, leaving through the door on the opposite side, where a set of stairs waits. I take it down, past the two floors of prep rooms, past the floor that holds the beehive-like rooms where surrogates are knocked unconscious to be transported to their new homes, down, down, until the stairs end in a cold, concrete hallway. I quickly bring up the blueprints in my mind again.

Right.

I turn and run. There is a door, a big wooden one that will take me to the station, to Raven and the others. I pass an industrial-size elevator, used to transport unconscious surrogates to their prep rooms.

Then I see the door. I slam into it, turning the handle and pushing it open just as the last train crawls into view. There are no conductors on these trains —they run automatically. I hope the girls have managed to take out the doctors and caretakers. The Regimentals haven't arrived yet, just as Garnet said.

The train screeches to a halt, steam issuing from its chimney and creating a soft mist in the air. One by one, iron doors slam shut behind each of the four trains, echoing with a loud clang in the cavernous space. The roof arches into a peak, stones fitted together in a puzzle of slate and charcoal and soft gray. Thick iron chandeliers hang from the ceiling on sturdy chains, glowglobes emitting a rich yellow light.

I don't have time to be cautious. "Paladin!" I cry.

"Violet?" Raven's voice rips through me, a happiness more powerful than I thought I was capable of feeling in this moment. Her head pokes out of the plum-colored Southgate train. "Violet!" she cries, and jumps down off the carriage.

I can't stop the cry that escapes my lips, a tortured howl

really. I run across the station as she starts toward me and we collide into each other.

"You're okay," she breathes into my ear, her hands scrabbling over my back to make sure I'm whole.

"Lucien's dead," I say, and it hits me then, like a punch in the chest. Lucien is dead.

"What?" Raven gasps, but I don't have time to explain because heads are popping out of train cars and girls are filling the room, eyes wide as they take in the huge space.

"Violet," someone says, and then my name is picked up and echoes through the train station. "Violet! Violet is here! Violet!"

I want to cry. I want to gather them all up in an enormous hug. I want to shout orders, to tell them to forget the wall, we are taking this whole Auction House down right now, we are punishing the royalty for killing the man who was ten times the human any of them were or would ever be.

"Violet, you're all right!" Indi engulfs me in one of her hugs. "I'd forgotten about your hair and your face. You don't look at all like you!"

Sienna and Olive join us, Sil bringing up the rear.

"We heard about Coral," Sienna says, at the same time Olive asks, "Have you seen my mistress?"

"Lucien's dead," I say again, the words coming easier this time as my body begins to accept the reality of that fact.

Sil's face goes blank with utter shock. Indi gasps and Sienna covers her mouth with her hands. Even Olive looks upset.

"It's my fault," I gasp. "All my fault." I only have eyes

for Sil in this moment. "I . . . I did something stupid and he took the blame for it. I should never . . . I didn't mean . . ." The tears begin to fall thick and fast.

Sil strides forward and takes my chin in her hands.

"Stop crying," she says sharply. "Look at me." She holds me in her steely, silver gaze. "That man loved you more than anything in this world. You can't do a single damned thing to bring him back, but you can honor who he was and what he did, right here, right now. These girls need you, Violet."

She sweeps a hand out over the seventy-seven girls who were meant to be unconscious, sold into slavery, but instead have gathered around me, faces bright and determined.

"They are here, and alive, and they need *you*," she murmurs. Seventy-seven pairs of eyes stare at me, waiting for instructions. Girls ranging in age from thirteen to nineteen, looking to me for guidance.

Sil is right. I take a deep breath.

"We've got to divide up," I say. "Raven, Sil, Indi, Olive, you'll be in charge of each team. Make sure you've got every element. Sienna, you're with me."

Sienna flicks her lighter open, making the flame burn bright.

Then I turn to the waiting faces, and for the first time, I really see them. Amber is there, looking at me with a clenched jaw and resolute face. Tawny, Ginger, and Henna are right beside her. I see Sloe, a beautiful girl with russet skin and dark, arching eyebrows, the leader of the Northgate girls. She throws her hair over her shoulder in her typical haughty fashion. Little Rosie Kelting, a fourteen-year-old from Eastgate, chews her lip as she awaits instructions. So many faces, so many names.

Strong, beautiful girls. Paladin.

"Southgate to Raven!" I call. "Northgate to Sil! East-gate to Olive! Westgate—"

I'm interrupted by a flat piece of stone wall sliding open. A Regimental steps out and for a second I panic, but the glint of blond hair under his cap makes my chest swim with relief.

"What are you doing here?" I demand, walking over to greet Garnet. "You were supposed to—"

But all my panic returns when I am close enough to see his face.

It isn't Garnet.

Hidden doors are all around us, clicking like insects as they slide open, Regimentals pouring out of them, a wall of red.

We are surrounded.

Twenty-Four

SURPRISE SEEMS TO BE OUR ONE ADVANTAGE.

The blond one is staring at me, mouth open, like he's never seen a girl before.

The room is a powder keg, waiting to explode. The instant someone moves, the spell will be broken. My knees bend slightly as I prepare myself to light the spark.

There is stone all around us. Water beneath us. Air everywhere. Sienna has her lighter.

"Who in the Exetor's name are you?" the Regimental says.

"I am Violet Lasting," I say calmly. Then I take a deep breath and cry, "Paladin!"

I join with Air instinctively, gathering all the molecules

of air in this room toward me, condensing and compacting them. Then I release them, like a stone from a slingshot, at the blond Regimental still gaping at me. The force of it is so powerful, he is slammed into the far wall and slumps to the ground unconscious.

"Sil, Earth!" I shout. "Indi, Water!"

There is a rumble underfoot as the floor begins to shake. Sil shouts for the girls who can to join with Earth, but the Regimentals are running toward them, despite the unsteady ground. I send two flying, but a third has drawn his gun and is pointing it straight at my head.

This is it, I think. *Maybe I'll get to see Lucien again. And my father.*

Then the Regimental is engulfed in flames. His screams stun everyone temporarily as I turn and see Sienna, lighter in hand, a murderous expression on her face. We nod to each other as a crater opens up at our feet, Sil and Amber and five other girls focusing on the ground. Two Regimentals fall into it as the crater deepens, searching for the water down below. Sienna sends a snaking coil of fire toward a Regimental aiming his gun at Sloe.

"Don't shoot to kill!" one of them calls out to the others. "The royalty need them alive!"

"Are you crazy?" one shouts back as another cries, "What's happening?"

The crater hits water—I can smell it; I can feel its writhing, fluid force.

"Finally," Indi sighs. She's with seven other girls, and they condense the water the way I've condensed Air, forming it into a thick white jet and shooting it across the hall.

It hits one Regimental hard in the face and his neck snaps back. Others raise their hands to cover their eyes as the jet splits into seven, and Regimentals start slipping on the wet floor.

I'm still connected with Air when I hear the bullet. I don't know if I make the conscious decision or somehow the element does it for me, but it whizzes by my ear, nicking my lobe, and then sharply shifts direction, landing in the shoulder of an oncoming Regimental. I ignore the sting of pain and the feel of blood dripping down my neck.

My eyes land on the chandelier hanging from the ceiling.

"Earth!" I cry. "The walls!"

Sil and I make eye contact and I jerk my head to the light fixture. Sloe joins us, then Amber, adding her own force to our might, so that cracks begin to snake up the walls and then across the ceiling.

"Back up, back up!" I shout, and the Paladin scatter toward the door as the chandelier sways precariously over the main force of Regimentals.

There is a loud crack and it falls, delicately at first, a beautiful swirl of light and metal. I grab Sil's hand and run, barreling right into Sloe and getting all three of us out of the way just as the chandelier crashes down.

The noise is deafening. It bounces off the walls, magnified tenfold, so that my eardrums feel as if they might pop. Hunks of stone and iron fly everywhere. Sil and I use Air to deflect the larger stones away from the girls. Sloe is trembling underneath me.

"You're okay," I say. My ears are ringing faintly, and I'm reminded of how I felt after the explosion in the Bank.

I lift my head and survey the damage.

It seems as though most of the girls made it to the door. But there are bodies littered around and under the rubble. A girl with curly hair lies a few feet away from me, her neck twisted at an unnatural angle, a bullet hole in her chest. I don't recognize her—she must have been one of the last ones in the holding facilities to gain her powers, when I was already in the Jewel. Regimental bodies are everywhere.

"Raven," I croak, sitting up. Dust settles in my hair and on my eyelashes. "Raven!"

"I'm all right!" She stands up, shaking the dust from her hair.

"Sienna? Indi? Olive?" I call.

I hear a cough and Sienna's braided head emerges from behind a chunk of rubble. "We're fine." Indi pops up beside her, her pale skin smudged with gray. I see Olive rubbing her eyes blearily.

"That was a very good idea," Indi says.

"That was only the beginning," I say. "This number of Regimentals is a fraction of what's guarding the Auction House."

As I look around the ruined station, though, I think, *We may be small in number. But we are a force to be reckoned with.* Then I add, *Lucien, wherever you are, I hope you're seeing this.*

"Sil, Raven, Indi, Olive," I say. "Get everyone to the wall. You remember the way, right?" They nod in unison. "Fire won't do much but maybe you can use the water here. Earth and Air will be crucial. This wall is thick. Really thick."

"We know," Sloe says. "We saw it."

"Where will you go, Violet?" Amber asks.

I catch Sienna's eye. "We're going to signal to the rest of this city that it's time. Let's show the royalty that they can't control us anymore."

Several girls whoop and cheer, but Sil shouts, "Quiet!"

"The Countess," Raven says to me with pleading eyes.

"She's here," I promise her. "With Frederic. Don't worry. You'll have your chance. But these girls need you now. They'll follow you." I turn to Sienna. "Let's go."

I lead everyone out the door and back to the stairs I took to get down here. As we climb, adrenaline pumping through me with each step, I wonder if the royalty felt the earth shudder as the chandelier crashed down, or if they are still blissfully unaware of the danger that is about to befall them.

There is a door to the outside on the lower floor of prep rooms, right at ground level. "Be careful," I whisper to Raven. She beckons to Indi to follow. The other girls are so quiet, even the ones who look frightened. They file out into the hall, determined and alert. Sil is the last to leave.

"We'll see you up there," she says, pointing above us, where the spire waits. I grip her shoulder for a brief moment, then she's gone.

Sienna and I climb up another floor to the top level of prep rooms. There will be Regimentals here for certain—the lower level is used only when lots of surrogates are being Auctioned, but this level is in use every year. I pause behind the door and listen. I can make out at least three different voices—Regimentals.

I grab the handle and nod to Sienna's lighter. We need a distraction. The flame bursts up, a fiery orange. I open the door and she sends the fire racing down the halls. We hear screams and cries as the Regimentals guarding prep room doors run from the blaze. We wait a few seconds, then enter the hall. Flames devour the carpet and climb the walls, but the hallway is empty. Sienna and I quickly put the fire out together.

I see the door we need and throw it open with Air, the handle too hot to touch. This staircase is narrow, with slitted windows, and it curls up in a spiral. We start to climb—up and up and up . . . and when we reach the top of it, I can see the pink curve of one of the smaller domes of the Auction House a few feet below us out the window. If I crane my neck, I can see the wall. There is a short hallway that takes us to a long ladder.

I go first, tying the skirts of my lady-in-waiting gown so I don't step on them. Sienna wears pants; the rungs pose no problem for her.

Halfway there, my arms are aching and my breath comes out in heavy pants. I can hear Sienna gasping behind me, but neither of us complains or slows our pace. I know we're close when I hear the wind whistling shrilly above us. We climb out onto a tiny, round landing made of the same golden material as the spire that surrounds us.

As I stand up and look around, I find myself grateful that I'm not afraid of heights.

The spire is hollow, thin strips of gold shooting up into a point and forming a sort of cage around us. We are a few feet above the top of the wall, and can see its vastness stretching out before us.

"Whoa," Sienna breathes. I agree. The wall is immense, and maybe fifty yards away. I look down and see the figures of the Paladin on the swath of green lawn that separates the Auction House from the wall. Indi's blond hair is easily identifiable and I watch Raven lining girls up on the grass.

"It's so big," Sienna says.

"It is," I say.

"Are we really going to bring it down?"

I grit my teeth. Ash promised me he'd be behind that wall, with Ochre and so many Society members. Lucien was counting on me. I can't fail them now. I won't.

"We will. Come on," I say, motioning to her lighter. "First things first."

It's time to give the Society members the signal to set off the bombs.

She flicks it and the flame shoots up. "Brighter," I say, and the fire glows until it hurts to look at it. The wind whips Sienna's braids around her face and tugs at the strands in my bun, stinging my eyes.

I connect with Air and it plucks the lighter from her hands, carrying it through the slats of gold. I lift it up, high into the sky, where it hangs like a tiny sun. Then I feel along the cracks in the lighter, and in a burst of dazzling light, it explodes.

I hold my breath. Ten seconds pass. Twenty. I watch as the last embers die, whisked off by the wind, scraps of metal from the ruined lighter falling to the lawn below.

Another twenty seconds pass. Nothing. I wasn't sure what to expect but I assumed there would be an immediate answer to the flare. My stomach begins to sink, fear seeping in. Sienna voices my concern.

"Do you think they didn't—"

Suddenly, there is a deafening boom, and a fireball blossoms far away in the center of the Bank. Glass sparkles like fireworks in the sun. The Society's bombs are going off. Thirty seconds later, I think I see a plume of black rising up from the Smoke. The Farm is too far away to know whether the bombs went off or not.

I reach out and grip Sienna's hand. "Ready?" I ask her for the second time.

She squeezes mine tight, no snarky comment on her lips, only hard, cold resolve mingled with a hint of fear.

I connect with Air again and shout, "NOW!" pushing my voice down so that it swoops around the line of girls waiting on the lawn below. Then I release my hold on Air and switch to Earth.

I can feel the heat of Sienna's hand in mine, a comforting warmth at odds with the heavy pull in my chest from the wall. These stones are old and they've been standing for a long time. I feel as each girl who can connect with Earth joins us. I think I hear Raven's shouts of encouragement, but maybe I'm just imagining that. The wall is heavy, so very, very heavy. I try to break cracks into the stones. I can feel Sienna fighting with me, and Sil, and Amber, and all the other Earth girls, but it's so hard. As the minutes tick by, I begin to fear the wall *is* impenetrable. My shoulders ache with effort.

Lucien was wrong. My plan was doomed. I am not the leader he thought I could be. It doesn't matter how many Paladin I convinced to join us. I've led them to failure.

Don't you give up, honey, Lucien's voice whispers in the back of my mind, as crystal clear as if he were standing right next to me. *I know you can do this. I knew from the day I met you.*

I think . . . I think I love you. Ash's words ring out alongside Lucien's.

You found me, Raven murmurs, the salty tang of the ocean filling my nose.

Let's hope she's everything you think she is, Sil growls, *or we'll be living like cockroaches under a rock for the rest of our damned lives.*

My heart begins to beat faster, swelling with each new voice I hear. These people are the air I breathe and the blood I bleed. They are my courage. I will not let them down.

I know you can do this.

Lucien believed in me, always. I hold that thought close, and for the first time, I try to believe it, too. No, not try.

I *can* do this. I am stronger than I think I am.

My legs and arms are filled with the heaviness of the rocks beneath me. My torso is made of stone, my eyes tiny pebbles that grind against my skull. My heart beats out a powerful rhythm in my chest, swelling with each new thud, and I grip Sienna's hand even tighter.

The power flowing in my veins feels as ancient as this very wall as I accept it into me, as I believe in it. I spread it out to Sienna, filling both of us with a heat like fire and a drive like flowing water and the force of a windstorm. I am all of the elements, and I can sense each of the girls below me, the little lights of their magic glowing like candle flames. I pour everything I have into them, the way I did that night I saved Raven. I pour out all my love, my hope for a better life, a better world. I infuse them with my belief that they are strong enough. I am the strongest of them all and I radiate that might out to them.

We are the Paladin. We are more powerful than rock and stone. I know it now.

We are the protectors of this island.

I brush the last cobwebs of fear from my mind. I focus everything I am into this huge swath of wall, and Sienna does, too. So do the girls on the ground.

The first crack appears, and though I can't see it, I feel it in my chest. Sienna gasps, accepting this raw, pulsing power. I have never felt so strong or so alive. And I see that Lucien's original plan, of using only me to tear down this wall, never would have worked. It takes all of us, working together. No one Paladin could do this on her own.

With a great groan, a whole section of the wall begins to collapse. As hunks of rock and clouds of dust rain down, I release my hold on the element and grab one of the golden spires. The thunderous avalanche of stone drowns out the sound of my panting. Sienna covers her ears, crouching beside me.

But we're not done yet. I join with Air and scream, "AIR!" my voice swooping over the girls below.

Air is ready and eager to help. Sienna watches as we lift chunks of stone and rubble, heaving them into the remaining parts of the wall, clearing the way for the fighters standing by in the Bank. I see Indi raise her hand and then a wave of water bursts up out of the ground, pouring over the opening we made, a vast river clearing away the royalty's main defense.

The wind picks up a faint cheer rising from the other side of the wall. I release my hold on Air as the cheer grows louder. People climb through the opening, braving the water, which slows at their entrance. I catch glimpses of white fabric tied around arms.

I look for Ash but there are too many people and I'm too high up.

But I do see Sil turn and shout something. I follow her gaze—at least a hundred Regimentals are swarming out of the Auction House as a volley of gunshots rings out. Men and women fall to the ground and don't get up.

"We have to get down there," I cry. Sienna and I quickly climb down the ladder, jumping the last several feet onto the landing. Then back down the spiral staircase until we reach the first floor of prep rooms. Regimentals are everywhere, streaming down the hall to the fight. We crouch in the doorway as they rush past us. Sienna's lighter is gone, so we can't use Fire as a distraction again.

But I am one of the Paladin. And I am not afraid.

I take a deep breath and join with Air, gathering it to me in a gust so strong it blows the hats off the Regimentals' heads. Then I push it out, more forcefully than I ever have before, toppling them like dominoes, and Sienna joins with Earth so that the ground shakes and pieces of the ceiling cave in. We crash out into the hall, climbing over prostrate Regimentals, dropping more pieces of the ceiling on them with Earth and throwing them back with Air. Sienna is stronger than she was, too. It's as though bringing the wall down imbued us with more power than we ever thought we possessed.

The doors to the lawn have been blown off their hinges

and we dive through them, into the fray. The rosy façade of the Auction House is pockmarked with bullet holes. A bullet whizzes by me and I deflect it, still connected with Air, into the leg of a nearby Regimental.

Bodies litter the ground, staining the green lawn a dark, rusted red. Regimentals, Society members with white armbands, Paladin . . . I see little Rosie Kelting's body, her eyes vacant in death. Indi is swirling water this way and that, blasting the enemy out of the way, while Sil tosses huge chunks of rock with Air. Garnet has tied a band around his arm and is leading a group of rebel Regimentals fighting hand to hand with Jewel Regimentals, Raven by his side, holding her own, her body strong and fluid as she fights. I search for Ash desperately in the melee, but there are too many people and too much chaos.

Rye is a black-and-white blur. He moves so quickly it's hard to keep track of him. A few other companions are fighting with him, also dressed in tuxes, looking beautiful and terrifying. One has gotten his hands on a sword and he slashes the throat of an enemy Regimental, a bright red spray splashing across his tuxedo shirt.

More white-banded rebels pour through the opening in the wall, forcing the Regimentals back toward the Auction House.

One of them points his gun at Sil and Indi hits him with a blast of water so forceful he slams into the Auction House wall.

Suddenly, a shot rings out. It's one of so many I'm surprised I can identify it specifically through the din. I feel it, more than see it, as it speeds across the lawn toward Indi.

In a flash, I push a gust of Air toward it, but I'm too late.

I can't make sense of the way her head tilts backward, or the spray of red that explodes out of her beautiful blond hair.

She falls almost gracefully to the ground, her tall, lithe body twisting and swaying. She lands with a thump and doesn't get up.

"Indi!" I scream, pelting across the grass. Bullets are flying but my anger makes me strong and with a wave of my hand, Air sends them all shooting in another direction, scattering into the wall and Regimentals behind me.

Indi's eyes are open. She stares up at the clear blue sky with a slightly surprised expression, lips parted, hair tumbled about her face. A pool of blood begins to ooze out from the back of her head, turning her golden strands crimson.

Twenty or so Regimentals are approaching me from the Auction House. I stare them down with a fury unlike I have ever known, one that grows with every pulse of my heart.

"BURY THEM!" I shriek. My rage is white-hot fire. I join with Earth so quickly and completely that I feel as if I have been built into the very foundation of this palace, into the roots of the grass and down below, to where this island meets the ocean. I will destroy each and every one of them.

I feel Sienna join with Earth as well, then another girl, and another. Clicking into place like puzzle pieces, our power increasing as more of us are focused on the same thing. The Auction House makes a strange groaning sound. The Regimentals are bewildered. One shoots another girl connected with Earth in the chest and as she falls I feel the loss of her, her bright light snuffed out so quickly.

Bury them, I think again, and the entire south wall of the Auction House collapses.

The Regimentals have a split second to run. Not nearly enough time. The rose-colored stone crashes down on top of them, glass windows shattering, so that an entire side of the Auction House is nothing but a gaping hole. I can see the remnants of the amphitheater where I was sold. It's been broken in half, the fancy chairs and chaise lounges toppled, ruined. There is nothing left but dust and bodies.

And still the members of the Society swarm through the open wall.

Sienna runs over to where I'm kneeling beside Indi.

"No," she murmurs. She cups Indi's cheek in one hand, a remarkably tender gesture. Other girls are gathering around the bodies of their fallen friends, some crying, some rocking the dead back and forth as if it will soothe them, as if they could be soothed. I watch numbly as a squad of handsome young men splashes through the ruins of the wall, through the river Indi made only half an hour ago.

Then I hear a voice, so achingly familiar, it's the only sound that could reach me in this well of anger and despair.

"Violet!"

"Ash?" I gasp. I'm on my feet and running, pushing people out of the way to find him.

And there he is. His hair is even longer, and rough stubble covers his cheeks. He wears a black shirt, the white band standing out starkly on his arm, a rusty, dented sword in his hand. He is facing the wrong way, still calling my name, searching the crowd.

For a split second, I wonder if he'll even recognize me, if

he'll remember I look different. Then he turns and his gaze lands on me. The sword drops from his hands and falls onto the grass.

"Violet," he says, and I can't hear him but I know it's my name on his lips. He walks toward me, slowly at first, then faster, then I'm running, too, and we crash into each other in a tangle of arms and tears.

He smells like blood and sweat with a faint tinge of gunpowder. The stubble on his jaw is rough but I press my face against it, holding him tighter than I need to, feeling his chest rise and fall against mine, drinking him in, almost delirious with joy.

"You're alive," he whispers in my ear, breathless with the same elation I feel.

"I'm sorry," I whisper. "I'm so sorry, Ash. I should have believed in you."

"It's all right," he murmurs. "You're alive . . ."

And then he starts laughing, his chest heaving, and I'm laughing, too, though I don't know why.

"Ochre," I gasp, pulling away from him. "Is he—"

"He's fine," Ash says. "He and a few other boys have been confusing the Regimentals in the Bank, leading them to the wall where the Society was waiting."

Relief washes over me. My brother is safe.

Now I need to help my sister.

"Lockwood!" a companion in a tux comes running up to him, Garnet by his side. "The Regimentals have fled. Some are still inside the Auction House, but we fear others are shoring up the rest of the Jewel. We think many of the royals are dead or in their safe rooms, but we don't know how many more could be hiding in the palaces."

"Search every floor," Ash says. "Imprison as many as you can, but anyone who resists, we shoot to kill." He gazes through the opening in the wall, toward the Bank. "We need more help."

"You need Paladin," I say. I turn and call out to Sienna, Sil, and Olive. "Sil, take as many girls who can connect with Earth and Air as you can. We need the rest of this wall taken down. Sienna, get your own group together. Go with our Regimental force and search the Jewel for more royals. Olive, you gather some girls and go with the companions to clean up the Auction House."

Sienna immediately rushes off to find Sloe and a few other girls she knows. Olive claps her hands and says, "My mistress might be in there!" before forming her own little group.

"We're going in there, too," I say, turning to Ash. "I think Hazel is still inside."

Ash is staring at me with a look of wonder on his face.

"What?" I say.

He flashes me my favorite, secret smile. "You're incredible."

"You're pretty impressive yourself," I say, nodding toward the companions gathered around us. "You'll have to tell me everything once this is all over."

"Once this is all over," he agrees. "Let's get your sister."

He turns to the waiting companions, Regimentals, and Society members and begins giving quick orders. I move toward the Auction House, impatient.

"Where's Raven?" Garnet asks suddenly. I look around,

but in the swarm of bodies, I can't find my best friend anywhere. Then I look up.

I know exactly where she is heading, because we studied
these blueprints for months and the only place she made
sure she knew the location of backward and forward and
every which way was the Countess of the Stone's safe room.

"There," I say, pointing to the turret that holds the
Founding House safe rooms. "That's where she'll go."

Garnet swears under his breath. "Is she crazy?"

I look at him, then Ash.

I'm not leaving my sister abandoned in that awful
place or my best friend to face the Countess on her own.
"Let's go."

Twenty-Five

THE MAIN DOORS ARE HANGING OFF THEIR HINGES, AS IF a stampede of people blasted through without bothering to open them first.

Olive's group follows us inside, along with a crew of companions. Ash has his sword in hand again and Garnet keeps his pistol at the ready.

The main foyer is a mass of death and destruction. The fountain has broken in half, water spilling across the mosaic of tiles, carrying the blood of the fallen royals, Regimentals, and servants in delicate red swirls. We cross the foyer and I see the Electress is among them, still on the dais. She looks so young in death. There is a gaping wound across her chest.

But the Duchess and my sister are nowhere to be found. Neither is Raven.

Suddenly, there is a shriek from across the room.

"Mistress!" Olive cries. The Lady of the Stream is huddled behind the orchestra stand with a few other frightened royals. "Mistress, it's me! Oh, I found you at last."

"Get away from me!" the Lady screams, and just as Olive reaches her, arms outstretched, the Lady grabs a cornet off the platform and swings it hard. It connects with the side of Olive's head and she drops like a stone. One of Olive's friends wails. The next second, the water rises up, as her handpicked group of Paladin retaliates, blasting the royals while the companions surge forward to finish the job. Olive's face still has the remnant of a smile, her joy at seeing her mistress one last time forever etched on it.

So much death. So many lives ended today.

I turn away to face Garnet and Ash. "Raven will try to get into the Countess's safe room. And Hazel might be with the Duchess in her own safe room."

"So they'll be right next to each other," Garnet says.

I close my eyes, picturing the dotted lines and patterns that I worked so hard to memorize.

"This way," I say, and we take off, leaving the carnage behind us.

We barge through a door made of blackened wood, then down a hall lined with pretty sconces and papered in gold and white . . . when we come upon Raven, grappling with a Regimental.

Garnet lets out a strangled yell and barrels forward, knocking both Raven and her attacker to the ground. Raven rolls to one side and is on her feet as Garnet hits the Regimental in the temple with the butt of his gun. The man falls unconscious.

"What are you doing?" Garnet demands, standing up to face her. She stares him down.

"I have to," she insists.

"I know," he says. "I just don't understand why you didn't wait for us."

Raven opens her mouth as another Regimental comes running down the hall. I slam him into a wall with Air.

"The safe rooms are up this way," I say, opening a door to reveal a set of curving stone stairs. Two Regimentals are guarding it and I deflect their bullets, still connected with Air, as Ash takes them out with his sword.

As we climb, we pass other safe rooms, for lesser royals—the Founding House safe rooms are in the very top of this turret. Every room is sealed tight, keeping the royalty inside. Hopefully, these ones won't trouble us any longer, won't try to fight now that their precious Regimental force is being battered and their wall is destroyed.

We reach the top, where there are five doors, each with a crest. Scales, Royal Palace, Rose, Lake, Stone.

I focus on the House of the Lake first. Get Hazel, then help Raven.

"Stand back," I say. I gather all the air here to me, then expel it like I did to open the door with the hot handle. The door bursts open, revealing a small, beautifully decorated room behind it.

It's empty.

"She's not here," I gasp. "She's not—"

"The Countess," Raven begs. "Please."

My head spinning, I focus Air on the door with the House of the Stone's crest, a gray square crossed with two bronze hammers. The blast hits the door and rips it off its hinges. I send it flying across the room and there is a loud crash as it bursts through a window on the opposite wall.

Why do they even have *windows in these safe rooms?* I think, as the inhabitants inside cower and cough. Glass is littered around on the floor of a room as pretty as the one with the Duchess's crest.

We charge inside. The frail man I saw briefly at that last royal dinner cowers behind the door.

"P-please," he stammers, "d-don't hurt me."

"What do you want?" the Countess demands. Her eyes widen. "Garnet?"

"At your service," Garnet says, touching his cap.

"What is going on here?" Frederic demands, rising up from behind a sofa. "How did you—"

But Raven has stalked over to him and in one swift movement winds up and punches him hard in the face.

I can hear his nose break. Blood spurts out from between his fingers as he clutches his injured face, howling and stumbling backward.

Then she turns to the Countess.

"Hello, Ebony," she says.

I love my friend. I saved her life once and I would do it again in a heartbeat. But the look on her face as she stares down the Countess of the Stone is frightening. It sends a chill up my spine and makes the hairs on the back of my neck stand on end. There is a bruise swelling on Raven's left cheek and several long scratches down her neck, giving her a slightly wild appearance.

The Countess looks, very appropriately, as though she is

staring at a ghost. "You're dead," she gasps.

Raven gestures to herself. "No. I'm not."

The Countess pulls herself together quickly. "When this whole thing is over, I am going to have you dismembered, 192."

"My name," Raven says, carefully enunciating each word, "is Raven Stirling. And your time of torture and mutilation and cruelty is at an end."

I see Frederic move out of the corner of my eye and am about to cry out a warning. Garnet moves with me, raising his pistol, but Raven is faster than both of us, almost as if she anticipated this. She ducks and whirls, so that where once he was behind her, now she is behind him.

She grips his head between her hands. "Oh, Frederic," she says. "I have been thinking about this reunion for such a very long time."

Then with a sharp twist, she snaps his neck. He crumples to the floor like a rag doll, his head bent at an odd angle.

"No!" the Countess shrieks.

Raven steps over his corpse without giving it a second glance.

The Countess glares at her. "You don't honestly think you'll win this, do you?" She looks around the room. "What is your revolution made of, a handful of disgruntled servants, disgraced companions, and farmworkers? And one pathetic royal?"

"Have you looked out that window?" Raven says. "Your forces are scattered. Your wall is broken. The circles will be integrated. The people of this city will take it back from you tyrants."

"The people of this city would be lost if it weren't for the royalty," the Countess says. "They need us to survive."

"No," Raven says. "We don't." She touches her scalp, feeling each scar one by one. "You gave me such a gift, Ebony. And you didn't even realize it."

"Do not call me by my given name," the Countess snarls. Raven ignores her.

"I can hear things now, you see. I know you are afraid. More afraid than you were that time your mother starved you for a week because you still hadn't lost weight. She locked you in the dungeon and wouldn't let you out. You cried yourself to sleep every night."

There is an evil gleam in Raven's eyes at the look of terror on the Countess's face. "Oh yes. I've heard your secrets. I know your thoughts. You can't go digging around in someone's brain and not expect there to be repercussions. Especially not a Paladin brain." The Countess's brow furrows and Raven cocks her head.

"That's what we are," she says. "Not surrogates. Not slaves. But you knew, didn't you? That we were different. You were smart to fear us. Of course, you wouldn't call it fear. You called it, what . . . curiosity? Experimentation? But deep down, you knew there was something about us, something about the Auguries, that was dangerous if unleashed." She takes another step closer.

The Countess stumbles back toward the broken window. "I am not afraid of you."

"Yes you are," Raven says, her voice as deadly as a snake's hiss. "And you should be."

Another step forward for Raven. Another step back for the Countess.

Then she closes the distance between them in a flash. The Countess's eyes widen in surprise, her large mouth dropping open as Raven shoves her out the window. She disappears with a shriek, falling to crash into the ground far below.

The room is silent except for the whimpering of the Count. Raven stands in the window, staring at the spot where the Countess vanished, her chest heaving.

"She's gone," she whispers to no one, or maybe to herself, confirming it aloud so she can truly believe it's real. Her knees give out and she falters. Garnet is by her side in an instant, sweeping her into his arms.

"She's gone," Raven sobs into his chest.

"She is," he murmurs into her hair. "She can't hurt you anymore. She can't hurt anyone ever again."

Raven takes a deep, shuddering breath and looks up into his eyes. They stare at each other for a long moment. Garnet gently traces a line around the bruise on her cheek with his finger. It's such a deeply personal thing to witness, I have to look away, out the door to where the empty safe room for the House of the Lake reminds me this day isn't over yet.

"The Duchess still has Hazel," I say.

Ash nods. "Where would they go?" he asks. "To the palace of the Lake? One of the palaces nearby?"

"No," Garnet says with grim resignation. "I bet I know exactly where she's gone. Follow me."

We run back down the stairs, into the bloody foyer, and out the ruined front doors.

"This way," Garnet says, pointing to where lines of motorcars wait to pick up royals who are never leaving this Auction House again.

We sprint to a car, Garnet and Raven in the front, Ash and I in the backseat. Garnet rips out the ignition and plays with the wires until the engine roars to life. We speed through the mostly empty streets of the Jewel, catching glimpses of befuddled servants and bursts of fighting among Regimentals and Society members. Many of the palaces, I note, are being looted, their gates broken down, their windows smashed.

"Where are we going?" Raven asks.

Suddenly, the earth shakes beneath us, the motorcar skidding on the paved road. In the distance, smoke and dust rise up; then a few hunks of rubble are lobbed through the air.

"Sil," I say with satisfaction, and Ash's fingers close around mine.

"You can bring them all down," he says. "Every wall in this city. Lucien will be so proud."

My throat closes up.

"Lucien's dead," I say. Ash looks confused for a second, like those two words don't make sense together. Then his lips form a thin line and he blinks very fast.

"Oh," is all he says.

"Garnet, where are we going?" Raven demands again.

"The Royal Palace," Garnet says through gritted teeth.

The home the Duchess always wanted but was just out of reach. The place she felt she was destined to have as her own.

"Of course," I murmur.

Twenty-Six

GARNET SLAMS THE ACCELERATOR DOWN AND WE PEEL through the streets.

The palaces whip by until we are in the forest, a blur of greens and browns, then past the topiary, until finally, he pulls up in front of the fountain of trumpeting boys.

The doors of the Royal Palace are open. When we get inside, the halls are empty.

"I'll bet my entire inheritance she's gone to the throne room," Garnet says.

"Which way?" I ask, and he takes off down the opulent main hallway. We pass the ballroom where I played cello at the Exetor's Ball, and I glimpse the garden where I spoke to Ash in the gazebo that same night, before we make a sharp left.

The sound of voices stops us in our tracks. Garnet holds up a hand and we creep to the end of the hall, the plush carpet muffling our footsteps. He peers around the corner, then pulls his head back quickly.

"Seven Reg," he mouths. Ash withdraws his sword as Garnet unholsters his gun. Raven crouches into a fighting stance. I join with Air, and for one second, I allow myself to revel in the blissful freedom of the element.

Then I focus it, calling the wind to me from the hundred halls in this palace, and it comes whistling and shrieking. Garnet, Ash, and Raven whirl around the corner as I send it flying at the Regimentals.

What happens next is a blur. Crunches and shouts and thuds, Ash's sword sings through the air, guns go off, and all the while I fill the room with wind so fierce and biting it makes my own eyes burn and water.

When I hear Ash shout, "Stop!" I release my hold on the element and everything settles. Regimentals are splayed out everywhere, some dead, some only unconscious. The room has an arched ceiling painted with murals depicting the four seasons, and stained-glass windows as tall as Garnet, their jewel tones spilling across the black-and-white tile floor. In the center of the room is a dais on which sit two immense, opulent thrones. The arms are scaled and end in snake heads with rubies for eyes. Enormous golden wings spread out from either side of each throne, and their seats are covered in crimson velvet.

The Duchess sits in one, her skirts tangled about her legs, looking utterly nonplussed at this latest development. Her fingers grip the snakes like claws when she sees her son.

"Garnet?" she gasps. Hazel is on the floor beside her,

still leashed. Her face lights up when she sees me. Cora and Carnelian are behind her—Cora gapes at Garnet, but Carnelian only has eyes for Ash.

"Hello, Mother," he says, as if they've just sat down to breakfast. "Not your typical Auction Day, is it?"

"You . . . you're with *them*?" The Duchess spits out the word. Her gaze lands on Raven, then Ash, then me. "Fighting with whores and servants?"

"You mean fighting alongside human beings?" Garnet says. "Yes, Mother. I am."

The Duchess sneers. "I shouldn't be surprised. You're more like your father than you ever were like me."

Garnet pretends to consider for a moment. "I'll take that as a compliment."

"You'd rather be a weakling?"

"Better a weakling than a murderer," I say, stepping forward.

The Duchess stands and I see she holds a dagger in one hand, presumably the same one the Exetor gave her. Its handle is studded with gemstones, its blade engraved in swirling lines of silver. "I will not suffer a mere lady-in-waiting to speak to me in such a manner. When this ridiculous rebellion is over, I will have your tongue cut out. I will have your head on a spike. I will—"

"You will have nothing," I say, walking forward slowly. "You have no power in this city. And I am no *mere lady-in-waiting*."

I will not be afraid of her anymore.

And she will see me for who I truly am.

Once to see it as it is. Twice to see it in your mind.

Thrice to bend it to your will.

My scalp tingles as my hair turns from blond to black. My nose aches as it returns to its normal size, my forehead shrinking. I save my eyes for last. They burn like hot embers sizzling in my skull, but I force myself to keep them open while they revert back to their natural violet. I want to see the Duchess's face as she realizes it's me.

I am not disappointed.

Her mouth falls open. The dagger clatters to the floor, just out of Hazel's reach—she makes a grab for it but the chain holds her back. The Duchess snatches the dagger away and grabs Hazel by the hair, yanking her upright and pressing the blade against her throat.

"Stay back," she says.

"Violet," Hazel croaks.

"You will *not* hurt her," I hiss. I consider joining with Air and throwing the Duchess off the dais, but that could end in Hazel with her throat cut.

"So," the Duchess says, looking more comfortable now that she's got my sister's life to hold over me, "you have returned. I wondered if you would. That's part of the reason I took her in the first place. I thought perhaps you might get caught trying to save her." She raises one eyebrow. "You disguised yourself well, I'll give you that."

Ash, Raven, and Garnet have formed a loose half circle around me. Cora watches my every step eagerly, waiting for her own revenge.

"And the rest of the reason?" I ask.

The Duchess shrugs. "Well, I was hoping she'd have your abilities, of course, but it became evident rather quickly that she was not the surrogate you were. A child was not possible." Something flickers in her eyes—regret maybe?—but it vanishes before I can make sense of it.

She pulls Hazel's head back farther. "When you escaped with the whore, I thought I was finished. I thought I would never get the thing I truly wanted, for my daughter to rule as I should have. But . . . what is that quaint saying you have in the lower circles? When all you have left is lemons, make lemonade? I saw an opportunity. Why give a child the life that should have been mine? The Electress is so simple and stupid, so easy to manipulate. Why not use that to my advantage? After all, she did such a lovely job of shouting to anyone and everyone in the Jewel about how she hated me, how she did not wish a match with my House. She was jealous. Jealousy is a petty emotion. It pollutes the mind. It makes you rash. Because she had everything and she did not *appreciate it.* Even worse, she did not deserve it in the first place."

"So you stole my sister and went over the Electress's head to make a match with the Exetor?"

"Well deduced," the Duchess says with a sneer. "And once Onyx realized there was a chance to be together again . . . well, we would do anything for each other. Even kill his Bank-trash wife. That is the depth of our love."

"Where is he, then?" I ask, gesturing around. "It looks like he's abandoned you."

"Oh no," the Duchess says. "He will never abandon me again."

Something in her tone makes me uncomfortable. Cora looks unnerved as well—she glances about the room, but it's empty except for the eight of us.

"But he did once," I say, trying to find a weak spot. My eyes flicker to the dagger still pressed to Hazel's neck. "He left you. He married the Electress."

"Don't speak as if you know anything about him," the Duchess snaps. "He never chose to leave me. We were forced apart." She raises her head proudly. "We love each other. More than any two people have ever loved before. We made something beautiful together and they took it, they ripped it from me even as I begged them not to. They called it a monster, the life that was growing inside me." There is a wild look in her eyes. "It's not fair!" she cries. "You poor, stupid, useless surrogates can bear a child and I cannot."

I am stunned. The Duchess was *pregnant?* Royal women are sterilized upon marriage, but clearly, the Duchess and Exetor slept together before that. I hear a gasp from Garnet. Even Cora seems shocked. It would have ruined the Duchess's House forever if the news got out.

Her eyes are bright with tears even as her hands shake with anger. A thick drop of blood oozes from the point of the blade and drips down Hazel's neck.

"What a little fool I was," the Duchess whispers. "To think they'd let me keep it."

For a moment, I can see her, the Duchess, young and in love. Who might she have grown into, had things gone differently?

"I'm sorry that happened to you," I say. Carnelian tears her eyes away from Ash to give me a shocked look. It exactly mirrors the expression on the Duchess's face, and for the first time since I've known them, I can see that they are related.

The Duchess's shock melts away to scorn. "I don't need your pity," she says. "Nor do I want it."

"That's the difference between us," I say. "You see pity. You see weakness. I see compassion. I see strength. But when *you* suffer, you feel you must make others suffer around you. You allowed this tragedy to turn you into something cold and cruel. You murdered Dahlia, a girl whose name you didn't even know, who had done nothing to you. You poisoned her out of spite. You killed Annabelle for no reason except to punish me. You took away a beautiful life on a whim, to make a point. You might have become something great, Pearl," I say, taking a note from Raven's book and addressing the Duchess as an equal, "and instead you are just another petty, sniping royal."

"She is infinitely more than that," a low voice says. The Exetor steps out of the shadows as his guard files into the room, marching in unison, their red jackets matching the seats of the thrones.

"Onyx," the Duchess says with relief. "I was wondering where you were."

No less than twenty Regimentals surround us, all carrying rifles.

We are trapped.

~ Twenty-Seven ~

THE EXETOR SAUNTERS OVER TO KISS THE DUCHESS ON the cheek, ignoring Hazel struggling between them.

"I was going to send these men out into the city," he says, "but then I heard voices and thought I should check on you."

"I'm so glad you did, my darling. You remember my old surrogate, 197. She's come back to rescue her sister."

"Just as you suspected," the Exetor says. His gaze lands on Garnet. "What is he doing here?"

"He's with them," the Duchess says. "Always such a disappointment."

The Exetor traces the line of the Duchess's jaw with a finger. "You deserved better," he says.

They don't even look at us. Garnet's lone pistol is nothing against all those rifles. Neither is Ash's sword.

"So," the Duchess says, turning to me, "how long were you working with the eunuch?"

My brain is spinning furiously, trying to come up with a solution to get us out of this. The best thing to do is keep her talking while I figure out a plan.

"He had a name," I say.

"I'm fully aware of Lucien's name, I simply don't—"

"He had a name and it wasn't Lucien. Do you even understand why all of this is happening?" I gesture out a window depicting a sunset in a blaze of color. "Can you even conceive of what you have done to the people of this city? To the island itself?"

The Duchess's smile is icy. "You are a foolish little girl. This island would be nothing without us. We made it great. We created something where there was nothing before."

"There wasn't nothing," I say. "There were people here, and your ancestors, the ones you are so proud of, killed them all. Or at least, they thought they did."

The Duchess stiffens and the Exetor looks confused.

"What is she talking about?" he asks.

"I have no idea," the Duchess replies.

It's my turn to smile. "What did you think Lucien was doing in your library? Catching up on royal history? You people. You haven't changed at all. Taking whatever you want. Did you really think you killed all the Paladin?"

"All the what?" Carnelian asks, but no one answers her.

"How do you know about that?" the Duchess hisses.

"Because I am one of them," I say. "Who do you think

brought that wall down? You have no idea what I'm capable of."

"Prove it, then." The Duchess yanks Hazel's head back farther so that she cries out in pain. "All I've seen from you thus far is a little bit of wind. Prove your strength. Kill me now, if you can."

I think about it. I think about the ceiling collapsing on her head, Air snapping her neck, drowning her in the water I can sense in a garden just outside.

But I am not the Duchess. I do not solve my problems the way she does, with violence and blood.

"I could," I say carefully, "but I won't."

The Duchess laughs, a high, echoing laugh. "*I could but I won't,*" she says, mimicking me. "Oh, that is rich."

The Exetor joins in. Cora is livid. She takes a step forward.

"You promised you would kill her!" she cries.

"I'm sorry," I say, at the same time the Duchess says, "I beg your pardon?"

"You murdered my daughter," Cora cries, whirling around to face her mistress. "Did you think I wouldn't care? Did you honestly believe I felt nothing for her?"

The Duchess levels Cora with one look. The lady-in-waiting withers. "I should have drowned that runt when she was born," the Duchess says. "You were lucky you got to know her at all."

"Can you even hear yourself, Mother?" Garnet says. "Annabelle was . . . she was the best person in that entire palace. She was wholly innocent. She was *good.*"

"No one is wholly innocent," the Duchess says. "If you

believe that, you are even more stupid than I thought." Her eyes flash to something behind me. "Let's start with the companion, shall we?"

We have all been so focused on what's in front of us, that none of us have looked back. I whirl around now, just as three of the Exetor's guard descend on Ash, two grabbing his arms and throwing his sword aside as another holds a gun to his temple.

"No!" Carnelian and I scream together.

The Regimental holding the gun has a broad, ugly face and a gold tooth that glints at me when he smiles. He has a brutish look, as if he enjoys hurting people.

Ash keeps his eyes trained on mine and mouths one word. *Hazel.*

I know what he means but I can't. I can't make that choice. His eyes drink me in as if it's the last time. As if he'll never see me again.

"Take me!" Carnelian offers. "Kill me instead. Please! Just don't hurt him."

It is such a brave statement. I tear my gaze away from Ash to look at her face, stricken with fear but sincere. She would truly die for Ash. I can't believe I once thought her annoying, small-minded. I hated her for all the wrong reasons.

"Carnelian, stop, you're embarrassing yourself." The Duchess doesn't even spare her niece a glance. She looks gleeful at this turn of events. More blood drips down Hazel's neck. "What could anyone possibly gain from that? Alive or dead, you are nothing to me. This companion risked his own life to be with a surrogate. Do you see that? He *does not love you*. Even your own mother preferred death to your company. What will it take for you to grasp the concept that *no one wants you?*"

Even I feel the sting of her words, how they cut right to Carnelian's core, a place that has been slashed by grief and cruelty a hundred times over.

Quick as lightning, I join with Air. It's like it's been waiting for my call.

The Duchess gives me one last disdainful glance. "Kill them all," she says in a bored tone, but I am ready and I will not let her hurt me or my friends.

The rifles go off almost in unison, filling the room with sharp pops.

You can do this, Lucien whispers in my ear. *I believe in you.*

I feel every single bullet slicing through the air in this room and I sweep them upward, circling them around the ceiling like a swarm of flies.

Hazel slams her foot down on the Duchess's instep, causing the Duchess to let out a strangled howl and release her. The dagger falls off the dais.

I raise my hands. The Regimentals are all staring at the bullets in a daze of wonder and confusion. Slicing my hands through the air, I send the bullets flying back toward their owners, dropping the Regimentals one by one. One I send through the chain binding my sister to the Duchess—it snaps in two.

I sense, rather than see, the ugly Regimental fire at me. I hear Ash cry out, and then there's a crunch behind me, and I send the bullet shooting away from me, not caring where it lands, as Hazel plummets into my arms.

"You're safe now," I say as she sobs against my shoulder. "I've got you. You're safe."

"NO!" The scream that issues from the Duchess's throat is wild, guttural, like the cry of a dying animal. And I see why—the last bullet I sent astray went right through the Exetor's chest.

She gathers him up in her arms, tears streaming down her cheeks. "Onyx, no, no, please . . ."

Blood trickles from his mouth. "Pearl," he says, reaching up to touch her cheek. Then his hand falls, limp and lifeless, and his head rolls to one side. The Duchess falls over him, clutching his body. Then her head whips up.

"I will kill you slowly for this," she says. She lays the Exetor gently on the floor and rises to face me. I push Hazel behind my back and prepare to join with Earth, to open up the ground beneath her feet. "Do you understand me? I will ki—"

Then she gasps, her back arching. A horrible, choking sound comes out of her throat. Red begins to seep through her blue dress, staining it, changing its color like an Augury.

Carnelian stands behind her. In one swift movement, she pulls the dagger out of the Duchess's back and holds it up triumphantly. She must have picked it up when the Duchess dropped it.

"You're such a disappointment, Carnelian," Carnelian hisses in a mockery of the Duchess's voice, stabbing the dagger into her back again. "No one cares what you have to say, Carnelian." The dagger hits its mark for a third time. "No one loves you, no one loves you . . ." She stabs the Duchess

again and again and I can only watch, stunned and horri-
fied.

The Duchess falls to the floor beside the Exetor. Carnelian looks like she's about to keep stabbing her, when Ash
rushes over. He holds her wrist gently. Carnelian is shaking.

"It's all right," he murmurs. "You can let it go now.
She's gone. It's all right."

She blinks and looks at him. "She . . . she was so . . . I
had to . . ."

"I know," he says. The dagger clatters to the floor. She
falls into him, sobbing, and he holds her tight. Our eyes
meet over the crown of her head. The scene does not make
me jealous as it once would.

Hazel is gripping my arm and I turn to face her.

"Let's get this stuff off of you," I say. Raven helps me
with the leash and I rip the veil off her face. Garnet has gone
over to help Cora. Hazel steps out of her high heels so she
is her normal height again and together we unstrap the fake
belly from over her stomach. She kicks it away viciously.

"Is it over?" she asks.

"It's over," I say. She collapses into me and we hold each
other tight.

"All those things you did," she says, pulling away to
look up at me. "With the wind and the bullets and . . ." She
gazes around the room, dazed. "You told me you could do
things but . . ."

"You can do those things, too," I say.

Hazel blinks. "I can?"

I smile. "This is Raven," I say. "She's my best friend. She
can show you, if you want."

"You want me to take her to the cliff now?" Raven asks.

"What?" Hazel asks.

"Maybe not right this second," I say. "Maybe it's too soon. Hazel needs to rest. She—"

"I've been doing nothing but rest for months," Hazel says, stepping back and crossing her arms over her chest. "Show me whatever it is. I can handle it."

My chest swells with pride. "I know you can," I say. "Come on."

We leave the throne room and exit out into a garden filled with butterflies and rosebushes. The sun is molten gold in a perfect blue sky. I feel an overwhelming sense of exuberance. We did it.

Raven grips my hand as I take Hazel's.

"What are we doing?" she asks.

"We're going to show you who you really are," I say. I've said it so many times before, at Southgate, Westgate, at all the holding facilities. I've given girls something to believe in, showed them what they were capable of.

But it's never meant as much to me as it does now.

The cliff is perfect when we arrive.

The sky mirrors our sky, cloudless and bright blue. The air is warm and bees buzz lazily around the monument. The trees are lush and green, and the gentle roar of the ocean is soothing below. How I long to see the true ocean.

I turn to my sister. She stares around, captivated by the beauty and wonder of this place. Her violet eyes are filled with awe.

I sigh.

Change her back, I whisper silently to this space, to my

ancestors who linger just beyond, in a place between living and dead. *Please.*

Change her back, Raven whispers beside me. Our pleas drift into the air and swirl around the silvery blue monument and it's as if I can hear a hundred voices taking up the cry.

Change her back, change her back . . .

Hazel has run to the edge of the cliff, gazing out across the ocean. Suddenly, she grabs her face, dropping to her knees. I start to run toward her but Raven stops me, keeping a tight grip on my hand. Hazel rocks back and forth for a few moments, then goes still.

When she turns back to me, my heart leaps to my throat, and if I could make a sound, cry out in this place, I would.

The magic of this cliff has worked. The Paladin have returned her to who she once was. Whatever the doctor did was no match for the power that exists here.

Hazel's face is the one I remember, the one I grew up with. Her eyes are back to their original color, her nose and mouth and cheeks all the same as they used to be. She stares the same wide-eyed stare I've seen on the faces of so many girls now. Raven and I join her at the edge of the cliff. We look out at the ocean, letting the salty tang fill our nostrils, and I feel a sense of wonder, of curiosity. I feel as if I am a very small part of something so large, it cannot be contained in one island, one city.

I wonder what is out there.

Me too, Raven thinks. *Want to find out?*

Yes, I think back. *But there is something I have to do first.*

Twenty-Eight

WHEN WE RETURN FROM THE CLIFF, WE FIND THAT Hazel's flowers are white, like mine were.

She bends down and they grow taller, reaching toward her fingertips, their cheery faces brushing her skin before withering to die, even as new ones grow to take their place.

"What do you feel?" I ask, wondering which elements she can connect with.

"Everything," she whispers. "I can feel the grass growing and hear the wind whispering and there's something shimmery and flowy, like . . . like water."

I clasp her shoulders in my hands. "Stay out here for a little while. Everything is going to be different from now on. Enjoy this moment. It's the beginning of your new life."

In so many ways, I think. It's a new city. It's a new world.

I don't want to leave my sister but there's something I have to do. Or, more accurately, a place I need to visit.

I turn to Raven, but she's a step ahead of me. The benefit of having a best friend who can sometimes read your thoughts.

"Garnet and I will stay with her," she says. "Go."

I wonder if she knows where I'm going, or just that I need to go. Either way, I smile and embrace her, squeezing her tight. "We did it," I whisper.

"We did," she whispers back. Hazel has sunk down to the grass and is staring at a rosebush with a look of wonder on her face. A bud blossoms suddenly, a swirl of color unfolding as its petals grow. I leave her to the awe of nature and head inside.

Garnet and Cora have moved the Duchess's and Exetor's bodies aside and are stacking the rifles up in a pile in the center of the room. Carnelian sits on the edge of the dais beside Ash, still looking shell-shocked.

Ash stands as I enter.

I sway a little on my feet, suddenly overwhelmingly tired. But this day isn't over yet.

"Hazel?" he says, coming over to grip my elbow.

"She's fine." I keep my eyes on his, not wanting to look at the bodies on the floor. "I have to . . . I have to go someplace. In this palace. A secret place. I have to . . ."

I don't know what I have to do. All I know is that I want to go back to Lucien's workshop. I don't need to destroy it anymore, now that the Society has won. But I want to see that there is still some piece of him left in this world.

Ash's arm snakes around my waist, as his lips press against my temple.

"Wherever you need to go," he says. "I'll be with you."

We leave the throne room and walk back down the empty halls to the front doors, hand in hand. I take a right and am about to lead him to the antechamber when I stop.

"I want you to see," I say to him, the guilt surging up in a hot wave inside my chest. "I want you to see the awful thing I did."

I open the door to the room of mirrors. Ash gasps and steps inside, his face alight with astonishment, fractured in the broken mirrors. Some have been removed so there are blank spaces, as if servants stopped cleaning up halfway through. But there are still plenty of keys lining these walls.

"You did this?" he asks.

"The night before the Auction. There was a royal dinner and I came with Carnelian. I was . . . I was mad, frustrated, ready for this to be over. I didn't think anyone would see it. There are hundreds of rooms in this palace. I thought I was being so clever."

My throat swells up and I stop talking. I wasn't being clever. I was being foolish and Lucien lost his life because of it.

Ash looks at me as though he can read my thoughts, my guilt printed clearly on my face. "So what should your punishment be?"

"I don't know," I murmur. I stare at myself in an oval mirror. One of my eyes is fractured, my mouth a diagonal slash.

Ash tucks a stray lock of hair behind my ear and cups my face in his hands. "Do you really think Lucien would want you punished for this? Don't you think he'd be proud? You made his mark on the place where he was enslaved for most of his life."

"I killed him," I croak.

"No," Ash says firmly. "The royalty killed him." I can see he knows I don't believe him. "You made a choice, Violet, one that had consequences. Like saving me. Like saving Raven. Not all choices result in what we want, or even what we expect. But what you've done, what Lucien has done, what me and Raven and Garnet and everyone at the White Rose and everyone in the Society has been trying to do, is give everybody, no matter their station or their status, a chance at making choices for themselves. Some things are bigger than just one person." He enfolds me in his arms and whispers into my ear. "But that doesn't mean it doesn't hurt. To lose him. To feel pain. And that's okay. Just . . . don't hate yourself for it."

A fat tears drips down my cheek and bleeds into the fabric of his shirt.

"Come with me," I whisper.

I open the picture of the dog in the antechamber and climb through the hole to the staircase. Ash doesn't ask any questions, he just follows after me, and we climb the stairs. Lucien has left markings, as he said, white Xs that tell me where to turn and which halls to take. After what feels like an hour, we are standing outside the door to his room.

I open it with trembling hands. Lucien's bedroom is a mess. This must have been where he was when he was arrested. Blankets and clothes are scattered about and the dresser has been knocked over. But the closet is untouched, hiding the workshop behind it.

It's only a few feet away, but it may as well be a mile. It may as well be on another planet.

My legs have turned to stone and melted into the floor. I can't move. I can barely breathe.

Ash has no idea what this place is, what it could mean, and yet he threads his fingers through mine, not hesitating to stand by my side. And in that moment, I know that while I may have lost Lucien, the effects he has had, on me, on my life, on my friends and the people I love, will last forever.

Keeping Ash's hand firmly in my grasp, I take a step forward. Then another. Then I'm walking—no, almost running to the closet. I throw the doors open, push aside the lady-in-waiting gowns, and pull the arcana out of my hair. I press it into the indentation in the door's center.

It opens with a click. I stand on the threshold, my skin tingling. The lights flicker on inside.

"Violet?" Ash asks again.

"Wait here," I say. "Please."

I open the door wide and leave Ash behind, knowing he'll listen to me, knowing that even if he doesn't understand why, he trusts that I'm asking him for what I need.

I step into Lucien's workroom and the memory hits me like a blow to the stomach. The clocks on the wall tick casually, unaware that their owner is never returning. The books, the papers, the beakers . . . all of it is as it was that day Lucien showed this place to me, back when I was Imogen and Coral was still alive.

My gaze lands on the easel in the corner and I let out a

tiny cry, somewhere between a gasp and a sob. The picture Lucien was painting, the one that was just the outline of a girl. The one I thought was of Azalea.

It's me.

Lucien has drawn my face in perfect detail, right down to the little point of my chin. I'm looking slightly to the left, smiling in a way that is at once sweet and mischievous, like perhaps I'm about to do something reckless. My hair tumbles over my shoulders, and my eyes . . . he got their color just right. I see tubes of various shades of purple scattered across his worktable.

I gaze at it, guilt and grief and love warring inside me. The tears are falling thick and fast and I don't bother to wipe them away. My head spins and my legs weaken, so that the room swirls in my vision and I know I'm about to collapse.

A pair of strong arms grabs me, pulling me upright. Ash's familiar scent is like its own embrace, but it only makes me cry harder. The weight of this whole day crushes me and I sob until there is nothing left to cry. Ash doesn't say a word. He just lets me get it out.

Finally, I straighten up, gulping for air. I smile at him blearily and he wipes the tears from my cheeks.

"This place is . . . incredible," he says. "And so very *him*."

I swallow hard. My hands snake down his arms, gripping his wrists. I look around the room one more time. "He told me to destroy it. If we lost. He made me promise."

"Well," Ash says. "I'm glad that's one promise you don't have to keep."

The exhaustion hits me again, and suddenly all I want is to be with my sister.

"Let's go," I say. But as we turn to leave, my eye lands on something shiny. The copper spring that Lucien was toying with when he talked to me about his wall of clocks, the one he unwound and tossed aside on the table. I pick it up and slip it into my pocket.

Then I take my arcana out of the door, and Ash and I and walk back to join our friends and my family.

Twenty-Nine

WE BURY OUR DEAD THE NEXT DAY.

The Royal Palace has become the new headquarters for the Society of the Black Key. People started filtering in yesterday at sunset—servants, Society members, friendly Regimentals, Paladin. Sil came with her group after "making neat work of that damned wall," as she put it. Sienna followed later, and I was so relieved to see her I hugged her tight and she actually hugged me back.

Ochre arrives in the morning with a group of boys around his age, and Hazel and I tackle him, falling to the ground in a mess of hugs and laughter and tears.

"Why didn't you tell me about the Society?" Hazel asks, punching him in the arm.

"I did!" Ochre protests, holding up his hands to block her. "You didn't believe me."

"Wait till you see what I can do," Hazel brags.

"Is it like what Violet can do with water and stuff?"

"When did you see that?"

"I've been part of the Society for ages, Hazel," he says importantly.

"Stop it, you two," I say with a wide grin, wrapping my arms around both their shoulders. "I'm just happy we're all together again."

There is a meeting that night about what to do with the remaining royals. Many, as Lucien had said, want executions across the board. Others, like Sil, insist the royals should pay with hard labor.

Finally, an agreement is reached. A tribunal will be set up, with representatives from each circle present, and the royalty will be judged for their crimes.

I sit apart from the main crowd, with Ash, Raven, Garnet, Ochre, and Hazel, an idea chewing at the edges of my mind.

I get up and motion to Sil to follow me. She does, without question, and I take her to Lucien's workshop.

"Well," she says after several long moments of silence. She shakes her head. "If anyone were to have a place like this, it would be him."

"I think maybe there are things here that could help the Society. Or the new government, whatever it will be called." I run my fingers across the prototype of Annabelle's slate. When I glance up, Sil is looking at me strangely.

"You know," she says, walking over to the bookshelves

and peering at the various titles. "I've known Lucien for almost five years. The first day I met him, I blew him off my porch with Air."

"You did?" I say.

"What would you do if a lady-in-waiting showed up at your front door? In a place you thought no one could find?" Sil says, but her mocking is gentle. "He didn't like me much after that. Of course, we had to get along, for Azalea's sake."

"I know," I say.

"But Azalea never brought us together the way you did," Sil says. I stare at her, dumbstruck, but she's refusing to look at me, flipping through an old, leather-bound tome. "I saw a change in Lucien, even before I met you myself. The way he used to talk about you . . . if I heard one more damned Violet story, whether he was proud or worried or just bothering me with that arcana to complain about you . . ." She chuckles at the book. I'm having difficulty breathing. "He'd lived in that circle for so long. I don't think he realized how much it had affected him, even if he never wanted it to. But you did. You held up a mirror and reminded him that he was just as worthy of saving as the surrogates."

"Of course he was," I whisper.

"You say that like it's an easy thing to believe," she says with a snort. "And then he showed up at my door again, with not one but two surrogates, a companion, and a royal." Sil lets out an exasperated sigh. "I was so mad. Well, you know, you were there. That wasn't the plan. Saving those people, a pregnant surrogate, a companion, it was such a risk. Lucien and I, we were so wrapped up in what we were supposed to be doing, we forgot *why* we were doing it. I thought it was just revenge—that's all I wanted at first, and I think he did, too. Revenge for Azalea. Blood for blood."

She finally meets my gaze. Her eyes are red and glassy. "We were wrong. You showed us what really mattered. You changed us both. I wish I could make you see that, Violet." She turns away, wiping her nose with her sleeve. "He was a fool, to be sure. But you can't say he didn't love you."

I sink into the armchair. Sil quickly busies herself with examining papers and looking at beakers and saying things that don't make sense to me, like, "The Apothecary will be very interested in this," or "Got to make sure the Feroner gets a look at these."

Lucien is gone. The revolution is over. It's time for me to exercise the freedom we fought so hard for.

"Sil?" I say hesitantly.

"Mph?" she replies, not looking up from a beaker filled with simmering blue liquid.

"I . . . I want to leave. There's something I want to do. I know there's so much work to do here, and things to figure out, but . . ."

She gives me her most penetrating stare.

"Spit it out," she says.

"I want to see the ocean." It's been tugging at my heart, the desire to see over the Great Wall, to see what's out there. To get to the edge of this little piece of my world and climb the wall the royalty built. To see what hasn't been seen in centuries.

Sil's pale eyes soften with understanding. "You do what you have to," she says, patting me on the shoulder, before turning back to Lucien's table.

* * *

WE BURY THE FALLEN IN THE LAWNS SURROUNDING THE
Auction House, the Paladin burying our own separately,
under a little copse of trees.

Twenty-five in all. Indi, Olive, little Rosie Kelting . . .
Ginger died, too. As we cover them with earth, a myriad of
flowers grow up over their graves, each girl's flowers sprout-
ing from the earth one last time. I see Indi's lemon-yellow
blossoms entwine with Olive's dark green ones.

"I want to see the ocean," I say to Raven.

She grins at me. "So do I. We're all coming with you."

"We?" I ask, startled. She glances over to where Ash and
Garnet stand, a little apart, watching this private funeral
from a respectable distance.

Raven sighs dramatically. "If we left without them,
they'd just follow after us anyway." She throws an arm
around my shoulder. "When do you want to leave?"

IT'S ANOTHER DAY BEFORE WE ARE READY TO SET OUT.

I expect Hazel and Ochre to come, to be eager to go
home to the Marsh, but to my surprise, they both staunchly
refuse.

"I can't go back," Hazel says. "Everything is different
now. I . . . I *mean* something. I matter here. I can't go back
to the Marsh like everything is the same because it's not.
I'm not."

"Yeah," Ochre agrees. "Besides, the Society needs me."

Stubborn, Lucien's voice whispers.

Just like me, I think.

"All right," I say. I won't argue with them. They need to

make their own choices now.

"Be safe," Sienna says.

"Don't do anything stupid," Sil adds. "It's still dangerous out there. There's fighting in the lower circles."

"I wouldn't worry about us, Sil," Garnet says cheerfully, clapping her on the back. "Don't you know we've got the most powerful Paladin in recent history as our guide?"

"Second most powerful," Sil grumbles, and we all laugh.

We leave through the ruined south part of the wall, the one by the Auction House. It takes us the better part of the day to make it across the Bank, which has surrendered rather quickly to the fall of the royalty, though there's a hefty amount of destruction all around us. Many stores have been looted or burned.

When we reach the wall, Garnet glances at me. "Can you get us through?" he asks.

"Of course she can," Ash says, and I grin.

I join with Earth and welcome the thick, mighty sense of being rooted in something deep and ancient. I feel the stones of these walls, greeting them like old friends, and when they begin to break apart, I fill up with a blissful power. This one isn't nearly as thick as the wall that surrounded the Jewel. I make only a narrow fissure, just wide enough for us to climb through.

The scene that meets our eyes is one of widespread devastation. Maybe because there were more things to explode in the Smoke. Factories have been leveled. There are bodies in the streets and constant outbreaks of fighting.

I'm grateful when we reach the wall to the Farm. At first, this circle seems untouched by the violence. Until we come across the first burned-out farmhouse, the fields sur-rounding it dead and blackened. It takes several days to cross the Farm.

We reach the wall to the Marsh late at night. My feet are sore and my back aches, but when I draw on Earth, my strength returns. The wall is black against the night sky, but I don't need to see it to break it. It is too dark to continue into the Marsh so we camp in the shadow of the wall.

I wake at dawn. The air is chilly, drops of dew forming on my hair like crystals. I stare at the pearlescent strip of gray in the distance that grows lighter. Then a streak of orange appears, underscored with slashes of pink and gold. Slowly, a symphony of color plays out in the sky, nature welcoming the beginning of a new day.

I have always loved sunrises. There is something hope-ful about them.

After a quick breakfast, we set off again. Raven and I agree to visit our families on our way back—I fear if I see my mother now, I may never leave her.

At first, the Marsh appears to be deserted. But then I realize that most of the laborers must have been in the other circles. We see the elderly, and children with young mothers, or children with no mothers at all. The Great Wall looms in the distance, but it never seems to come any closer.

Until suddenly, the mud-brick houses end and we stand at the edge of a vast expanse of dry, cracked earth. The Wall rises up before us. It is larger than I imagined, larger by far than any of the other walls in this city, and I know I would never be able to take it down on my own.

It grows more massive the closer we get to it. The wind

blows sharply across the empty plain, whipping specks of dirt and dust up around us. We walk and walk and the Wall looms higher and higher. By the time we reach it, it hurts my neck to look up to the top.

I turn to my companions. "I can't break this one down."

Garnet's eyes are wide.

Ash looks slightly stunned. "It's . . . so . . ."

"Big," Raven finishes. *Big* doesn't seem like enough. The stones are gray and murky brown. Some are covered with lichens or moss. She reaches out and runs her hand over its rough surface, then gasps.

"Follow me," she says, taking off at a jog. Garnet rushes to catch up to her and Ash and I take up the rear.

Whatever Raven's looking for, she doesn't find it for nearly half an hour. "There!" she cries triumphantly, pointing at what appears to be just more wall.

But then I see the contrast, the shadows, the place where steps have been carved into the stony surface.

Up, up, up they go, to a dizzying height that sets my head spinning. But I have to see.

At first, the stairs are wide and smooth, but the higher we go, the narrower they become. By the time we are halfway up, my thighs are in agony and there's a painful stitch in my side. The drop below me is terrifying, worse than in the sewers when we had to climb that rusty ladder to get into the Bank, worse than the top of the golden spire in the Auction House where Sienna and I sent up the flare. Three-quarters of the way up and everything below has turned miniature—minuscule houses, baby trees. I can see straight across the Marsh, to the wall of the Farm.

"How long . . . do you think . . . it took to build this?" Ash pants.

"Twenty-five years," Garnet says.

Raven gives him a surprised look.

"What?" he says. "You think I could have lived with my mother all my life and *not* known that? She loves to—" He stops himself and clears his throat. "She loved to say how our family 'built' it. Funded it, yes, but I'll be damned if a single member of the House of the Lake ever touched a brick or stone."

"They are now," Raven points out.

Garnet looks at his own hands like he's never seen them before. "Yeah," he says. "I guess you're right." Then he shrugs. "Well, there isn't a House of the Lake anymore. So I'm no one, really."

"Don't ever let me hear you say that again," Raven snaps. "After all you've given up. After everything you've done."

"Can we keep moving, please?" Ash says. He stands with his back pressed against the stone, his skin taking on a grayish tinge.

"You didn't have to come," I say as we plod forward. Each step makes the muscles in my legs burn.

"Yes, I did," he says through gritted teeth. "I want to see what's out there, same as you."

"I didn't know you were so afraid of heights."

He lets out a breathy laugh. "I didn't either. This isn't just high up. I feel like . . . I don't know, like we're walking straight into the sky."

When we reach the top, it truly does feel as if we've

emerged into some other world. The top of the Wall is easily twenty feet wide, the stone pockmarked. The wind is vicious up here, but something about it pricks at me, like little fingers, pinching and nibbling as if to get a sense of who I am. I walk to the other side, shaking with trepidation.

The lip of the Wall comes into view, and then there it is. The ocean. Exactly as we saw it on the cliff. I hear a gasp, and Raven's hand slips into mine.

It is gray and blue and endless. White-capped waves crash onto a long strip of beach, hundreds of feet below. The Wall stretches away in every direction, and for a moment, I could easily believe there is nothing else out there, that this island is the only thing in the world besides water.

Then I see the ships.

Their hulls are rotting, their masts splintered, the sails eaten by wind and water and time. But they are there. Maybe a dozen of them, gathered together in a cove near the Wall. Perhaps the royalty kept them for sentimental reasons. Or they have simply been forgotten, lost to time. The only thing that matters is, they are here. Which means the royalty came from another land, as Sil's book said.

"I've only ever seen ships like those in pictures," Garnet says in awe. Ash has collapsed on the ground, staring out at the ocean with greedy eyes, as if he can't see enough of it. I sit beside him.

"I never thought I'd see it," he says.

"Me neither."

"But you have seen it."

"Not like this."

"It's incredible," Raven says, wrapping an arm around

Garnet's waist as he kisses her temple.

The briny tang fills my nose, sharp and sweet all at once. The crash of the waves mixes with the wailing of the wind, and in it I hear something else, too, something that might be singing, in a strange language that I don't understand. It lifts my heart and makes me sad at the same time.

We are taking this island back, I think, wondering if these ghosts of the Paladin can hear me, can understand my thoughts. *For you. For us.*

The singing swells up around me before fading into the wind, the dying echo of a race that was nearly extinguished.

But survived.

We sit on the Great Wall and watch the sun sink lower toward the horizon. Ash's hand is warm around mine. I feel complete here. The rebellion, the royalty, the city itself all seem so far away. There is only the rich blue of the sky, the gentle bite of the wind, and the dim roar of the ocean. I look at my friends and think about who we all once were, and how far we have come.

I am Violet Lasting again.

I am home.

Acknowledgments

I CAN'T BELIEVE THIS SERIES HAS COME TO AN END. AND it would not be what it is without the help of so many incredible people.

Karen Chaplin, my wonderful editor, thank you for your passion, your endless supply of wisdom, and your unwavering belief in me. Your guidance has made this story better than I ever thought possible, and I am eternally grateful for just how much you got me and this world and these characters.

Charlie Olsen, thank you for being a sounding board, a protector, a champion, and for believing in me even when I didn't. I will hold all the doors for you, my friend.

To everyone at HarperTeen, especially Rosemary Brosnan, Olivia Russo, and Olivia Swomley—you are all wonderful, and I am so thankful to be in such capable hands. And massive hugs to Heather Daugherty, Erin Fitzsimmons, and the design team for yet another exquisite cover.

Huge thanks to everyone at Walker Books, particularly Gill Evans and Emily Damesick, for their brilliant editorial insight, and to Jack Noel for the wonderful UK cover.

Thanks to Lyndsey Blessing for being a master in all things foreign rights, and to everyone at Inkwell Management for their knowledge and support. And to Philippa Milnes-Smith for taking care of Violet so well across the pond.

Jess Verdi, I don't even want to think about how I would have survived this series without you. You were there for every word, every scream of frustration, every eureka moment. Thank you for always telling me to keep going and for always being there when I felt like I couldn't. I love you to pieces. Moonstone.

To my incredible betas Caela Carter, Alyson Gerber, and Corey Ann Haydu—you guys are quite simply the best. Thank you for all your wisdom and enthusiasm.

Riddhi Parekh, friend of friends, thank you for all the hugs, flowers, roosters, wise words, patio laughs, and for just being an amazing person.

So many incredible friends have supported me on this journey—Matthew Kelly, Erica Henegen, Jill Santopolo, Lindsay Ribar, Alison Cherry, Mindy Raf, Rory Sheridan, Jonathan Levy, Tori Healy, Maura Smith, Mike Hanna,

Melissa Kavonic, Ali Imperato, Carly Petrone, Shilpa Ahlu-walia, Nina Ibanez, Marissa Wolf, and Jared Wilder, thank you all so much. I value your friendship more than you know. I wish I could give each of you a palace.

My family has been a bottomless well of support throughout the years. Thank you to both Ewings and McLellans—Jean and Dave, Don and Sandy, Tim, Sadie and Reed, Craig and Vicki, Sam and Sophie, Jennifer, Jonathan, Martha, and Mike. Enormous hugs to Kristen and Molly. As always, extra special thanks to Ben, Leah, Otto, and Bea.

To my parents, who every day remind me of the power of following your dreams. Thank you for believing in me, for trusting me, and for helping me become the person I am.

And to Faetra. I wish you could see your name on the dedication page. I wish you could have seen this story go from those few chapters I emailed you to these three actual, real live books. I wish for so many things that will never happen. But as E. E. Cummings said, "I carry your heart with me (I carry it in my heart)." You will be in my heart forever.

A RIVETING TRILOGY FROM
AMY EWING

In the Jewel, the only thing more important than opulence is offsprin

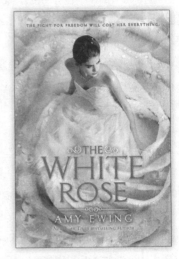

Don't miss
Raven's sto
in this digi
novella!

05640 7928